# FRIDAY BEFORE BANK HOLIDAY

*A witty novel of theft, murder, arson, fraud and double-cross.*

Two events, which cost the insurance companies a lot of money, took place on the Friday before Bank Holiday. Charles Hammersley had a horse-riding accident in Knightsbridge, and the Continental Diamond Exchange in Hatton Garden were relieved of the Yellow Fire Diamonds. These events came together to lead to Operation Safe-Deposit. Charles believed the cause of the trouble was his chance meeting with Tim Tweedy in the White Hart at Esher, for if that meeting had not taken place Simon Good, chairman of Roag's Syndicate, would not have been suspected of being behind the diamond robbery...

# Friday Before Bank Holiday

*by*

George Davis

**Dales Large Print Books**
Long Preston, North Yorkshire,

British Library Cataloguing in Publication Data.

Davis, George
    Friday before bank holiday.

    A catalogue record of this book is
    available from the British Library

    ISBN   978-1-84262-802-7 pbk

First published in Great Britain in 1964 by Collins

Copyright © 1964 by George Davis

Cover illustration © Clayton Bastiani by arrangement with
Arcangel Images

The moral right of the author has been asserted

Published in Large Print 2010 by arrangement with
George Davis, care of Watson, Little Ltd.

Dales Large Print is an imprint of Library Magna Books Ltd.

Printed and bound in Great Britain by
T.J. (International) Ltd., Cornwall, PL28 8RW

# CONTENTS

1 Proximate Cause 11

2 Ontploffingen in Hatton Garden 21

3 Accidents Will Happen 32

4 Pragmatic Lucubrations 47

5 Bad Samaritan 60

6 Blinded With Science 69

7 Tenuous Threads 80

8 Sour Grapes 90

9 Do Be My Enemy 98

10 Million Pound Objective 114

11 Blank Astonishment 143

12 Neutralising the Position 158

13 The Cobbler of Theilt 171

14 Milk Bottle Tops 191

15 Artists in Crime 215

16 Birth Of An Operation 237

17 Letters To Lingard 255

18 A Couple Of Heels 268

19 Blake's Jerusalem 284

20 Operation Safe-Deposit 294

21 Dear Lady Veronica 303

22 Operation Police-Benefit 319

23 Die For Your Country 326

# 1

## Proximate Cause

Two preordained events happened on that Friday before Bank Holiday. Charles Hammersley had a horse-riding accident in Knightsbridge. The Continental Diamond Exchange lost the Yellow Fire Diamonds. Both events cost the insurance companies a lot of money.

One sultry summer's evening, a few weeks previously, there were three worried men in the saloon bar of the White Hart at Esher. There were in fact a large number of worried men present, but we are concerned with only three of them.

Charles Hammersley, a professional insurance claimant, was worried. Funds were getting short. Roag's Syndicate, of which he was a member, had dispersed like fog-wraiths when the activities of their organising genius, Simon Good, had been suddenly curtailed by a legal system designed to do just that. It will be recalled that the Syndicate was founded under heavy fire in World War II, and that its leader, Major Peter

11

Meek, who had received a posthumous decoration for bravery in the field and had vanished in the process, had turned up years later at Tyburn & New York Insurance Company under the name of Simon Good; and with the aid of some of his wartime cronies – Hammersley (his ex-batman), Sergeant Blake, Dutch and Rip Stookman – amassed riches by a series of complicated insurance frauds, investing the proceeds in Tyburn & New York stock, a company in which he had every confidence. Roag's Syndicate was doing very nicely, thank you, when Simon Good was unfortunate enough to be caught out using an 'ice-shilling' in his electricity meter, and was sent down for twelve months on the instructions of Mr Justice Meddlisome, who was not amused. The full story of that, however, is the subject of another chronicle...

Tim Tweedy, horse-doctor of Esher, was worried. His trouble was hard facts and a soft heart. Hard facts – money, or the lack of it. Soft heart – all over a circus horse, Fiddler...

Lew Gabbitas, artist with secrets he preferred to forget, was worried. Middle-aged, of good physique, dramatically handsome, vain, wealthy – his main trouble was woman-trouble. He was violently in love with a young lady half his age who had set him a startling objective which had to be attained before she would marry him...

The White Hart was crowded on that thun-der-in-the-air evening. Hammersley, clutching an ice-cold lager, pushed his way over to a window seat which overlooked a pleasant garden at the rear. He was a short, plumpish, round-faced gentleman with grey, watery eyes which peered out with a slightly bewildered expression through National Health lenses; people naturally made way for him, for somehow he gave the impression that he was doing his pathetic best at great odds, and to impede him would be like kicking a dog.

He had read somewhere or the other that the law does not concern itself with the cause of causes, that it was concerned only with the proximate cause. Every event, no matter what it is, is the last link of a chain projected back into the past, and if every event had to be considered in the light of what had happened previously, it would be necessary to trace things back to birth and even to the question of why one was born; and although a number of people had in fact asked him that very question, he was assured that the doctrine of *proximate cause,* laid down centuries ago by Lord Bacon in his *Maxims of the Law,* still held good.

He was inclined to believe that the proximate cause of Operation Safe-Deposit was

13

his chance meeting that night with Tim Tweedy...

He was sitting gently quaffing his lager, when he was joined by a sad, horsy-looking gentleman with a pint tankard.

'A beautiful evening,' ventured Hammersley.

The other nodded gloomily.

Hammersley watched him for some minutes. He was a kindly soul and it distressed him to see a fellow creature in trouble. 'It would appear,' he said diffidently, 'that you have something on your mind.'

'I've got a horse,' said the other, taking a moody swig.

'I seem to have heard that before,' said Hammersley.

'This is a special one.'

'They all are,' agreed Hammersley, who knew the form. At any moment now the rubicund gent opposite would inform him that he had just left Lord Marberry's stables, where he knew the stable boy, and that he had a dead cert for to-morrow and one for Friday. Coupled with other secret information and presented in the form of highly intricate mixed doubles, it would be possible to win a fortune for the very modest outlay of two pounds. If the gentleman had a scrap of paper he would write it all down – no, no, he didn't want a penny for the information himself, just a couple of bob to buy a drink for the man in the horse-box...

'This one dies for its country,' said the other morosely.

'Eh?'

'And then gets up when the war's over.'

'I'm afraid I'm not quite with you,' confessed Hammersley.

'My name's Tweedy. I'm a vet – not a surgeon, just a plain, unvarnished horse-doctor. Practised all my life, always loved animals, right from a boy. Know all about 'em. I know my stuff, but I have no letters after my name – except what I've made up myself. Some people even prefer me to the more polished article,' went on Mr Tweedy with a flicker of pride. 'I've got a couple of permanent jobs with two small circuses that winter in the neighbourhood, and quite a number of private clients. Worked up a good connection one way and another. Got a small office in the High Street. Do a bit of racing on the side.'

'Tell me about the horse that dies for its country,' said Hammersley, and there was a gleam in his eye.

'Fiddler,' said Mr Tweedy.

'I beg your pardon.'

'Fiddler. The horse.' Mr Tweedy cleared his throat with a gill of cold beer. 'You wouldn't want to buy a horse, I suppose?'

Hammersley was startled. He was prepared to give two shillings to the man in the horse-box for erroneous information on the sporting qualities of any animal, for he had been approached on a number of occasions by intimate friends of the aristocracy, but this was the first time he had been asked to buy the horse as well. 'I wouldn't know where to keep it,' he said defensively. 'I live in a flat, and they don't permit pets, not even a cat. I mean, a horse is a bit unusual.'

'Pity,' growled the other. 'If I don't find a good home for him I shall have to put him down.'

Mr Hammersley was concerned. He was a gentle soul, a rogue, but he wouldn't harm a fly.

'There's a tumbledown cottage and a field going with it for a mere song,' said Mr Tweedy temptingly.

Hammersley's mind slid back to the cherry-blossom days of boyhood, to the farm where there had always been the spare horse to ride. A cottage, a field and a horse which died for its country. Might be worth looking at. It might even be the chance for which a professional insurance claimant was waiting.

Mr Tweedy pressed on with his story. 'The boss of Alberto's Wonder Circus asked me if I could find a home for one of his speciality horses, Fiddler. Getting a bit old for the act. They've trained up Son of Fiddler to take its place. Like a fool I said I'd buy it – I was always a sucker for poor old Fiddler. I put it to grass at this place of mine at Marlow. But now money's a bit tight, I want to realise on the cottage – needs must when the devil drives, as they say, I'm lumbered unless I can find another home for Fiddler. Or sell the whole caboose. I should hate to put him down. Intelligent, friendly creature. Almost human.'

Hammersley leaned forward. 'What precisely does it do?' he prompted.

'Dies for its country.'

'So you said. What does that mean?'

'Isn't patriotism enough?' jerked the other, his face crinkling in a sudden toothy grin. 'I'll tell you. Imagine a miniature war in the ring, with redcoats falling left, right and centre, until Fiddler alone is galloping around with the gallant Captain of Horse in the saddle. The ring-master suddenly shouts *"Wounded soldier!"*, Fiddler receives a sly tap on the flank and immediately rears up on its hind legs and staggers about in an alarming fashion, finally falling over, hooves flailing the air. The Captain of Horse, who has fallen off base over apex, staggers over to his wounded charger, squeezing a plastic bag of tomato ketchup in his breast pocket to look like blood. *"Die for your country!"* roars the ring-master, and the captain, making much of his horse, administers two more pats in the right place; and Fiddler, rearing up in a last sad gesture, collapses and dies. And there the two of them lie, absolutely motionless, right into the middle of the next act, until the ring-master suddenly flicks his whip and cries *War over!* Fiddler's up like a shot in a mad gallop round the ring, the gallant captain leaping up into the saddle the second time round. The kiddies loved it.'

Charles Hammersley looked very thoughtful. His mind wriggled with possibilities. 'When can I see Fiddler?' he said.

'Run you down to-morrow morning?'

That suited Hammersley very well. He first wanted an opportunity of consulting one of his numerous insurance textbooks, although these had not been issued for the purpose of circumnavigating the policy conditions.

'You could look at the cottage at the same time,' added Mr Tweedy hopefully.

'At the moment I'm only interested in *looking* at Fiddler,' said Hammersley firmly. 'You know the legal maxim – *caveat emptor.*'

'Of course,' said Mr Tweedy, out of his depth.

'Is it possible for one to buy a *dead* horse?'

The other showed his surprise. 'You could get one from the knacker's yard. Or from me.'

'I wouldn't want to buy one from you,' said Hammersley. 'No offence, of course! If

18

you could recommend the right sort of – um – knacker's yard, I'd willingly pay you a small over-riding commission – if what I have in mind ever comes to fruition.'

Tim Tweedy was completely at a loss, but things looked promising. 'Shall we say to-morrow morning, then?' he said briskly. A little to his surprise Mr Hammersley said yes, to-morrow morning, and bidding Mr Tweedy good night took his leave...

As Hammersley vacated his seat some-body else slid into it, and Tim Tweedy looked up in recognition. 'Why, Mr Gab-bitas!' he exclaimed. 'How nice to see you!'

'Tweedy! Fancy seeing you here! I'm merely passing through, as they say.'

'How many horses have you got now, Mr Gabbitas?'

'Just a pair.'

'I bet you don't get 'em looked after like I did for you. I missed your custom since you moved down to the West country.'

'How is business?'

'Not too brisk – although, did you see that joker who just left? I've been trying to sell him an ex-circus horse – Fiddler. I think I've almost landed him.'

The night was yet young and Mr Gabbitas wanted to relax, he had had a busy day.

'Tell me about it,' said Mr Gabbitas plea-santly.

The following morning Charles Hammersley reached agreement with Tim Tweedy over Fiddler and the cottage and certain other matters of a highly confidential nature, and the first link in a chain of events leading to Lew Gabbitas and violence was forged.

Hammersley already had a Personal Accident Policy with the Wyvern Insurance Company and he called at their office in Pall Mall to extend the cover to include horse-riding. He also made inquiries regarding taking out a bloodstock policy in respect of a magnificent horse he had just acquired named Ambiguity. He had in mind a sum insured of £650, but was very anxious in case the company thought the figure excessive. The Wyvern, always on guard against over-insurance, sent down an expert who came to the conclusion that Ambiguity was worth at least £850. It was pointed out that if Ambiguity was worth £850 it would have to be insured for that amount, otherwise the company would not be getting an adequate premium. Hammersley regretfully broke off negotiations on the ground that at the rate quoted the premium cost would be too high, and he conveyed the impression that he would have to seek a quotation elsewhere. The matter was left in abeyance for about a fortnight, until an inspector followed it up and induced him to take out an insurance for a compromise figure of £800. 'You've talked me into it,' said Hammersley admiringly

# 2

## Ontploffingen In Hatton Garden

The main entrance to the Continental Diamond Exchange is in Hatton Garden itself, and most of its trade drifts in apparently casually through a pair of well-worn swing doors. No particular precautions appear to be taken, although it is safe to assume that the tough-looking gentlemen who stand on the steps when a special delivery is made are not there for the fun of it. There is an alternative way into the premises by way of a door at the end of Flinder's Court, a narrow paved alley at the side of the building. This entrance is really an emergency exit, and is used only very occasionally when an assignment of exceptional value is being carried. The change of procedure is known only to a select few, but, it was to transpire, not few enough.

Flinder's Court, which reaches back for some fifty yards, is a cul-de-sac, and merely gives access to the fire exit on the one hand and, on the other, to a couple of grimy doors which have not been opened for half a century.

Along the middle of the court there runs a curious metal gutter to take away the rain waters urged there by the slightly canted paving stones; a gutter which is not open enough to be classed as an open drain, nor yet closed enough to be called a closed drain. At first glance it appears to be a long tessellated metal strip, some six inches wide, with an inch gap down the middle. It was probably an ingenious compromise under an early Public Health Act which required that whilst open drains must be closed to prevent fouling, rain waters must nevertheless be carried away. Honour was saved by devising what was virtually a pipe with a gap along its length, the gap being set flush with the level of the paving. Further to satisfy the requirements of the Act, the metal strips either side of the gap could be removed to facilitate periodic cleaning, although this tiresome procedure had probably not been carried out since the Boer War.

It seemed reasonable to suppose that sooner or later someone would be sent along to scavenge the gully, if only in belated compliance with Clause 47 of the long since rescinded Health Act, and that moment arrived one fine Tuesday morning when two workmen arrived with a handcart emblazoned with the insignia of the local council.

They set up a Gothic canvas shelter at the blind end of the alley, unloaded their gear, made a can of tea and drank it, and then set to work unbolting the slats of metal and prising them off in a highly professional manner. The filth of generations was removed with the aid of wire brushes and was carefully swept up before the metal strips were replaced. A circular metal grille some two feet in diameter, situated half-way along the passage, was also lifted and the main drain subjected to keen scrutiny.

Little notice was taken of the workmen because very few people came that way. If anyone had paid particular attention they might have wondered what the precise tie-up was between the local council and the War Department, since the stores removed from the handcart were all marked with broad arrows and the initials W.D. There were two large canisters, each with four nozzles, and a drum of what looked like thin black cable. One canister was painted green and bore the letters S(RD); the other, black and with white bands, carried the letters KSK(RD); and stencilled on the drum was FID.

The men casually erected a low canvas

screen round the central drain, not so much to protect passers-by from any stone chippings that might fly as a result of their labours as to give a certain amount of cover from prying eyes.

There was a certain degree of work involved in wedging in three iron bars across the open drain, some two or three feet down, as these had to be sufficiently rigid to take the weight of the two canisters. Working slowly and carefully, they lowered the Smoke (Rapid Dispersal) and the tear gas KSK (Rapid Dispersal) into position. Whilst one kept watch, the other linked the canisters together with a short length of fuse already cut to size. They replaced the grille temporarily, and whilst one of them strolled casually to the Hatton Garden end of the court to assess the right moment, and to remove one loosely-bolted strip of metal from the gutter, the other gave attention to the drum of Fuse Instantaneous Detonation. At a signal, he hurried forward without particularly appearing to do so, and in a trice one end of the fuse – with a black bakelite igniter-set already attached – was pushed down in the gutter. Whilst the first man swiftly bolted the metal strip back into position, the other rapidly unrolled the fuse-cord back to the central drain, pushing it down through the one-inch gap as he did so.

The length of fuse was precise. '
circular grille was removed once more ε
connection made to the igniter-set already
attached to the match-head of the Smoke
canister. About a yard from the end of the
main fuse was a carefully spliced-on length,
and this was expertly linked with a slab of
plastic explosive on the underside of the
grille. The grille was replaced securely, and
the empty fuse-drum and the canvas screen
removed leisurely to the canvas shelter.

The men breathed freely again. They
made another can of tea.

A little urchin ran home and told his
mother he had seen two men laying a telephone wire.

The workmen drank their tea and tidied
up. They pushed their handcart back against
the end wall, buckled up the flaps of the
shelter, and went to lunch, taking the fuse-
drum away with them in a sack.

The shelter would be required on Friday,
the Friday before Bank Holiday, and it was
essential that the few people who used
Flinder's Court should get used to the idea
of its being there...

Apart from the activities of the big diamond
houses, much of the diamond trade in and
around Hatton Garden is carried on in a
peculiarly casual fashion in doorways and
street corners by swarthy gentlemen who

look as if they have not got the price of a cup of tea. They haggle over the contents of intriguing little chamois leather bags, exchanges are made, and wads of notes pass hands as though they were bus tickets. This sporadic trade only comes to life from about noon onwards, and at ten o'clock on that fine Friday morning one could say that Hatton Garden was not yet fully awake.

It was for that very reason that the special delivery of the Yellow Fire Diamonds was timed for ten-fifteen.

A man stood kicking his heels by the iron post at the end of Flinder's Court, and he had been waiting there for at least half an hour for the car which was to bring the courier and the two guards detailed for this very special consignment.

He stiffened suddenly as a powerful car swept by, the driver attracting his attention by lightly touching the horn. The car accelerated round the block and a few minutes later came slowly back up Hatton Garden, the driver watching for the all-clear signal.

The look-out man glanced back along the passageway. It was empty, as it had been ever since he had stood watch. Hatton Garden itself was almost devoid of humanity, most of the employees of the big diamond houses were hard at work inside. The only other person in the immediate vicinity was a well-dressed young lady of obvious charm who was pacing up and down outside the main entrance of the Continental Diamond Exchange. From time to time she glanced impatiently at her watch. She was obviously a harmless bystander, although as the car approached she was actually moving towards Flinder's Court. She arrived at the mouth of the alley at the same time as the car drew up in response to the look-out man's signal. Idly she watched the three men get out and walk well-bunched together down the alley. The car drew away immediately; it was no part of the security measures to advertise unnecessarily the side entrance to the premises.

The look-out man remained where he was, as a rear-guard, and at that moment Lady Veronica Tuke, fumbling for a cigarette, spilled the contents of her handbag. Gallantly, the guard came to her assistance in collecting some of the curious paraphernalia that young ladies carry...

There was a vicious explosion and two minor ones in rapid succession. Wide-eyed, almost thrown off balance by the blast, they both whipped round. Twenty yards away, the narrow confines of Flinder's Court were rapidly being obscured by a swiftly expanding wall of smoke and tear gas, as eight high-pressure nozzles burst into life after being dormant for twenty years. For one sizzling split-second the rearguard was shocked into immobility. Then:

'*Ontploffingen!*' he bellowed, startled into the tongue of his birth, for he was a Belgian, born a few kilometres from the Dutch frontier. Running forward he plunged into the sinister swirling cloud which came out to meet him, only to stagger back a moment later choking and holding his eyes. In the brief moment he was in that devil's brew he glimpsed one guard lying prone on the pavement and the other staggering round in circles; the courier was struggling frenziedly to open the side door of the Continental Diamond Exchange.

Lady Veronica Tuke hastily scrabbled up her belongings and remained where she was in considerable agitation and doubt.

Suddenly a man broke cover from the wraith-mass. Staggering drunkenly and gasping for breath, holding a handkerchief over his eyes, he crashed into the girl, all but knocking her over. Knuckling his eyes and grasping the look-out man for support, he strove to regain his breath. 'Explosion!' he gasped. 'Gas main! Get – ambulance – fire brigade – police! Side door's jammed – can't get in that way! You phone – I'll try to reach the courier through the building. Quick – phone!' He pushed the other towards the telephone booth on the corner of the alley, and then staggered off up Hatton Garden in the direction of the main entrance to the

Continental Diamond Exchange.

A mixture of smoke and gas was creeping out evilly and quietly into Hatton Garden, and a number of people from nowhere were hurrying over to see what it was all about.

Veronica Tuke watched the rearguard totter into the phone-box. She turned and watched the other man hurrying along to the main door; she saw him slow up and straighten his clothing; she saw him walk slowly *past* the entrance and proceed leisurely to the next corner. And vanish round it.

A sudden higglety-piggle of doubts rip-roared through her agile mind. She wondered if the man in the phone-box had registered such a clear impression as she had of that wild-eyed apparition who had raced out of the ever-thickening pall to leisurely escape. She lost her indecisiveness. At that moment nothing would have induced her to leave the spot until the police arrived...

The man in the phone-box had dialled 999 and was having difficulty with the operator. The operator was having difficulty with him.

'Emergency services. Which services do you require?'

'*Ontploffingen!*' gasped the guard.

'Speak more slowly, please!'

'*Ontploffingen!*' yelled the other desperately.

'Fire? Police? Ambulance?'

29

'All three!' shouted the rearguard, tears streaming down his cheeks. 'Hurry! Hatton Garden.'

'What was that you were saying about popping 'em, or something?'

'*Ontploffingen!* Explosions! Can't you speak English – or do I have to spell it out?'

Whilst Lady Veronica Tuke had a sneaking regard for the hunted (coming from a hunting shire where little such regard was held) she gave a rather more precise description of the man who had almost knocked her over than that given by the rearguard, and Superintendent Lingard was confident the criminal would soon be apprehended.

He was right. At least, they picked up a man not a quarter of a mile away in a tavern in Ely Court, a narrow passage which links Hatton Garden with Ely Place. The Mitre, as patrons are aware, is famous for the cherry tree which thrusts its way up through the very corner of the tavern, and when they tapped Lew Gabbitas on the shoulder he was holding a glass and reading with avid interest the notice over the now glass-enclosed trunk.

He expressed great surprise and fierce displeasure when he was invited to accompany two plain-clothed policemen to Gray's Inn Road police station for questioning. They searched him, but failed to find what they were looking for. They put him up for identification and the rearguard, faced with an actual line-up, his eyes still smarting and bloodshot, was doubtful to the extent of not committing himself. Lady Veronica Tuke, quietly confident, emphatic to a degree, picked out the wrong man – a policeman in mufti – and they felt obliged to let both him and Mr Gabbitas go...

She did not then know that the courier was critically injured and that one of the bodyguards had been killed by a flying fragment of the metal grille.

Mr Gabbitas left the police station and strode in a highly pressurised, artery-bursting state along to Chancery Lane by way of Staple Inn. Even the ancient notice under the arched gateway failed to amuse him, a notice which informed the public that the porter had Order To Prevent Old Clothes Men & Others From Calling Articles For Sale, Also Rude Children From Playing &c.

He found a self-service teashop, purchased a cup of tea, and sat down to cool off.

A few minutes later, a young lady, parallel with him at the next table leaned over, cigarette poised between two elegant fingers.

'Could you oblige me with a light?' asked Lady Veronica Tuke...

# 3

## Accidents Will Happen

That afternoon found Lew Gabbitas pacing anxiously up and down in the vicinity of the Continental Departures platform at Victoria, and with the passing of each minute his edginess became more and more apparent. He was ultimately forced to the conclusion that the Belgian gentleman for whom he was waiting was not going to turn up, and this worried him considerably, for Victor Pajot was not one to let him down. Perhaps Pajot had misunderstood him and had gone down to Exeter, as he had been told to do on a previous occasion. But no, the instructions had been explicit, this was to have been a quick job. Something had evidently gone wrong.

The Dover train pulled out and Gabbitas strode irritably over towards the buffet, pausing to get a newspaper at the bookstand. The inch-high headlines leapt out at him with a sickening jolt. £250,000 DIAMOND THEFT. GUARD KILLED.

For a moment he stood stock still. A nerve began to flutter in his jaw and his hand shook a little as he fumbled with the paper. He skimmed down the account with growing apprehension, and found himself from time to time glancing furtively over his shoulder. So a guard was killed from a flying fragment of metal! And the stop-press said that the courier was not expected to live. No wonder Pajot had suddenly got cold feet!

Gabbitas thought swiftly. The police would be asking him further questions – if they could find him. It became more imperative than ever to get rid of the packet in his pocket. Where was the best place to leave it? Left luggage office? No, someone always remembered the packet and the person. Hide it? Yes, but where? His mind skeetered round for a solution. And then suddenly it came. Tim Tweedy. Tweedy didn't ask questions.

He hurried over to a telephone booth and rang an Esher number. Tweedy was not available. A girl gave Gabbitas a Belgravia number and said Mr Tweedy might be contacted there. This time he was lucky and he put the position briefly to his erstwhile vet.

'Can you do me a favour, Tweedy? Someone was to have met me here at Victoria Station to collect an important parcel and take it over to the Continent for me to-day, but he's let me down. I wondered if you could help me out and take it down to Exeter for me on Monday instead.'

'Exeter!' exclaimed Mr Tweedy.

'Yes, it's an alternative. I know it's a long way to go to deliver a parcel, but it's most important, and there's somebody there who will oblige me.'

'But aren't you going back to the West country yourself next week, Mr G.?'

'Unfortunately I've received a telegram to the effect that a close friend of mine is seriously ill in Scotland,' said Gabbitas smoothly. 'I shall go up on the night train, and I don't know how long I'll be away. If you could collect the packet immediately I should be more than grateful.'

'I'm sorry to hear about your friend, Mr G, but I'm already tied up over the holiday.' There was genuine regret in Tweedy's voice; Mr Gabbitas was not ungenerous in the matter of expenses. 'I'm doing a job for that fellow Hammersley.'

'Hammersley?'

'Yes, the chap I sold Fiddler to.'

'Oh.' Lew was disappointed. 'What sort of a job?'

'He's trying out a little joke in Knightsbridge with Fiddler. He's having an "accident" to fool some friends, and I'm helping him. Might be worth watching. Although if you ask me,' added Mr Tweedy injudiciously, 'it's beyond a joke.'

Something began to click in Gabbitas's brain. He said curiously, 'What does Hammersley do for a living?'

34

'Something to do with insurance, I think. Seems to know a lot about it.'

'Does he now!' said Lew flatly. The gears were meshing smoothly. Hammersley might be just the man he was looking for. 'What time is this – accident – due to take place?'

'About six-thirty this evening. Near Hyde Park Barracks. There's a set of traffic lights at a crossing by that narrow alley of shops which links Brompton Road with Knightsbridge. Why?'

'I'll be there,' said Gabbitas. 'But please don't recognise me...'

He rang off and found the nearest post office. There he dispatched a telegram addressed to himself at his hotel in Albermarle Street. Then making his way to a small café in a side-street, he ordered some tea and toast, and settled down to read all about the Yellow Fire Diamond robbery. At six o'clock he was at the traffic lights in Knightsbridge waiting for Hammersley's accident to happen.

Another link in the chain of events was being forged.

Things began to move at six-twenty when Hammersley came thundering madly along Knightsbridge on Fiddler, clinging on for dear life. What had happened a few moments previously was something of a mystery. The policeman at Alexandra Gate, noticing a gentleman on a horse patiently waiting to cross over into Exhibition Road, had very kindly held up the main stream of traffic. What had caused the horse to take fright and bolt almost out of control towards Sloane Street was inexplicable, for the gentleman sat well, toes up, heels down, apparently in full command. The horse was beautifully groomed, restful, had a sensitive mouth, no snaffle, leathers just right, was a pleasure to behold. Perhaps a little old for those who knew their horses.

The insurance claim-form later submitted by Hammersley indicated that either a pistol shot or a car back-firing had caused the animal to panic; the policeman, who knew something of the traffic at that point, was inclined to think the latter.

Traffic heading in the opposite direction pulled in to give horse and rider a wide berth; pedestrians drew back from the edge of the pavement in alarm, marvelling at the way in which the rider kept his precarious seat as the horse snorted and lunged towards the spot where Lew Gabbitas was waiting in keen anticipation.

Hammersley was by now well forward. He began to tense a little; he was now fast approaching the point of no return, being only fifty yards from the traffic lights. Warning shouts went up as a sudden surge of people started to stream across the road.

Hammersley's eye took in the lively scene with sharp appreciation.

'Steady there!' he grunted, and the animal checked. It knew the routine so well that it almost anticipated the precise command.

'*Wounded soldier!*' said Hammersley urgently. '*Wounded soldier!*' He was back in the saddle, exerting pressure with his knees. The horse reacted to the signal. It stopped suddenly – throwing Hammersley over its left ear – reared up on its hind legs, staggered about pawing the air, snorted vigorously and then collapsed slowly in the middle of the gaping throng. Making a couple of valiant efforts to get up, the creature rolled pathetic-ally over on its side, tentatively stroking the air with its right foreleg.

It was no part of Hammersley's plan to part company with the horse so suddenly. Having got over the sudden shock of parabolic flight through the air, the battle-training reflexes of old got to work and he found himself gripping each end of his crop and neck-rolling over it with the careless abandon of the expert. The forward finishing movement on the feet in the firing position did not quite come off, and he finished flat on his back. He got to his feet and ruefully held his shoulder. And Lew Gabbitas, standing in the crowd, watched very carefully.

Fiddler feebly flicked a hoof and twitched a muscle or two in the flank. The intelligent head flopped back on the asphalt; the enormous eyes closed gently. (That was the part that always *got* them in the old days!)

Hammersley knelt by the animal's head, opened its mouth and looked in. He had no reason for doing this, but it seemed to go down well with the crowd. 'Please keep back,' he said with an air of authority. 'We don't want anyone to be kicked.'

'What abaht you, guv – you all right?' asked a little man in a cloth cap.

'I think so, thank you. Please keep back.'

He bent over Fiddler once more and gave him three distinct pats on the flank. People in the know said he was making much of his horse. He whispered, *'Die for your country!'* Fiddler gave a violent shiver, neighed, lay perfectly still.

'I must get a vet,' pronounced Hammersley at length. He scribbled a telephone number on the back of a used envelope and asked someone in the upper income bracket if he would mind ringing the number and asking the vet to come. People in the upper income bracket made better witnesses. 'Ask him to bring the horse-box,' he said. 'I'm afraid it's...'

He wisely left the sentence unfinished, but the precise trouble was soon diagnosed by a gravely judicious crowd whose equine knowledge was limited to show-jumping on television.

Fiddler, in fact, was perfectly happy, dreaming of lump sugar and green pastures. Actually this was the difficult part of the act, lying perfectly still, so still that people really did begin to have doubts, until finally, when everyone was truthfully worried, especially the kiddies, the ringmaster would shout *'War over!'* and one could scramble up and gallop madly round the ring and take a graceful bow to thunderous applause. And then a bag of oats. Circus days were over, but life was still very sweet, brother. Sweet lump sugar. Green fields, lush grass, kind friends. Corn, oats and sugar, brother, who would wish to die? Fiddler gave his finest performance ever.

Two mobile policemen were trying to sort out the traffic, and a third was looking round for witnesses. In a remarkably short time a horse-box arrived and down stepped Tim Tweedy. He examined the horse and pursed his lips doubtfully. He tried to move its head but it flopped back on the road lifelessly. 'If we could only get the animal to his feet we might be able to get it up into the box,' said Mr Tweedy, renewing his efforts.

'Let me try,' suggested Hammersley. *'Wounded soldier!'* he coaxed softly, carefully giving the requisite number of pats.

Fiddler started to move and then stopped dead. It should have been *'War over!'* He opened an enormous right eye and gave Hammersley a conspiratorial look. *'Wounded soldier!'* hissed Hammersley anxiously.

Fiddler struggled up and lurched round in a drunken fashion, snorting and neighing alarmingly.

Tim Tweedy hurriedly manoeuvred the ramp into position and Hammersley gently encouraged the horse up into the box. The relief of the crowd was short-lived, for Fiddler, having made the top of the ramp, stepped into the box and immediately collapsed as Hammersley muttered *'Die for your country!'*

Mr Tweedy turned down a thumb and went round to the driving cab. He came back with a sack and a curious chromium-plated instrument which could have been a humane-killer. Screening Fiddler's head with the sack, he made some adjustment to the gun-like instrument and bent down. It was a pity Hammersley obstructed the view. The horse became very still ... Lew Gabbitas watched with cynical amusement.

'Sorry it had to be done,' said Mr Tweedy, a moment later.

'Not your fault,' grunted Hammersley.

'You all right?' asked Mr Tweedy with sudden concern.

'Bit dizzy,' said Hammersley bravely. 'My shoulder.'

'Came a regular purler,' declared the little

man in the cloth cap, with satisfaction.

Hammersley had reached a vital stage in his accident. A telegram to the Wyvern Insurance Company. He searched in his wallet for another scrap of paper and was obliged to resort to the back of another envelope. It looked better than having the telegram already written out. He was putting the finishing touches to the text when Lew Gabbitas came over, and Tim Tweedy did not bat an eyelid.

'Can I be of assistance?' inquired Gabbitas. 'I'd get that shoulder seen to if I were you – you came a nasty cropper. I saw the whole thing.'

The policeman moved in. 'Then perhaps I could have a brief statement from you, sir. You'd be surprised how few people see anything when there's an accident – you'd think they were all wearing blinkers.'

Gabbitas hesitated for a split second. He had not bargained for publicity, but there was no escape. With a show of co-operation he gave the required information and his name and hotel address. Hammersley gave his own somewhat confused version of the event, concluding, 'I was just writing out a telegram to my insurance company.'

'I think you should see a doctor,' said Gabbitas firmly. 'If this officer has finished with us, I'll take you to one in a taxi. We can attend to the telegram on the way.'

Hammersley was capable of making lightning decisions. It had been no part of his original scheme to have a personal accident, but Gabbitas was almost talking him into it. It required no high-powered advertising campaign to impress on Hammersley the security that insurance provided, for as a professional claimant he was well covered in every direction with a number of unsuspecting companies. Only his old O.C., Simon Good, knew of his ability to dislocate a shoulder at will – he had once been a contortionist in a circus act – and Simon Good was not due to come out of Wormwood Scrubs till the following week. The money would come in handy. After all, he paid away enough in premiums, he might just as well keep his hand in and his shoulder out, and collect.

'You're too kind,' said Hammersley, and permitted himself to be led over to a waiting taxi.

'St Anthony's Hospital,' said Mr Gabbitas to the driver, as they climbed in and settled back in their seats. 'And now, Mr–'

'Hammersley.'

'Ah– If you'll allow me to have the text of your telegram, which I believe I saw you writing out, I personally will see that it goes.'

'That is most generous of you, sir,' declared Hammersley, who saw in the other a witness that the professional claimant prayed for. He handed over the envelope and felt for some money. Lew Gabbitas waved aside the movement and Hammersley did not press the matter, especially as the other was glancing at the text. It read:

WYVERN INSURANCE COMPANY, PALL MALL. LIVESTOCK POLICY 1212 REGRET ACCIDENT KNIGHTSBRIDGE FRIDAY EVENING STOP HORSE AMBIGUITY COLLAPSED STOP DISPATCHED WITH HUMANE KILLER STOP WRITING.
CHARLES HAMMERSLEY

Gabbitas said: 'Is there any desperate urgency for this? There won't be anyone at the insurance office at this time of night, surely? They may even be closed to-morrow, it's Saturday. I doubt if it will be dealt with till Monday morning...' His voice trailed off. 'Not even on Monday morning – it will be Bank Holiday. So even if you send this now it won't receive attention till Tuesday.'

Hammersley was well aware of this fact – he would have been very worried if it were otherwise. He was aware that the Pall Mall office of the Wyvern Insurance Company closed at five p.m.; he was aware that the telegram would be accepted that evening by the housekeeper; he was aware that the office did not open on Saturdays; he was aware, too, that Monday was August Bank Holiday. He had made it his business to be aware of these things. He said firmly, 'I feel the telegram must go off this evening without fail. The policy conditions are very clear on the point. "Immediate notice of accident must be given." As I see it, immediate notice means immediate notice, and if I don't do anything till Monday or Tuesday, that's not immediate notice.'

'You are perfectly correct, of course,' said Gabbitas. 'How is your shoulder?'

'Quite painful,' said Hammersley stoically, and it was quite obvious from the pull of his jacket that something was wrong.

And something else was wrong, but Gabbitas couldn't put a finger on it. Something didn't quite add up, and it irritated Lew. He liked things to be shipshape, even if not square.

As the taxi proceeded Hammersley reviewed the situation. The accident had happened more or less as planned. There were a number of witnesses, not forgetting the friendly-looking policeman at Alexandra Gate. The horse had behaved superbly and was now being taken away in the horse-box. The text of the telegram was in able hands. The wording was neat; there *had* been an accident – not to the horse, but to himself; the horse had certainly collapsed – had it not subsided in the road, and what was subsidence but collapse? And the horse had certainly been dispatched *with* the humane-killer – they were both in the horse-box. In all, a truthful telegram without a vestige of truth.

Hammersley was well satisfied with the way things were turning out, and he was about to ask Gabbitas if he would kindly sign a statement in support of his insurance claim, when Gabbitas said, 'I'll attend to the telegram whilst you're with the doctor. Then I'll see you safely home.'

'My dear sir!' expostulated Hammersley. 'There'll be no need for that!'

'We'll see what they say at the hospital first,' said Gabbitas firmly. 'They may even keep you in – you look quite pale.'

And Hammersley would have perhaps turned a shade paler if he had known that Lew Gabbitas, in a sudden flash of clarity, had spotted the one mistake he had made, and that Lew liked to keep in touch with people who made mistakes. The links were forming into a chain from which there was to be no escape.

A staff nurse in Casualty at St Anthony's Hospital informed Mr Gabbitas that Hammersley's shoulder was dislocated and that manipulation was necessary. Gabbitas said that he would go and perform an errand and then come back and see his friend home. He found a post office open for the receipt of telegrams, and before throwing away Hammersley's envelope he took a careful note of the Marlow address on the front.

Tim Tweedy brought the horse-box to rest in a quiet side street near Sloane Square. He lit a cigarette and climbed down from the driving cab. The horse-box was a fine modern vehicle, and reaching up, he opened a side door and clambered into the rear portion.

'Come on, Fiddler, here's some sugar for you!'

Fiddler lay still as death.

'Come on, Fiddler, what's the matter with you! Sugar!'

Fiddler opened a wary eye but otherwise didn't move, and Mr Tweedy suddenly remembered. He tapped the horse lightly on the flank. *War over!* he said.

Immediately Fiddler struggled up, shook himself and nuzzled up for the reward – an immediate handful of lump sugar and, later, the bag of corn.

They were soon on their way to Mr Hammersley's newly-acquired cottage.

# 4

## Pragmatic Lucubrations

Late that evening the commander (Crime) New Scotland Yard rang for Superintendent Lingard. 'Sit down, Lingard, and tell me what you know about the Hatton Garden robbery. The Home Secretary's getting worried about this new wave of violence that's sweeping the country.'

'He's not the only one,' growled Lingard, rebellious after a harassing day. 'Even if we catch the culprits, what will he do about it? Tell 'em to be good boys?'

'Just tell me what you know about the Hatton Garden robbery,' suggested the commander mildly. 'Have a cigarette and relax. Think of your blood pressure.'

'Relax!' seethed Lingard. 'It's the criminal who relaxes – everyone's much more concerned with the welfare of those gentlemen than that of the victims. What about this man who was killed to-day at the Continental Diamond Exchange? What'll they do about *him?* Or his relatives? I'll tell you – sweet Fanny flipping Adams!'

'Do you know who he was, Lingard?'

'His name was Larbeeck, he was a Belgian, he was employed as a guard for this special assignment. And he bought it doing his job.' The superintendent was grim.

'Your information is incorrect, Lingard. His name was Johnson, he was an Englishman, he was undergoing training at Interpol, and he was seconded from the Leicestershire Constabulary. I agree he bought it.'

Lingard's jaw swung round. 'One of our blokes!' he jerked.

'Yes.'

'Single?'

The commander looked away. 'Married and two.'

Lingard growled a fearsome oath, and for a moment the commander contemplated the pigeons outside on the window sill. 'The man responsible must be brought to book, Superintendent,' he said softly. 'There's too much of a tendency nowadays to shrug off the killing of a public servant as an occupational hazard. You'll hear people saying, "Oh, he did it in the line of duty, his dependents will be recompensed".'

'Recompensed!' snarled the superintendent. 'Recompensed? Out of the Police Fund? Out of the Poor Box? They'll be lucky! First there's a wife with no breadwinner–' He broke off. 'She's been told, of course?'

'This afternoon.'

'And two nippers without a father – what

a Bank Holiday for them! It's not just for now – it's for ever! If I could put my hands on that – that – I'd tear him apart bit by bit! I'd put the clock back, all right. Recompense! Huh! A wave of public sympathy, a fund started by the neighbours amounting to sixty-two pounds one-and-a-penny, a wife striving to keep her head above water, and then, likely as not, finding herself kicked out of married quarters. From then on it's a losing battle. Everybody conveniently forgets – didn't they put a shilling in the collection-box? And meanwhile some hoodlum is laughing his head off whooping it up in a luxury flat with his current floosie.' A tiny pulse was hammering away in the superintendent's jaw.

'I know, Lingard, I know. You don't have to tell me. We've had it all before and we'll have it all again. But there's something big in this recent rash of crime, this is not ordinary hit-and-run stuff perpetrated by young delinquents out for kicks – this is well-organised crime with big prizes in view. We've had arson on a highly selective scale where firemen have lost their lives; there have been train robberies where signals have been altered and guards and drivers attacked with callous indifference – and without regard to the lives of hundreds of passengers; policemen are being shot down if they get in the way – to-day one is killed by flying fragments from an engineered explosion. There was a time in this fair land of ours when it was safe to leave a bag of gold on the King's highway.'

'Before my time!' seethed Lingard.

'Yes, and it was just after the time when they used to hang men for stealing sheep. One can only assume the nation got the message.' The commander looked absently out of the window again. Then, very gently, 'Superintendent. I personally don't care very much about the fate of the Yellow Fire Diamonds. But the man responsible for the Bank Holiday misery of that family in Leicester must be brought in. And if he happens to resist arrest and you are obliged to use a little – persuasion – I don't suppose for one moment I'll be able to see the bruises. My sight isn't so good as it used to be. I no longer see black and white, I get a sort of blurred grey. Now. What do we know about the Yellow Fire Diamonds? What do we know about *any* yellow fire diamonds?'

With an effort Lingard dragged his thoughts back into the room. 'The Press reports are largely accurate, sir. Yellow diamonds of the weight and depth of colour of those stolen are very rare indeed. Much of the value is in the matching. These were in the form of a rivière, or necklace, and were reputedly once part of the Austrian Crown

50

Jewels. They'd been in an Austrian duke's family for about a hundred years, and although they were known by the family to be valuable, their true value was never really appreciated. How the original duke got hold of them is lost in obscurity. With the death of the last of the line just after the war, the remains of the estate were disposed of, and the Yellow Fire rivière was bequeathed to a faithful old manservant. He, too, had no idea of its true worth, regarding it as something of a sentimental trinket. Falling on hard times, he decided to realise on it in Berlin, where a slick Swedish firm instantly appraised its intrinsic value and secretly purchased it at a knock-out price. They farmed it off to a Belgian subsidiary in Antwerp, and after careful re-appraisal it was decided to put it up for resale on the London market at its present inflationary price.'

'Which is–?'

'About a quarter of a million sterling.'

'A lot of money.'

'The fourteen deep yellow *brilliant*-cut major stones were unique. They were to be exhibited with replicas of other known tinted diamonds at Burlington House next week. The subsequent sale was to have been negotiated by the Continental Diamond Exchange.'

'What publicity was given to the business?'

'Regarding the original purchase by the

Swedish firm – flash-in-the-pan Press reports, a one day wonder. Regarding the proposed resale in London, secrecy was maintained so far as concerned the transference from Antwerp to London, and as to which London firm was involved. There was, of course, advance publicity of the proposed exhibition of rare geological wonders, of which they were to form part, at Burlington House next week.'

'And the security measures for the transference from Antwerp?'

'On the face of it, adequate – in view of the general secrecy with which the whole operation was surrounded,' said Lingard. 'The courier was accompanied by two guards, one a Belgian and the other, so you tell me, an Interpol man. All went well until they reached the Continental Diamond Exchange. The intention was for the trio to enter the building by a little-used door in Flinder's Court, a cul-de-sac which runs at the side of the building. The time of arrival was planned for ten-fifteen. They arrived on time in a fast-moving car which was to circle the block until the driver received an all-clear signal from a man stationed at the mouth of the court, a man named Verdoen, who was an employee of the Diamond Exchange. His function was to act as a "backstop" when the others passed him.'

'And what happened?'

'Verdoen gave the signal, the trio got out and went towards the side entrance, the car went on. They reached half-way along the alley, when there was an explosion – or explosions – in a drain in the middle of the paving stones, and in a matter of seconds the three men were enveloped in a swirling cloud of tear gas and smoke. The Interpol man was killed by a splinter of metal from the fractured drain, the other guard was temporarily blinded and all but suffocated, and the courier rushed chokingly to the side door a little farther on.'

'And failed to make it?'

'He made it, all right,' said Lingard grimly, 'but he couldn't open it – it was secured by a new padlock and hasp, screwed on outside, presumably overnight.'

'And Verdoen – what did he do?'

'He immediately rushed forward into the smoke and gas but was forced to come out into the air again.'

'And the courier?'

'The courier, gasping, but alert and realising there was a trap, was dimly aware of a man streaking towards him through the smoke from a canvas shelter at the blind end of the court, gun in hand. He turned to defend himself. He was ruthlessly shot down for his pains and had to relinquish his precious packet. He made a short statement, but now he's critically ill in Bart's.

The gun – complete with silencer, and a pair of gloves, were found in the court when the smoke cleared.

'And the other guard – what did he do?'

'He was kaput – he'd received a direct jet of KSK in both eyes, and couldn't see a thing. You may remember, sir, that KSK is a liquid tear gas with a persistency of about two hours.'

'I don't, but I'll take your word for it. And how did the gunman make his getaway – didn't Verdoen make any attempt to stop him?'

'Verdoen knew by sight only the courier, and he thought the man who came streaking out of the smoke was one of the guards.'

'H'm! And then?'

'The gunman calmly instructed him to ring for an ambulance, the fire brigade and the police whilst he himself would try to reach the courier from inside the building – he said the side door had jammed. And that was the last Verdoen saw of him.'

The commander remained silent for a moment. Then, 'This Verdoen – is he a reliable employee?'

'The secretary of the Diamond Exchange gives him an excellent write-up.'

'Was he able to give a detailed description of the gunman?'

'Not exactly detailed – he could hardly see or breathe. But quite good in the circumstances, I suppose.'

'So that leaves Lady Veronica Tuke. What about her? Was the description she gave at variance with Verdoen's?'

Lingard frowned. 'Not really at variance – no two people see the same thing – but the funny thing is she must have got quite a good view of the man, she was as near to him as anyone could have been – in fact, she was quite indignant at being almost knocked over by him – and yet when we pick up this man Gabbitas who seems to fit the description, she has to go and select a policeman in mufti.'

'Then Gabbitas wasn't your man. I gather Verdoen wouldn't commit himself at the line-up. You should be looking for someone more like the policeman, Lingard. Doubtless he bore *some* resemblance to the man described.'

The superintendent hesitated. 'Yes,' he said doubtfully. 'Superficially, I suppose.'

'Then what about the policeman?'

Lingard stared disbelievingly. 'You mean–?'

'Yes. Did he do it? After all, he was picked out by the young lady who saw it all happen.'

'No, sir,' said Lingard firmly, 'he didn't do it. As it is, he'll never live the incident down – he daren't show his face in the canteen! The inspector says that if ever there was a man whose heart was right in the service,

55

then this is the man.'

'I know, and when he dies, that golden heart will have one word engraved thereon – "Copper." But don't you see, Lingard, with a reputation like that he's just the joker who could get away with it. After all, a quarter of a million sterling is better than a police pension.'

'Apart from the management of the Continental Diamond Exchange few people knew of the delivery of the diamonds,' objected Lingard. 'Is it likely he would know?'

'H'm, I suppose not. It rather looks like a leak in Antwerp. Would you say "Gabbitas" is a Belgian name?'

'It's not particularly English,' flannelled Lingard.

'Where does Mr Gabbitas live?'

'In the West country, at a place called King's Barton. He's on holiday at present, staying at the Lincoln Hotel in Albemarle Street.'

'He must have money to stay there. You had to let him go, of course?'

'There was nothing to hold him for, sir. His explanations were perfectly reasonable, and coupled with the fact that someone else was picked out on the line-up, it seemed we'd got the wrong man. He had nothing on him, of course.'

'H'm. Tell me, what is this Lady Veronica Tuke like? A bit of a thigh-slapping country type with a face like a horse?'

Lingard was shocked. 'To the contrary, sir, she's a very tasty dish.'

The commander cocked a highly disconcerting eyebrow. 'And what was this – um – tasty dish doing in London?'

'Doing, sir?'

'Yes. The directory says she lives in Somerset.'

'Oh. Well, I don't think they asked her what she was *doing*. She gave the address of a hotel in Dover Street.'

'It seems everyone is on holiday except us, Lingard. Tell me a little more about the gas and the smoke.'

'Ex-W.D. stores, sir, probably sold in error with other surplus gear. Two rapid-dispersal canisters had been lowered into the main drain in the middle of Flinder's Court, with detonation sets timed to go off at ten-fifteen.'

'How could that be, Lingard?' objected the commander. 'If the courier had been five minutes late, or early, the whole object of the exercise would have failed. They must have been detonated by the man who was hiding in the canvas shelter.'

'There was no trace of fuse cord leading either up or down Flinder's Court, sir. The Explosives boys are working on it now. There was evidently a pretty powerful charge under the grille of the drain, to shatter it so that the gas escaped more rapidly, and evidence of the precise method of detonation has been destroyed. It could even have been taken away by the criminal himself.'

'And yet he left his gloves and gun lying there?'

'They were found near the drain, sir, so perhaps the actual firing device was more important to him and he stopped to pick it up. Something quite small – a transistor radio-control, for example.'

'I think it's something simpler than that, Lingard. Didn't anyone see these canisters being put in position – that must have been quite a job in itself.'

'We haven't found anyone yet, sir, and nobody else seems to have witnessed the actual robbery. We're making inquiries in the premises which look down Flinder's Court from the other side of Hatton Garden, but everyone appears to have packed up for the Bank Holiday, and I'm afraid we won't get much farther till Tuesday.'

'Get something out on the radio, it may help. And what about Identikit and television?' The commander brooded for a moment. Then, at a tangent, 'I'll tell you something, Superintendent, that will restore your wilting faith in humanity. A moment ago you were very critical of public reaction to the dependents of personnel killed in the line of duty. It may interest you to know that recently I have had brought to my notice several instances where dependent families have received, from anonymous donors, large sums of money by way of solatium.'

Lingard became very still. 'Conscience money?' he breathed.

'Ah, I wondered if that would be your reaction,' said the commander. 'If it *is* conscience money then we have the first link, because all these cases are connected with big-time crime. I've given orders to collate every bit of information we can get on the subject.'

Lingard looked doubtful. 'It might be the work of a philanthropist who's shocked at public indifference – a sort of one-man vigilantes.'

'It might be,' agreed the commander, reaching for his hat, 'or it might not. And now I must be off, else we'll be continuing these pragmatic lucubrations all night. Let me know how you get on. Put a tail on Mr Gabbitas, ask the local force if they know anything about him – where he came from and so on. But treat him very, very gently for the time being. If he isn't all he should be we don't want to frighten him. And if he's perfectly innocent, we still don't want to frighten him – we have to keep up a reputation of being a very kindly force. And that reminds me. Don't work too hard over the holiday You seemed a bit tetchy when you came in...'

The police looked everywhere they could think of for Mr Gabbitas, but he seemed to have vanished into thin air.

# 5

## Bad Samaritan

When Gabbitas returned to St Anthony's Hospital he was asked to wait. 'Your friend will be with you in about half an hour,' said the staff nurse. 'He's just coming round.'

'Coming round? Is he all right?'

'Oh, yes, but he was a bit fractious and we gave him the needle. We had to perform some rather painful manipulation on his shoulder.' She added unexpectedly, 'Does he suffer from epilepsy?'

Gabbitas was surprised. 'I'm sure I don't know. Why?'

'It would have helped us to understand his case. His shoulder just wouldn't stay put, we had to manipulate it several times, it was most puzzling. With epileptics there is a marked tendency to involuntary dislocation of certain joints, that's why I asked. He must have been in the Army at some time or the other.'

'Oh?'

'Yes. When he started to come round he kept mumbling something about a wounded soldier and dying for his country. The casualty doctor said he was probably reliving some terrible battle experience – it often happens when a patient is regaining consciousness. Actually it was rather embarrassing – every time he said "wounded soldier" he wanted to pat me on the – er–' (she got round the predicament) 'the *gluteus maximus*. However, he suddenly said, "War over!" and stopped his tricks. He's still very muzzy, I think he might be suffering from delayed shock. You did say you were going to see him home?'

Gabbitas would not have missed seeing Hammersley home for all the tea in China.

'He'd better have some black coffee before he leaves,' said the nurse.

'My dear sir, so nice of you to bother!' said Mr Hammersley in a slightly slurred voice when at length they produced him, his right shoulder strapped into position under his loosely flapping jacket. 'Did you send my telegram?'

'As soon as I left you,' soothed Gabbitas.

'Most kind of you,' declared Hammersley, and there was a note of relief in his voice. 'I do feel that if one expects the insurance company to pay up one must make every endeavour to comply with the policy conditions.'

Lew Gabbitas should have been impressed by this fine spirit, but somehow he was not.

'And talking of insurance,' went on Hammersley, 'would you be kind enough, as you saw the accident happen, to write out a statement that I could forward to the company in support of my claim?'

'By all means,' agreed the other, smiling inwardly. 'If I see you home perhaps you would supply me with pen and paper...' He wanted to know a little more about this smooth Mr Hammersley who had definitely made one mistake.

At Hammersley's flat at Mortlake Gabbitas wrote out a statement which so far exceeded Hammersley's dreams that he asked his new-found friend if he would mind writing it out again, in case he wanted to make a personal accident claim as well as a claim in respect of the horse. Gabbitas obliged, and afterwards they sat for a few moments with cool drinks watching the television news.

It was then that Hammersley noticed the sharp edge of anxiety which extruded from the being of Lew Gabbitas, who glanced once or twice at his watch. With sudden concern Hammersley wondered if perhaps he was monopolising too much of Mr Gabbitas's time. He said: 'My dear Mr Gabbitas, I have completely overlooked the fact that you must be wanting to be about your own business. I do apologise!'

'Not at all,' said Gabbitas. 'It was impolite of me to have betrayed any anxiety to get away, but it has been an unfortunate day for me, too.' He was thinking of the line-up at Gray's Inn Road police station, of the young lady who had given too close a description of him, of the sealed packet in his pocket, and of the failure of Victor Pajot to relieve him of it at Victoria. And of his urgent need to dispose of it for the time being. He said, producing the packet from a side pocket, 'I've been let down by someone who promised to collect his from me and deliver it to a friend – it was very important. And now I am left with it, and I have to make an unexpected visit to a very sick person in Scotland. I had a telegram at my hotel this afternoon, and I am going up by the night train. I must not leave it too late.'

Hammersley expressed his sympathy. 'Can I deliver the packet?' he offered.

'I'm afraid not, thank you all the same. As it wasn't picked up to-day, my alternative was to deliver it personally to a place near Exeter on Monday, but now I just don't know how long I'll be in Scotland.'

'Let me do it for you,' pressed Hammersley. 'You've been very kind to me.'

'I wouldn't dream of it,' said Lew, '–not in your condition. You'll have to rest for a while.'

'I'll be all right by Monday,' said Hammersley, and only he knew how very true this would be. He would, in fact, be all right as soon as Gabbitas left the flat. 'I probably shan't be able to work for a week or two, but I'll be fit enough to travel. I could do with a day or two in the West country.'

'If it's not being too inquisitive, what exactly is your vocation?'

'I'm a factor,' said Hammersley smoothly. 'I work on commission. I have to do quite a lot of writing down – its unfortunate I've hurt my right shoulder; when I move my hand the pain up my arm is almost unbearable. But the hospital gave no reason why I shouldn't at least try to move around. I have to report back to them to-morrow – there's a possibility of subsequent electrical treatment – but if I can help you I shall be only too glad.'

'If you feel that way about it, it would relieve me of much worry,' smiled Gabbitas, relaxing. 'We could regard the journey as being in the nature of a commission – I would pay your full expenses, of course.'

'That's good of you,' said Hammersley, taking the packet. 'I know a nice little hotel near what used to be Moll's Coffee House. In the shadow of the cathedral.'

He spoke as if a cathedral were his natural environment...

But if Hammersley had made a mistake, so had Lew Gabbitas, and it was one upon which Superintendent Lingard was to pounce and worry at like a savaged tiger...

The express from Paddington arrived at Exeter dead on time. Hammersley made his way round to a car-hire firm near St David's Station, and, producing a card on which Gabbitas had written certain instructions, was soon heading west out of Exeter into the sunshine. It was not long before he lost his sense of precise location, although he noticed that the sun seemed to veer right round until it was almost directly behind them. At length they swung into the drive-way of a sleepy Elizabethan manor house, and the car crunched to a halt on the gravel in front of the studded oak door.

As Hammersley alighted his appreciative eye noted the ancient mounting-block and wrought-iron lamp, with bubble-glass, hanging under the porch. He learned from the hammered metal lettering on an oak plaque that he had arrived at a place called Four Chimneys. Tentatively he tugged at the antique bell-pull, and was almost surprised when there was a faint clangour in the depths of the house. A full two minutes passed before the door opened and he found himself face to face with one of the most beautiful young women he had ever seen.

'Oh!' she said, her face dropping. 'I – I was expecting someone else.'

'I'm sorry to disappoint you,' beamed Hammersley. 'I've called on behalf of Mr Gabbitas.'

Sharp anxiety flooded her expressive eyes. Hammersley answered her unspoken question.

'He was called away suddenly to a sick friend in Scotland. I volunteered to help him out by delivering something which somebody failed to collect on Friday.'

'That was very kind of you – it's a long way to come.'

'I intend to spend a day or two in Exeter – to capture something of the atmosphere of the first Elizabethan age.' (Hammersley was inclined to be lyrical at times.) He said cautiously, 'Do you know what it is I'm bringing?'

A secretive, almost sly expression came and went with the speed of light in those sultry eyes, and Hammersley was not sure at that moment if he liked her.

'Would it be a flat, sealed packet?'

'Right, first time!' He produced the packet,

and a sort of visual sigh of relief slicked across her face.

'Thank you.'

There was an awkward little pause, and Hammersley assessed that the handing-over process was not to be prolonged. He extended his hand. 'Glad to have been of service,' he said. 'Good day, madam.'

She wore the ghost of a smile as he turned away to the car.

'The Drake Hotel, near the cathedral,' he instructed the driver.

They swung out of the drive, and Hammersley noted the Jaguar parked almost out of sight at the side of the house. Mr Gabbitas evidently moved in a moneyed circle. He might be worth cultivating...

The detective waiting unobtrusively in the lane by Four Chimneys had taken careful note of Hammersley's arrival and had watched the handing over of the packet. He took a careful note of the car number and jotted down a reasonable description of Mr Hammersley. He noted down the direction from which the car came and that in which it left. He was also interested to observe that the eye-catching young lady with the provocative walk left the house a few minutes later in a Jaguar. From where he was standing he failed to get the number – the angle was against him and the number plates were dirty. This latter point in itself was one of the four thousand-odd offences which the motorist could commit without much effort.

Hammersley was taken back to Exeter by a completely different route, and it was not until later that he suddenly realised that it would be difficult for him to find his own way to Four Chimneys – not that he had any intention of trying, for he was looking forward shortly to removing his old O.C., Major Peter Meek (or Simon Good, as he now preferred to be called) from the tender care of the Governor of Wormwood Scrubs. We are not concerned here with Simon Good's astonishment at being met outside the prison gates by the judge who sent him there. Our interest lies in other events which were taking shape whilst Roag's Syndicate was crusading on behalf of Mr Justice Meddlisome in Portugal...

# 6

## Blinded With Science

Shortly after his return from Exeter, Mr Hammersley was visited by a personable young man from the Wyvern Insurance Company.

'Please come in, Mr Brockhurst,' said Hammersley, glancing at the other's card. 'I've been expecting someone to call, although you shouldn't have gone to the trouble of bringing the money round personally.'

'I haven't brought any money round, sir. I've come to have a chat with you.'

'Nice of you to call. Do sit down.'

Young Mr Brockhurst was looking forward to this interview. From the Tuesday after Bank Holiday onwards, he had spent an interesting but frustrating week, having been instructed by the Claims Manager to go and view the carcass of a horse named Ambiguity, to count the teeth and to see that piebald spots had not been painted on an old hack not worth a fiver.

The Claims Manager had in mind the regrettable practice of insuring a valuable horse for a large sum of money, and then having it whisked down to the country out of the way whilst having an accident necessitating the dispatch of a similar-looking but ancient animal destined for the knacker's yard. It was to combat such whimsical practices that the Wyvern's livestock policy contained certain conditions governing the final disposal of the carcass, one of which concerned a time factor of forty-eight hours. Much good clean fun has been nipped in the bud by careful examination of the animal's teeth, for the masticatory structure of a horse is particularly telltale. A knowledgeable claims inspector doesn't have to be a genius to discover that a horse has aged several years since its master signed the proposal form last Wednesday.

'...Actually I called on the Tuesday after Bank Holiday, but you weren't at home.'

'I was in the West country. The hospital advised me to take things easy.'

'We didn't know of your personal injury, then.'

'You didn't? I wrote you fully.'

'Yes, but the letter didn't reach the department from the management till after lunch, and by that time I was already out making calls.'

'Oh, I see. So when you say you didn't know, you don't mean that the *company* didn't know, you mean that your manage-

70

ment had failed to pass on the information to you. Seems a bad way of doing business.' Hammersley shook his head regretfully. 'I sent you a telegram, too, on Friday evening. You did get it, I hope?'

'Yes. Though you couldn't have expected us to do anything with it on Friday night, could you?'

'No.'

'Well, could you?'

'No.'

Mr Brockhurst strove to regain mastery of the situation. 'Obviously we couldn't do anything with it before Tuesday, could we?'

'You know your own business best,' agreed Mr Hammersley politely. 'I'm afraid I don't know your system.'

'Well, you don't expect us to have a staff waiting for claims all over the holiday, do you?' pursued the other.

'It would be most unfair to them,' conceded Hammersley. 'But your system must work by and large, otherwise I suppose you would have altered it before now.'

'What I'm trying to get at,' floundered young Mr Brockhurst, who was of a suspicious and impetuous nature, 'is that it was most unfortunate to have an accident on the Friday evening before Bank Holiday.'

'Yes, most unfortunate,' agreed Hammersley. 'It upset me no end.'

'I didn't quite mean that,' said the other,

rather more quickly than he intended. 'I mean that it was most unfortunate for *all* concerned. Perhaps the word I'm looking for is "unfortuitous".'

There was a wealth of meaning in his voice which was not lost on Mr Hammersley.

'Is there such a word?' he asked curiously. 'I think I see what it is you're trying to say.' He went on gently, 'These things actually do happen, you know, at most inconvenient moments. Fires break out on the day after someone takes out a fire insurance. I once had an uncle who broke his leg on his birthday and it upset all the jollifications. My aunt was furious, and he assured her he wouldn't have had it happen for worlds – if only because of the pain he was suffering himself. But nevertheless it did happen. At an inconvenient moment. Births and deaths go on quite contemptuously of any petty rules we like to make up concerning the bit in the middle called life. One day is as good as another for an accident, whether it's Wednesday, Good Friday, or the fourth Sunday in Lent.'

'Oh, quite, Mr Hammersley, quite,' galloped Mr Brockhurst. 'What I meant was that the whole chain of circumstances was – unfortunate. The car backfiring, the horse bolting and collapsing and having to be put to sleep, your own unfortunate personal injury–'

'I think the hospital were worried about secondary shock,' said Hammersley.

'–and then the delay before we could do anything–'

'Before you *did* anything,' corrected Hammersley smoothly.

'–and then, of course, you still weren't at home on Tuesday afternoon – I rang your flat–'

'I was still in the West country.'

'–so I went on to the Belgravia Riding School where you sometimes stable your horse, but they were completely in the dark and said they hadn't seen anything of you since Friday evening–'

'Doesn't anyone read the papers?' said Hammersley petulantly. 'The accident was reported in Friday's stop-press.'

'And then I rang up the farm at Hurley where you told us you had grazing rights in a field, to see if by any chance the carcass had been taken there, but they, too, were without information.'

'I hope I'm not going to have any serious after effects from this dislocation,' said Hammersley. 'It struck me the hospital staff were keeping something back – one can never get at the truth, nowadays.'

'And then, when your letter came to hand, we immediately phoned your vet – Mr Tweedy, who had dispatched the horse–'

'Yes, very sad,' said Mr Hammersley, 'very,

73

very sad.' He sighed. 'Ah, well, I suppose all's well that ends well.'

'All didn't end well, sir.'

'No?' Mr Hammersley was astonished. 'What was the trouble?'

'We had no carcass to examine, sir. It had been disposed of, *entirely* disposed of.'

'Well, you didn't expect *me* to keep it, did you?' frowned Hammersley. 'Come now, be reasonable, I know this is a luxury flat, but the refrigerator is really very small – have a look at it yourself, if you like. Nowhere near big enough for a horse – even if one could get it up the stairs.'

Brockhurst took a firm grip on himself. 'Mr Hammersley. The policy lays down certain conditions regarding the disposal of the carcass. These conditions are framed to safeguard the company against fraud–'

'Fraud!' Mr Hammersley was horrified. *'Fraud,* Mr Brockhurst? Is there any suggestion of fraud? Is *that* what you're trying to tell me? I must ring my lawyer immediately.'

'Whoa-back, Mr Hammersley – I shouldn't have put it like that.' (That's what comes of learning the text-book, thought young Brockhurst.)

'I nearly misunderstood you,' smiled Hammersley pleasantly, taking his hand off the telephone. 'You mean to say that the conditions are there to enable the company to see for itself that the dispatching of the animal was necessary and kind.'

'Yes, that's right, sir,' said Brockhurst, running a finger round the inside of his collar to ease the constriction. 'You see, we called on Mr Tweedy and found he was the consultant of two small circuses based on Esher. He has an office in the High Street–'

'Yes, that's right, near the White Hart, that's how I got to know him. Grand chap.'

'Er – yes.'

'And what did he have to say?'

'He told me he waited till Monday morning for your instructions, and as you hadn't contacted him he tried to get in touch with you on the telephone. Without success.'

'I was probably on my way to Paddington. On Saturday I was messing about for quite a while at the hospital, and in any event didn't feel fit enough to be worrying about insurance policies; and it didn't seem fair to bother him on Sunday – he needs time off, as well as your Claims staff.'

'H'm. So, being without instructions, he removed the animal from his premises and took it to a local knacker's yard for disposal.'

'Very right and proper,' agreed Hammersley. 'He's a man with initiative.'

'So we didn't get a chance of checking,' said Mr Brockhurst.'

'You could have gone to the knacker's yard,' suggested Hammersley brightly.

'We did. We were too late.' There was weary resignation in Brockhurst's voice. 'The carcass brought in by Mr Tweedy was disposed of on Monday.'

'But the teeth – I filled in particulars of the teeth on the proposal-form. Couldn't you have checked the jaw-bone?'

'There was no jaw-bone,' said Mr Brockhurst flatly. 'There was nothing. Just an entry in the book.'

'It seems your policy conditions aren't wide enough to cover an eventuality of this sort,' frowned Hammersley thoughtfully. 'Or else your system needs tightening up. That is, if you want to go round suspecting everybody.'

'Oh, we're not suspecting everybody, sir. The knacker's yard is one of high repute.'

'Mr Tweedy wouldn't be satisfied with a second-rate place,' agreed Hammersley.

'Mr Tweedy! H'm!' Brockhurst almost sniffed.

'What about Mr Tweedy?'

'Oh, we've nothing against him, but he doesn't seem to have any qualifications that are recognised in veterinary circles.'

'He knows his business from long practice. Some people prefer him to the more polished article. After all, you don't require a bedside manner with a horse. When did you go to the knacker's yard?'

'Last Wednesday.'

'Wednesday? Let me see – the accident happened Friday evening. Saturday, Sunday, Monday, Tuesday, Wednesday – so you didn't really get down to business until the fifth day after the accident? Doesn't your policy say that in the event of the demise of the horse the carcass need only be kept for four days?' said Hammersley, knowing perfectly well that it said nothing of the sort.

'Not "need only" – the expression is "at least".' Mr Brockhurst added reluctantly. 'But the period is forty-eight hours.'

'I knew there was a four in it somewhere – but that's only two days!' Hammersley seemed surprised. 'Then I haven't, so to speak, contravened the policy conditions?'

Brockhurst remained silent and unhappy.

'Now let's see,' went on Charles Hammersley. 'Friday evening to Saturday evening, twenty-four hours; plus Saturday evening till Sunday evening, that's forty-eight hours. So even if Mr Tweedy had disposed of it Sunday evening, he wouldn't have unwittingly broken the conditions of the policy.'

'Oh, I agree, you're within your rights.'

'If only you'd got cracking right away on Saturday morning instead of hanging around till Tuesday – everyone was available. Except your Claims staff. You know, it's most annoying, one makes a great effort to get off a telegram at a time when one can hardly bear the sadness and the pain, and the only thanks one gets is for the insurance company to send someone along to cast thinly-veiled aspersions. I suppose you've read the statement by a certain Mr Gabbitas?'

'Oh, yes.'

'Are you satisfied with his testimony?'

'As far as it goes, yes.'

'As far as it goes? How much farther could it go? I suggest you tread very carefully, Mr Brockhurst. Mr Gabbitas appears to be a man of considerable wealth, and I imagine he wouldn't take too kindly to the slightest hint that he was holding something back.'

'I'm sure we can iron this out amicably,' said young Brockhurst with a faint note of panic. 'But I think you will agree that it was very fortuitous that Mr Tweedy, of all people, should be on the scene of the accident so quickly.'

'Very fortuitous indeed,' agreed Hammersley.

'I mean that he should be almost *on the spot* at the time of the accident.'

'Yes, it couldn't have been a better man, he certainly has a nice way with animals.'

The grey eyes blinked out innocently through National Health lenses. Mr Brockhurst gave it up and reached for his briefcase.

'I expect you have other pressing engagements,' went on Hammersley, 'I mustn't keep you, it was nice of you to call. Please don't attempt to shake me by the hand, the pain is quite intolerable. Thank heavens I'm insured with a good, reliable company, one never knows when calamity might strike.'

Brockhurst said (and to Hammersley the question seemed loaded), 'Do you intend to make a personal accident claim as well?'

Hammersley looked as if the very idea was unthinkable. 'On top of the claim for the horse? What on earth would you think! If all goes well I shan't be more than partially incapacitated for a week or two.'

Mr Brockhurst was strangely silent.

'You do get the point about not keeping the horse for more than the two days laid down in the policy, don't you?' asked Hammersley anxiously.

Mr Brockhurst had got the point, and he made for the door. He vowed he would find out all there was to find out about this smooth guy Hammersley and his horse, even if he had to make a life work of it...

(The links were taking shape faster than ever.)

'There's no particular hurry for the money,' said Hammersley as he closed the door.

He had already put in a personal accident claim with another company. He did not believe in putting all his claims in one basket. As he understood it, the whole basis of insurance was to spread the risk.

# 7

## Tenuous Threads

'I've got a job that's right up your street, Lingard,' said the commander. 'The Claims Manager of the Wyvern Insurance Company came to see me about one of his claims.'

Lingard groaned inwardly; the commander seemed to think he liked these insurance cases.

'You'll be interested in this one,' said the other, reading his thoughts, 'so don't get fussed. The Wyvern have got their doubts about a claim and are wondering if the Fraud Squad might be interested in case it happens again – if it has happened at all, that is. On the face of it, it's straightforward enough, but these underwriters have a sixth sense. The Claims Manager left a file of papers – you might like to glance through it. Smoke if you wish – perhaps you could let me have a cigarette, I've left mine in my car.' (Lingard obliged; the commander's car must be stuffed full of cigarettes by now.) 'By the way, did you find out how those gas canisters were set off in Flinder's Court?'

'Yes, we've had a lead there, sir. A woman, who lives in some dwellings in Leather Lane, came forward and told us that on the Tuesday before Bank Holiday her little boy saw two men laying what he thought was a telephone line down the middle of Flinder's Court. She thought we ought to know, because they were laying it in a sort of half-open gutter which runs back to the drain where the explosions took place.'

'Smart woman! And I suppose this gutter runs to where that canvas shelter was?'

'No, sir, it goes back to the Hatton Garden end of the court. We found a burnt-out length of fuse.'

'Why wasn't it found before?'

'It seems that the force of the explosion ripped out a length of fuse-cord near the canisters and disintegrated it, and the Explosive boys had searched for the obvious, *back* to the shelter – rather like you originally thought,' said Lingard daringly. He added a quick 'sir' to soften the glint in the commander's eye. 'Further examination revealed the remains of fuse back along the gully to Hatton Garden.'

'I see. And where does this gully end – in the road in Hatton Garden?'

'No, by an iron post at the entrance to the court.'

'So it must have been set off by someone standing by the post. Did you find the igniter-set at this point?'

'No, only a broken-off terminal jammed in the gap in the gutter. Someone had evidently tried to wrench the evidence away and the thing snapped, leaving just a terminal nut and bolt set in a fragment of black bakelite. Initials on the bakelite suggest it was an old German igniter.'

'Interesting. So the man waiting in the shelter had an accomplice at the street end of Flinder's Court. And as there was nobody else about at the time, it all points to–'

'The Diamond Exchange employee – Verdoen.'

'Or Lady Veronica Tuke.'

'Lady Veronica Tuke!' Lingard was shocked. There was a hint of frost in his voice. The very idea of the nobility being involved in anything shady rocked him to the back teeth; he imagined that that sort of thing had been rooted out at Runnymede in 1215.

'We mustn't overlook the obvious, Superintendent,' said the commander mildly, 'even if she does have a pretty face. Did you ever find out what she was doing in Hatton Garden at the time of the robbery?'

Lingard shuffled. 'We – er – did make

some inquiries at the hotel address she gave, but they said they'd had nobody of that name staying there. It was assumed the constable had got down the wrong name or the wrong hotel.'

'He would hardly have guessed a name like Lady Veronica Tuke, would he?'

'We also tried the other hotels in Dover Street, but had no luck.'

'Then we'd better check with the Somerset Constabulary. I see that she lives at a place called The Mullions at Stoke Magna. She lives alone, both her parents were killed in a car accident. We'll see what she has to say.'

The superintendent was looking thoughtful. 'Stoke Magna,' he mused. 'That's not far from where Gabbitas lives.'

'If you're thinking there's a link, Superintendent, think again. Stoke Magna and King's Barton are some fifty-odd miles apart. To link dear Lady Veronica with Lew Gabbitas would be rather like linking half the population of Brighton with a bag-snatch in London. Anyway, what have you found out about Gabbitas?'

'The report from the local police indicates that he's well-liked in King's Barton, he's a great do-gooder in an unostentatious fashion – although everyone knows he's the one who's doing it – a pillar of the church–'

'Yes, yes, but what have you found out?'

'Very little, sir. When we lost track of him in London, they discreetly put a man on his house locally. He didn't turn up for over a week, and during that time only two people visited the place. It seems he'd been unexpectedly called up to Scotland to a sick friend. I checked with his hotel and they confirmed he had received a telegram. The reception clerk remembers handing it to him when he came in about ten-thirty p.m. on that particular Friday. Gabbitas was most upset. He paid his bill and left immediately to catch the night train.'

'Who were the visitors to his house?'

'One was a very elegant young lady who had a key to the place. She turned up on Bank Holiday Monday an hour before a man arrived by car. This man didn't go into the house, he merely delivered a small packet and left. The car was owned by a car-hire firm in Exeter. It took him back to a hotel near the cathedral. And the young lady left a few minutes later in another car, a Jaguar, which went off in the opposite direction. The plates were muddy, and from where he was placed the plainclothes man failed to make out the number, so we've no means of checking who she was. A week later, Gabbitas's housekeeper – who'd been on holiday –turned up. She knew nothing of his movements except that he'd gone to London on holiday, and she had received a telegram to say he was returning later that day, which he did.'

'H'm. Not very exciting. But it seems Gabbitas has a flair for being associated with presentable young ladies. You've done nothing to frighten him off, of course?'

'Following your instructions I told the local men to be circumspect to a degree. Fortunately Gabbitas had informed them that he was leaving his house unoccupied and asked them to keep an eye on it, so the local inspector was able to call on him quite naturally to see how he enjoyed his holiday. He got the story of the sick friend in Scotland all right, but no mention of the line-up at Gray's Inn Road police station.'

The commander looked thoughtful. 'H'm. If you'd been arrested and put up, Lingard, and were innocent, would you have considered the event worthy of mention to the friendly local force?'

'I think I would, sir.'

'So would I. It seems this Gabbitas doesn't mind advertising his saintly side, like visiting the sick, but is sensitive to anything that smacks of criticism. However, have a quick glance at that claims file – I think you'll find it interesting.'

Lingard skimmed down the report and suddenly stopped. He opened his mouth to say something, changed his mind and shot back to the beginning. 'Hammersley!' he breathed at length. 'Not our old friend Charles Hammersley of Mortlake again! Oh, lor'!'

'You don't know the half of it yet, Lingard. Read on.'

Lingard read on. 'Seems a straightforward enough accident,' he commented as he scanned the first of the witnesses' statements.

'It's what happened *after* the accident that's worrying the Wyvern,' said the commander. 'And anyway, you haven't yet reached the final statement.'

Lingard thumbed through the police report, but only for one moment. 'Gabbitas!' he exploded violently. 'Now this is a coincidence!'

'You once told me you didn't believe in coincidences, Superintendent, and in this case I'm almost inclined to agree with you.'

'I certainly can't believe in this one!' grated Lingard. 'Here's Gabbitas in the vicinity of the robbery and later he vanishes to Scotland after witnessing an accident of Hammersley's that stinks to high heaven. If Hammersley is involved with Gabbitas, then Roag's Syndicate could be tied up with this diamond theft!'

'You're assuming, Lingard, that Gabbitas was tied up with it in the first place. You've got to prove *that* before you start to get one of your hunches. Besides, you're not suggesting Simon Good had anything to do with the Yellow Fire Diamonds, are you? He's only just out of jail – you went along yourself to see what sort of a reception committee he had. There was only Hammersley and an elderly gentleman. Now, this man who delivered a packet to Gabbitas's place – do we know anything about him?'

'The police report from Devonshire gives a thumbnail sketch–' The superintendent suddenly stopped aghast, his jaw working wordlessly for a couple of seconds as a starshell burst in the recesses of his brain. He said, 'Excuse me, sir, I'll go and get it,' and rushed from the room like a gale-force wind, to return waving a buff form. He cleared his throat. 'The man is described as a short, plumpish, mild-mannered gentleman, middle-aged and wearing what are said to be old-fashioned National Health spectacles. Now, sir, who could that be?'

The commander (Crime) sat up, suddenly alert, 'Hammersley!' he ejaculated. He slumped in his chair again. 'Assuming it was Hammersley who delivered the packet, I think the most you can say is that Gabbitas is tied up with Roag's. That still doesn't mean to say that he stole the Yellow Fire Diamonds, or that Roag's had anything to do with it, or that the packet contained the diamonds. After all, Gabbitas had nothing on him when you arrested him.' The commander glanced at his watch. 'I've got to be over at the Home Office in ten minutes' time.' He squinted wolfishly at the superintendent. 'I can see the way your mind if working, Lingard. You *want* Roag's Syndicate to be tied up in this robbery.'

The commander was referring to the fact that Superintendent Lingard was the sixth man present in World War II when Simon Good put forward the embryonic wisp of an idea of a post-war syndicate. Lingard, then an interpreter attached temporarily to Major Meek's unit in an action against a German strongpoint, had made it clear to Meek that he wanted no part in the scheme, that as a law-man he would do his best to bring any wrongdoer to justice – as indeed he had been successful in so doing in bringing Simon Good to book, achieving the right results from the wrong set of circumstances.

He remained silent.

The commander went on, 'Do you think Hammersley would recognise you if he came face to face with you after all these years, Lingard?'

'I wouldn't care to guess,' said Lingard slowly. 'I recognised him, of course, along with all the others.'

'You didn't recognise Dutch.'

'Dutch had a new face after being badly burned by a flame-thrower near Bremen,' said the superintendent. 'Hammersley may not remember me, I was only with the unit for a few days and I've put on a good deal of weight since then.'

'You've put on a good deal even since I've known you,' agreed the other pleasantly. 'Would you like to go and have a chat with him?'

Lingard looked grim. 'I'd love it!' he said.

'Then study that claims file and go down to Marlow. Tread warily and let him do the talking. Don't go with an *idée fixe* that he's tied up with Hatton Garden business – or that Roag's Syndicate is, for that matter. We must keep our sense of proportion, Lingard. You once told me that Simon Good wouldn't indulge in violence. In this case a man was killed and another badly shot up.'

'There must be a first in everything,' growled Lingard.

'Let us examine two basic facts, Superintendent. The Yellow Fire Diamonds were stolen on the Friday before Bank Holiday – correct?'

'Correct.'

The commander reached for his hat and made for the door. 'Simon Good was still in prison on that day. So it couldn't have been Simon Good, could it?'

Superintendent Lingard wished he had the same childlike faith as the commander...

# 8

## Sour Grapes

'Mr Hammersley?'

Charles Hammersley stopped fiddling with a flowerpot outside his greenhouse and looked up. For an elusive second he thought he recognised the man standing at the gate, but the expression on the other's face slid away like quicksilver and the disturbing – disturbing? – moment was gone. 'Yes?'

'I'm a police officer, sir, and I'm making a few inquiries.'

'Yours must be an interesting life.'

'Yes.' Superintendent Lingard displayed his card in a carefully calculated, off hand manner, just long enough to prove authority and short enough for anyone not to be able to read it. 'I hope you're quite fit after your accident?'

'My shoulder still gives me trouble,' said Hammersley easily enough, although a warning flutter went through his system. 'I think the hospital were quite puzzled by the after-effects.'

Lingard was quite prepared to believe this. 'What I wanted to ask you, sir, was whether you happened to know the address of the man who witnessed the accident. This Mr – Mr–' (Lingard appeared to consult his notebook) 'Gabbitas.'

'I think he gave it to the policeman who took his statement,' frowned Hammersley.

'Yes – unfortunately he only left the address of his hotel in London. It was his private address we wanted.'

'Oh,' nodded Hammersley blankly. A sixth sense sent out urgent warning signals. It occurred to him that if the police had found out his newly acquired cottage so easily, they should not have had so much difficulty in finding out the address of Lew Gabbitas. 'I'm afraid I don't know his private address,' he said

Lingard seemed disappointed. 'Pity. Still, never mind – just a shot in the dark. I should take it easy with that shoulder – don't do too much gardening.'

'I've got to get the use back sooner or later,' said Hammersley bravely. 'Anyway, I've had a few days' rest down in the West country.'

'Oh, yes, sir? Whereabouts?'

'Exeter.'

'A nice town. What made you choose Exeter?'

'I like Exeter.'

'A good enough reason,' smiled the superintendent.

Hammersley was looking thoughtful. The vague feeling that he had seen the police officer somewhere before persisted to the point of irritation. He had the most transient of notions that it was somewhere out of context, some other role, some other place. That precise other role, that precise other place, had almost clicked into position when he had looked up suddenly a few minutes previously. But the filmy image had dissolved and it seemed he would never recapture that finger-snapping instant...

'Something worrying you, sir?'

'I was still thinking about that address. Mr Gabbitas signed a statement for me to send to the insurance company – you might try there – although I'm pretty certain the address he gave was a hotel in Albermarle Street.'

'Thanks very much, sir. We'll find it some-how or the other. When did you last see him?'

'See him?' Hammersley's grey eyes peered out through his lenses. 'On the Friday before Bank Holiday. He was kind enough to see me home after the hospital treatment, and after writing out a statement we had a drink and watched the television news at nine-ish. Then he hurried off to catch the night train to Scotland – a friend had been taken ill. He'd received a telegram at his hotel that after-noon. In all the circumstances it was very good of him to waste so much time over me.'

'There's good in everybody,' said Lingard. 'By the way, there was another small point. I understand you obtained a carcass of a horse from a yard at Boxted.'

'That's right,' said Hammersley keenly. 'I paid for it, I've got the receipted bill.'

'I don't doubt it, sir. And that was on the *Thursday* before Bank Holiday?'

'Yes.'

'On the day before your accident in Knightsbridge?'

'That's right.'

'Would you mind telling me why you purchased it?'

'Of course I wouldn't mind, why should I?'

Hammersley took Lingard by the arm and led him to the side of the greenhouse. (It seemed to be the horse, and not Gabbitas, that the officer was interested in; the warning signals worked overtime.) He pointed up into the angle of the glass roof. 'Now tell me, what do you see ripening up there in great big bunches against the glass?'

Lingard's eyes opened wide in admiration as he saw the grapes. He was about to reply when he was distracted by a low whinnying sound which came from the other side of an adjacent four-foot wall. An intelligent-looking horse stuck its head over and almost asked for a knob of sugar. A gleam came into Lingard's eye. 'I thought Ambiguity was put down in Knightsbridge?' he remarked, all too casually.

'Yes,' said Hammersley. 'Poor Ambiguity.'

The superintendent looked over the wall at the animal. 'From the description I have, this horse could well be Ambiguity,' he said slowly.

'Yes, how right you are,' beamed Hammersley, 'and I'm glad someone else sees the resemblance. I felt the loss so much. I just *had* to get another horse as near like Ambiguity as possible. This is Fiddler – there, did you see how he pricked his ears at the sound of his name?'

Lingard had indeed noticed the fact and was bitterly disappointed. Hammersley produced a few pieces of sugar. 'Come on, Fiddler! Sugar!' With a snort of anticipation the animal immediately sidled along to him and claimed the titbit. 'Good chap!' said Hammersley. 'Off you go!' He slapped the dappled flank affectionately.

The superintendent was dispirited. 'You were showing me your grapes, sir,' he said.

'Oh, yes. Here – try some. Those I've just cut, in the basket.'

Lingard tried a couple.

'What do you think of them?'

'Delicious, sir.'

'How do you think they get so big and luscious?'

'Depends on what you feed 'em with, I suppose.'

'Precisely.' Hammersley indicated a twenty-foot plot of well-dug-over ground between the greenhouse and the wall. It was liberally larded with some sort of compost and gave off what for some inexplicable reason is called a healthy country smell. 'The roots of my vine come out from under the greenhouse into the middle of that lot,' he said. 'And do you know what the main constituent is?'

'Haven't an earthly,' said Lingard, biting on a particularly fleshy grape.

'Blood,' said Hammersley.

'Blood?' The superintendent stopped chewing.

'Yes, it's the nitrogen. Now do you see why I bought that carcass? There's a spade over there, check if you wish.'

Superintendent Lingard choked and suddenly lost his liking for grapes.

'Ever been to Hampton Court, officer? They feed the Great Vine there in exactly the same way. Dead horses. You ask them. The attendants.'

'I will, next time I'm there,' promised Lingard taking his leave.

Hammersley, with a thoughtful expression, watched him go. He was glad his invitation to the other to go ahead and check had not been taken up. But then, the officer had been altogether too casual; he had not even asked the name of the insurance company...

The superintendent was not too happy with his brief horticultural excursion; sweet grapes had suddenly turned sour. Although he was reluctant to admit it, it seemed that Hammersley, with his flowerpots and grapes, his willingness to discuss anything and give away nothing, was for once being maligned. The vague seismosonic rumblings of the Wyvern Insurance Company were merely the hypersensitive jogglings of a delicately poised Claims staff.

Two things emerged, however – Hammersley did not appear to have recognised him, and he had frankly admitted to being in Exeter. The latter could have been bland ingenuousness. But two could play at being ingenuous, and for that reason Lingard had not pressed him too much. He made a mental note to get the Devon police to check with the car-hire firm in Exeter to see what name their client had given; and to check the register of the hotel where the driver had deposited him, to see under what name he had booked in there. The commander might have ideas about the saint-like piety of Roag's Syndicate in the matter of the Yellow Fire Diamonds, but Lingard had other ideas. It only wanted Lady Veronica Tuke to confirm that her name had been taken in vain, and the link with Simon Good would gather strength. For Simon Good knew a young lady called Quenella Mansfield who had been suspected of complicity in blackmailing Jullien Fane, the General Manager of the Tyburn & New York Insurance Company, Simon Good's post-war employers. Nothing was ever proved, all that was known was that Miss Mansfield was Mr Fane's very private secretary, that she worked in the same office as Simon Good, and that when she left her bank balance seemed to go up suddenly. It could have been *she* who was in Hatton Garden, using – for some reason as yet unknown – Lady Veronica's name. Perhaps the grapes wouldn't turn out to be so sour after all... Which reasoning was a pity, for Superintendent Lingard was not normally one whose only mental exercise was jumping to conclusions.

One thing irritated him. Something Hammersley had said had stirred up a vague, jangling discord in his mind, something which now he couldn't isolate, like a nagging tooth pain which would worry him until he put his finger on the spot...

The next concrete step was to interview Lady Veronica Tuke.

# 9

## Do Be My Enemy

By special arrangement with the Somerset police, the Yard sent down a London policeman to The Mullions. It was a hot afternoon when he arrived in company with the local chief inspector who was to perform the introductions. Lady Veronica, attired in an inadequately adequate bikini, was indolently reclining on a chaise-longue on the terrace. Without moving her body or twisting her head she watched their approach across velvet lawns which had taken a hundred years to get that way. The chief inspector she recognised; the plain-clothes man she did not, although she divined he was a policeman. She made no movement as they came up close to her, other than gently to close her eyes behind ornate sun-glasses.

For a moment the two men stood in silent homage, drinking in the disturbing display of pulchritude, until the chief inspector reluctantly felt obliged to cough.

Lady Veronica stirred lazily, opened her eyes slowly as if from a deep sleep, and then sat bolt upright with a jerk, nearly (as the

London policeman put it later) falling out of her flaming bikini. 'Why, hallo!' she exclaimed. 'You gave me quite a start!' (She'd given them one, too, but they were too polite to say so.) 'What can I do for you, Inspector? Where have I parked it wrongly this time?'

The chief inspector smiled in a fatherly manner. 'It's not the car,' he said tolerantly. 'Our friend from London is making some inquiries in connection with the diamond robbery in Hatton Garden on the Friday before Bank Holiday.'

'Oh, yes?' Lady Veronica looked vague. 'I remember reading about it in the papers.'

'You remember *reading* about it?' said the man from London gently, and the inspector shot him a swift look.

'You mean when those – what were they? Austrian Crown Diamonds? – were stolen. The guard was killed, wasn't he? Yes, I read all about it – or as much as they put in the newspapers.' Lady Veronica was suddenly very much alert. 'Why? What brings you *here?*'she jerked. 'Behind the sun-glasses her eyes were now wide open in astonishment.

The plainclothes man's interest quickened. This was something which Superintendent Lingard had warned him might happen, and the situation would require careful handling. 'Well, now, madam, the position is this. A young lady waiting near the Continental Diamond Exchange in Hatton Garden saw the robbery take place, and was able to give a description of a man thought to have had a part in the incident.'

'Good for her.'

'A man of that description was picked up, but later she failed to pick him out on an identification parade. In fact, she selected a perfectly innocent man.'

'Embarrassing for all,' said Veronica, reaching for a cigarette. 'And where do I come in?' She fumbled in her handbag for a lighter, and noticed that the two men were so absorbed in watching her reactions that they both failed to come to her aid.

'The young lady gave your name, madam.'

A butane flame sprang to life but three seconds passed before she applied it to her cigarette. '*My* name?' she said, mystified. She expelled a trickle of smoke. 'Now why would she want to do that?'

'I take it then, madam, that it was not you in Hatton Garden?'

'What on earth would I be doing in Hatton Garden on the Friday before Bank Holiday?'

'That's what we hoped to find out, madam. But it seems we're wasting our time. And yours.'

'But why should anyone give *my* name?' frowned Veronica. 'After all, if this woman came forward as a police witness, she apparently had nothing to hide. Why give a wrong name?'

'It could have been because for some reason or other – spite, for example – she wanted to incriminate, say, a friend of yours.'

'A friend? I don't understand. Who, for instance?'

'I didn't say he *was* a friend – it was just a suggestion. The description she gave fitted a man we picked up in a public house near the scene of the robbery. Not a one hundred per cent fit, but near enough. A man named Gabbitas. Do you know anyone of that name, madam? Gabbitas. Lew Gabbitas?'

'No. Certainly not.'

'You're absolutely sure?'

'Of course I'm sure. You don't have to strain your memory for a name like that.'

'We only wondered, as he lives in these parts.'

'He does? Where?'

'King's Barton.'

'King's Barton! That's fifty or sixty miles away! In Devon! Gabbitas, you say? That's a curious name – is it Continental?'

'I don't really know, madam. It does sound a bit foreign.'

'You say this young woman – after giving a description of the man – later failed to identify him?'

'That is so.'

'Then you picked up the wrong man. You had to let him go?'

'We had nothing to hold him for. She picked out someone else who had a perfectly good alibi.'

'So that even if Gabbitas was a friend of mine, she didn't incriminate him after all – in fact, she did just the reverse, she put him absolutely in the clear.'

'Could be,' agreed the other, non-committally.

'Was she the only witness?'

'No, madam. There was an employee of the Diamond Exchange, but as his eyes were filled with tear gas he wouldn't commit himself at the line-up.'

'I suppose,' said Veronica thoughtfully, 'there is no question about this man Gabbitas? With a name like that he sounds just the type to be at the head of a crime organisation – a sort of master mind.'

The man from London glanced with faint amusement at the paperback thriller which rested on Lady Veronica's lap, all but obscuring the bottom half of her bikini. 'Oh, I don't think Gabbitas is anything like that, madam,' he said. 'I imagine the answer is that the C.I.D. should have picked up someone more like the man who was actually selected from the identification parade.'

'Yes – what about that man? Did you charge him?'

'No, madam, he was a policeman.' The plainclothes man appeared not to notice

Lady Veronica's throaty gurgle. 'In view of what you've already told me, the question I'm going to ask you may seem an impertinence, but I'm obliged to ask it to eliminate you entirely from our inquiries.'

'Anything to do that!'

'Well, then, do you mind telling me what you were doing on the Friday in question?'

'Yes, I do mind. Very much so. The question *is* an impertinence.'

'It's entirely up to you whether you answer it or not, madam. It would help us – and you – if you did, though. Still, never mind. If the chief inspector hasn't any other business, we'll be on our way.'

'My dear good bobby, don't get huffy! How would you like to be pestered with fatheaded questions about what were you doing a hundred miles away from the scene of the robbery?'

'We're trying to establish that you *were* a hundred miles from the scene of the robbery, madam. If you weren't in Hatton Garden at the material time, then I'm told the Yard will follow up another lead. The Diamond Exchange employee got quite a good look at the lady before he was nearly blinded.'

Lady Veronica Tuke was very still for a fraction of a second, as though her heart had missed a beat, and this did not go unobserved by the London man, who was a clever policeman for all this casual manner. Veronica said tensely, 'Do I detect a threat?'

'Dear me, no!' hasted the other. 'My last remark was linked with the other lead the Yard will follow, if you'll only confirm that it wasn't you who saw the robbery.'

'I see.' Veronica frowned thoughtfully. 'If you have any doubts, you'd better bring this man down and let him have a look at me.'

'That's very kind of you,' went on the other suavely, 'we may take advantage of your offer – although I don't think such a step will be necessary. We've already taken the liberty of showing him some quite good photographs of you from the *Tatler*, but he seems very reluctant to make up his mind. We like to have a positive identification. Of course, the clothes make considerable difference.'

Lady Veronica Tuke made up her mind. 'If you really want to know where I was, I went down to Lyme Regis for the day, but I can't prove it. At least, I'm not going to – I have to protect the honour of the gentleman who was with me!'

The chief inspector burst into life. 'So it *was* you we saw speeding along the Chard road, m'lady?'

Once again she seemed to stop breathing. (Her suspicions that her chauffeur used the car, when she was away, for little jaunts with the Austrian maid, appeared to be well-founded.) 'Oh, I'm not going to tell you which road I took, Inspector. Didn't you get my number?' she added sweetly.

'You went by too quickly,' confessed the inspector. 'We thought it was your car, though.'

'Thought it was!' Lady Veronica radiated a smile. 'It seems I get caught either way,' she said mischievously. 'Which way do you advise me to jump?'

'The choice is yours,' grinned the plain-clothes man, 'but I'd say definitely not in the direction of Hatton Garden!'

The chief inspector touched his trim moustache. 'I don't think you'll hear anything more about the speeding, ma'am,' he said gallantly. 'After all, we have no definite proof it was you.'

'Thank goodness for that!' Lady Veronica Tuke took off her sun-glasses and swung them round by the frames as she got up. 'And now perhaps you'd both like a nice, long cool drink before you go...'

The temperature of the policeman from Gray's Inn Road police station rose violently, but not because of the animal attraction of the bronzed form now stretching before him. She was just the right height, he remembered that clearly. And although she had very emphatically picked him out at the line-up on that particular

Friday, she obviously didn't recognise him now. But he had no difficulty in recognising *her*, in spite of the fact that she was wearing considerably less than on that occasion. There was no doubt at all in his mind that she was the young lady who had failed to pick out Gabbitas after giving a slightly off-beat description of him. The mistake she had made was to remove her sun-glasses. There was one thing she could not disguise. Those beautiful green eyes... She looked the sort of young miss who would do anything for kicks... And perhaps she now regretted it.

He accepted the offer of a drink, although he felt something of a cad. Nevertheless, no unbelted member of the flaming aristocracy was going to take the mickey out of him...

Superintendent Lingard received the information with mixed feelings. If it *was* Lady Veronica Tuke the Somerset police had seen on the Chard road, then she couldn't have been in Hatton Garden. And if *she* hadn't been, someone else had, and Lingard's mind jumped once again to Quenella Mansfield, friend of Simon Good. It was just a hunch, but some of Lingard's hunches paid off. It was pursuit of a hunch that had ultimately put Simon Good away for twelve months, if for the wrong reason, and the superintendent decided to chance his arm and arrange for someone to call on Miss Mansfield.

A very young-looking policeman therefore called at a house in Shepherdess Walk and took Quenella by surprise.

'Good afternoon, miss,' he smiled shyly. 'I wonder if you'd mind very much answering a few questions?'

'Depends what they are,' said Quenella cautiously. 'But please come inside.'

'Thank you, miss.' The policeman removed his helmet and stepped into the hall. He caught a brief glimpse of a man who showed his face round the kitchen door.

'I shan't be a minute – er – Mark,' called Quenella, leading the constable into a small front room. 'Now what appears to be the trouble?'

'No trouble, miss,' the other assured her. 'Just a question of trying to eliminate certain people from a line of inquiry we're making.'

'Not with the object of including me in, I hope?'

'I hope not, too, miss,' said the young man sincerely, for he was very susceptible to a pretty face. 'Would you mind telling me what your movements were on the Friday before Bank Holiday.'

Quenella looked surprised, and she thought carefully before replying. 'So far as

I can recollect I had no movements at all,' she said slowly.

'No movements, miss?'

'No. I'd been to a late party the previous night and I slept it off till about midday. The party was at the Golden Web Club in Curzon Street – you'll want to know that, of course.'

'Ah. And what did you do on Friday afternoon?'

'Nothing.'

'Nothing?' The young man looked doubtful. 'Can you prove this?'

'I don't quite know how you prove you did nothing. It's easier to prove you did something.'

'Well, was there anyone with you who could bear you out?'

'If anyone was with me I'd probably be doing something. No, I was quite alone, doing nothing, and nobody was watching me do it. And there was nobody watching me doing nothing in bed till midday. You'll have to take my word for it.'

'Of course, miss,' blushed the constable uncomfortably. 'Didn't you go out at all?'

'Not till the evening. I just pottered around in the house all the afternoon.'

'And where did you go in the evening?'

'I had a meal at a restaurant in Shepherd's Market, alone. And then came back and watched television. Alone.'

'Well, thank you very much, miss. You've been most helpful.'

'Have I been eliminated or included?'

'I wouldn't know, miss. I was only asked to come and see you. Good afternoon...'

The very young policeman was not entirely dissatisfied with his visit. She had made only one mistake, but she had made it. The man who showed his face. She had called him Mark.

The policeman, who had been in court at the 'ice-shilling' trial, remembered him as Peter. Or Simon. Peter Meek or Simon Good. But not Mark...

The young man ambled round to the Golden Web in Curzon Street and asked to see the manager. He was shown into the presence of a Mr Blake, who was able, by consulting the club records, to confirm that a Miss Quenella Mansfield had indeed been a guest at a party given by Lord Amble-thorpe in the private rooms on the Thursday evening before August Bank Holiday.

'To tell you the truth,' said Blake, 'I was rather blessing it. It went on till the early hours, and I had a very full day before me on the Friday and I had to leave early Saturday morning for Brussels. Believe it or not, I can't stand late or early hours.'

'Well, thank you very much, sir. That bit about the party confirms what the young lady told me.'

'No trouble, I hope?' asked Blake anxiously.

'Oh, no, sir. Just a question of finding out where certain people were, with the object of eliminating them from our inquiries. If it was trouble, they'd send round somebody important...'

The young officer did not know that Blake was a friend of Simon Good.

It seemed to Lingard that although hard facts groped towards Lew Gabbitas and Lady Veronica Tuke, a circumstantial web of pure gossamer was gradually weaving itself around Simon Good & Co.; loose threads were forming into meshes which, coupled with what was already known about the Syndicate, would slowly but surely entangle them. For one delirious, golden moment he dreamed of the whole Syndicate standing in the dock together...

The commander acted as a cold douche.

'Let us add it all up, Lingard,' he said. 'Lady Veronica Tuke says she wasn't in London, our policeman says she was. She implies she didn't give that description of Gabbitas, our man says she did, although she failed to pick him out of the line-up. Gabbitas had nothing on him when he was picked up, and on the face of it he's the local plaster saint doing good at every flick of his little finger. He was even doing good when he got involved with Hammersley and his accident, about which the insurance company have their suspicions – but which you yourself think are without foundation. Hammersley, however, goes all the way to Exeter to deliver a packet on behalf of Gabbitas, whilst that gentleman clears off out of the way to Scotland in response to a telegram.' (The jangling discord started to echo again in Lingard's brain.) 'Off your own bat, you chase up Quenella Mansfield, who swears she didn't leave her house on that Friday till the evening, and we can't prove otherwise. She went to a party the previous night at the Golden Web in Curzon Street. The Golden Web belongs to our old friend Blake, who sees fit to leave suddenly for Brussels on the day after the Yellow Fire Diamonds were stolen. And when your man called on Miss Mansfield, Simon Good was there, and she called him Mark instead of Simon.' The commander lit a cigarette. 'Doesn't get us very far, does it?' he said, between puffs.

A bell suddenly rang loud and clear in Lingard's head. 'Got it!' he said triumphantly. 'That telegram! I knew there was a discrepancy! The hotel clerk said he handed it to Gabbitas when he came in at ten-thirty p.m., and yet Hammersley told me Gabbitas had received it in the afternoon –

anyway, he mentioned it to Hammersley *before* he had received it! Now how could he have done that?'

'He couldn't have – not unless he sent it to himself and was already aware of the contents,' said the commander mildly. 'It would almost seem that Gabbitas was using Hammersley.'

'Or that they're in it together and Hammersley mis-cued when he was chatting to me in that innocent way of his.' Lingard scratched his head irritably. 'There's something very mysterious going on here and I'll lay a hundred pounds to a penny that Simon Good's behind it!' he almost snarled.

'The trouble with you, Lingard, is that you've got a "thing" about Simon Good – it's almost an obsession. You'd be disappointed if he wasn't to blame. Rather like what Blake had in mind.'

'Blake?' Lingard jumped at the name.

'Not your old Army acquaintance. I mean William Blake – the poet chap. He wrote "Thy friendship oft has made my heart to ache: Do be my enemy – for friendship's sake..."'

Lingard's rosy dream of clapping Roag's Syndicate *en bloc* in the dock gradually faded, as most dreams do; the life-germ withered and died and the empty husk skittered away on the winds of change. For it was at this stage that Simon Good & Co. became tied up with Mr Justice Meddlisome and Toledano, and Simon Good's intentions were for once honourable, the Syndicate were for a while untouchable ... although Blake, it will be recollected, received a term of restraint from Judge Knott for trying to do Mr Meddlisome a good turn.

When Simon Good had been released from Wormwood Scrubs, Hammersley had seen fit not to burden him with details of his horse-riding activities, and their rather more pressing adventures in Portugal had pushed the matter from his mind. There was to come a moment, however, when he felt urgently impelled to place the facts before Simon. That moment arrived a short while before Blake was due to come out of jail, and it was not very long after Hammersley received his first letter from Lew Gabbitas...

# 10

## Million Pound Objective

The letter arrived one winter's morning and contained a pressing invitation from Gabbitas for Hammersley to spend a few days in Devonshire. Hammersley always reacted favourably to spending a few days anywhere at anyone else's expense, and whilst he thought it strange that Mr Gabbitas had forgotten to put his address at the top of the letter, he was nevertheless at St David's Station, Exeter, on time, looking out for the dark blue Bentley which had been laid on for his benefit.

He wondered if he would be going anywhere near Four Chimneys, but when the car left Exeter by a different route and swung off into strange country he decided that he couldn't be.

It was very dark when he arrived at Four Chimneys.

It was a very different Lew Gabbitas who welcomed him. There was no trace of the jagged edginess by which Hammersley remembered him, he was relaxed, genial, a would-be English gentleman.

'My dear Hammersley, so nice of you to come!'

'Nice of you to invite me,' responded Hammersley. 'But I had no idea Four Chimney's belonged to you.'

Gabbitas made an eloquent bow. 'My very own,' he said whimsically. 'Do come in, you must be tired. First, your room and a wash, and then a meal fit for a king. A leisurely evening by the fire, and we'll get down to business to-morrow morning.' (Hammersley's red corpuscles turned to leucocytes.) 'I have a little proposition to make. I want you to help me to reach an objective so that I can marry the woman I love.'

'I shall be only too delighted,' agreed Hammersley politely. 'And what is your objective?'

'A million pounds sterling,' said Lew Gabbitas...

Gabbitas was disinclined at this juncture to speak further of his startling objective, and by the end of the evening Hammersley wondered if his ears had deceived him.

The following morning was bright and cold. After a sizzling hot breakfast of bacon, eggs and mushrooms, Gabbitas suggested a cross-country gallop. 'I've got a couple of hacks,' he said, 'and the going's not too hard after the rain.'

Hammersley said he would be delighted, although privately he would have preferred to sit by the fire with a newspaper.

'You're quite sure your shoulder won't give you any trouble?' inquired Lew solicitously, although Hammersley wondered if there was a hint of amusement in his voice.

'I'm quite fit now, thank you,' he said.

'Good. You had a very nasty fall. It was most kind of you, in the circumstances, to have acted as my courier with that little packet. At the time, it was very important to me – I can't thank you enough. We'll have our exercise and then I'll tell you about my million pound objective.'

'It's difficult to make so much money honestly,' said Hammersley, who had tried both ways and failed.

'I didn't say anything about the way in which it had to be made,' said Lew Gabbitas.

They were soon cantering along well-worn rides in the wooded country at the rear of Four Chimneys.

'Sit down by the fire and relax,' said Mr Gabbitas afterwards. 'Restlessness is the curse of the age. Everyone is unsettled nowadays, nobody is content with what they've got – they must have something new.'

Hammersley discreetly eyed the mellow

opulence of the room. 'You're not doing so badly yourself,' he commented candidly.

Gabbitas shrugged off the simple comforts that only wealth could procure. 'I get by,' he agreed. 'I like a place to be homely. You must excuse the deficiencies.'

Hammersley gulped. 'I, too, am a man of ordinary tastes,' he acknowledged. He took a sip of his brandy. The bottle said Napoleon, and although it didn't say which one, it was nevertheless very good.

'Of course,' went on Mr Gabbitas, 'even living on this modest scale costs money.'

'That is very true,' nodded Hammersley comfortably.

'And I personally have to find the cash to provide for things. I have no union to look after my interests, no shop steward to ensure *I* get a tea-break.'

Mr Hammersley could not imagine that Lew Gabbitas would ever be in need of a tea-break, but he got the point. He took another sip. 'Poverty is a great thing to be without,' he said judiciously.

Mr Gabbitas lit an expensive cigar and his eyes slid back into the past. He said with sudden intensity, 'I've known poverty, Hammersley – every miserable, scrimping, petty, stinking aspect of it imaginable. I made up my mind at a very early age to avoid it at all costs.'

Hammersley was startled at the other's

unexpected venom. He said gently, 'At all costs?'

Gabbitas looked along the length of his cigar at him. 'That's a good question,' he said. He glanced out of the window and his eye was distracted by a figure in clerical garb coming up the gravel drive. 'Ah, the worthy vicar! An earnest young man who is continually trying to save me from my wealth. I wonder what it can be this time?'

If he felt any irritation he concealed it effectively from the churchman. His welcome was good-humoured and apparently sincere. 'Well, Vicar,' he said, as he brought the Reverend Theodosius Todd into the room, 'it's good to see you looking so fit again. This is my friend, Mr Hammersley. Will you have a small sherry?'

'Thank you, no,' smiled Mr Todd. At short range it was evident that the young man possessed a tough physique which belied his gentle calling. 'At least, we'll shelve the idea for the moment – you may regret having offered it. I'm on the cadge again.'

Mr Gabbitas poured a small sherry. 'I'll take a chance,' he smiled. 'Now let me see. I've paid for the repairs to the organ loft. I've given you a donation for the new church hall. I've contributed to the Un-married Mothers – if you see what I mean. I've sent my annual subscription to the Boys' Club, the Children's Holiday Fund and the Pensioners' Outing Fund...' He suddenly looked confused and unhappy. 'Oh dear, oh dear!' he said. 'Please forgive me! I didn't mean to sound pretentious, it seems you'll have to save me from myself, after all, Mr Todd!'

'I'm sure you were merely treating the matter humorously,' said the vicar smoothly. 'And I can assure Mr Hammersley that all your kindnesses are done without ostentation. You are entitled to rebel sooner or later at my constant begging calls in the name of charity.'

Concern suddenly replaced the look of discomfort on Gabbitas's face. 'My dear Vicar! How remiss of me! Your hands – are they healing?'

The Reverend Mr Todd looked down at his hands with embarrassment. The right one was bandaged. The left one was covered with a cotton glove. He waved the latter airily. 'The burns on this one have practically healed. And this' (he held out the bandaged one) 'is not so good. I have to go in for another skin graft next week.'

'Mr Todd is our local hero,' explained Lew.

'Oh, come!' growled young Todd, growing pink about the cheeks. 'The hero was the man who died.'

Lew Gabbitas drew in his breath sharply, and his reaction did not go unnoticed by

Hammersley's speculative eye. 'What happened?' asked Hammersley.

'The furniture depository over at East Lampton was gutted by fire about a fortnight ago. It is said to have started in the antique renovation department, although local opinion favours a more general reason – boys throwing fireworks. Much valuable stuff from Martock Chase – our local stately home – was in for renovation prior to opening to the public next season. It was all lost. What was infinitely worse, a fireman lost his life, and an elderly nightwatchman was trapped and severely burned. He too would have perished if it hadn't been for Mr Todd plunging into the inferno.'

'I happened to be passing, that was all,' growled the young man, endeavouring to dismiss the subject. 'Anyone would have done it.'

'There were three hundred people watching who didn't,' grunted Gabbitas.

'The fireman tried but gave his life,' said the other quietly.

'It was in his line of duty,' pointed out Gabbitas.

'I, too, am charged to save.'

'Souls.'

'Bodies and souls.'

'Have it your own way, only don't try too hard in my direction – I should hate to think St Anselm's had a frustrated vicar.'

'The tougher the case the greater the sense of achievement when victory is attained,' smiled the Reverend Mr Todd. 'However, I haven't come to save your soul, I've come with the more practical object of saving someone else's body.'

Lew Gabbitas slanted an eyebrow. 'Whose?'

'Mrs Bowling's.'

'By all means let us do that – but who is Mrs Bowling?'

'The widow of Jack Bowling – the fireman who died.'

Once again Hammersley was conscious of an inward shrinking in the manner of Mr Gabbitas. The East Lampton fire was an image Lew Gabbitas preferred to reject.

'She is left with three small children,' went on the vicar, 'to say nothing of having to meet various hire purchase payments in respect of furniture. I have started a fund to alleviate the position, and I felt sure you wouldn't wish to be left out.'

'I'm glad you called,' said Mr Gabbitas, feeling for his cheque-book. 'How much is outstanding for the furniture?'

'Er – rather a lot, I'm afraid.'

'How much?'

'Some seventy-three pounds.'

'Seventy-three pounds! Quite a lot!'

'Any contribution, however small, would be welcome.'

While Gabbitas wrote, Hammersley slipped a treasury note into the vicar's left hand.

'That is most kind of you, sir, most kind,' said Mr Todd gratefully, jotting down with difficulty the amount in his notebook. 'This is really a local affair, but I'm not going to refuse!'

Lew Gabbitas flapped his cheque about in the air to dry it. Folding it in half, he pressed it into the vicar's palm. 'Please don't find any more worthy causes yet awhile or you'll lose one of your flock,' he said.

'I shan't,' promised the Reverend Theodosius Todd. 'You've both been most charitable.' (He glanced at the cheque as he spoke, and folded it again.) 'I can't think you enough–' He stopped suddenly and fumblingly tore at the cheque. His eyes goggled with disbelief. 'My dear Mr Gabbitas!' he stuttered. 'You – you can't do this!'

'I have done it.'

'But this is for one hundred pounds!'

'I can afford it.'

'Nobody can afford one hundred pounds!'

'Surely that is the essence of giving? Or have I missed the point of your sermons?'

'But – but–' Mr Todd was speechless.

'I make one condition. I want to meet the whole of the furniture bill out of that money – no publicity, of course! You know I am interested in antiques, and I have a feeling that if Mrs Bowling has to pay for her furniture out of her own meagre resources it *will* be antique by the time it is hers. I understand the nightwatchman has no relatives, so please use the balance to ease his stay in hospital – I gather the poor man is not likely to live.'

Something about Lew Gabbitas didn't quite jell. Hammersley couldn't put his finger on it, but there was *something*.

'I must not detain you any longer,' said young Todd. 'Shall I see you in church on Sunday?'

'If you promise not to cut your sermon short,' declared Mr Gabbitas. 'I enjoy a good sermon. If it's not good, I still enjoy a good rest.'

'Most people complain I make them too long,' said the vicar regretfully. 'Everyone seems to be waiting for the commercials so that they can get up and make a coffee. Once again, thank you, Mr Gabbitas, thank you, Mr Hammersley–'

'I hope my contribution wasn't too much of a widow's mite,' said Hammersley apologetically.

'I shouldn't have embarrassed you by revealing the extent of Mr Gabbitas's generosity. I was taken off my guard. I must keep my wick trimmed.'

'A lot of fires are caused by faulty oil-heaters,' agreed Hammersley, a little out of his depth.

'Mr Todd was referring to the wise and foolish virgins,' said Gabbitas gently.

'Oh.' The brandy was insidiously strong, and this talk of oil-heaters and virgins rather confused Hammersley. It seemed to him that the vicar, estimable young man that he might be, was slightly off-beat.

Gabbitas escorted Todd to the door and watched him stride off down the drive with renewed purpose. There was a thoughtful look in his eye when he rejoined Hammersley a moment later. He stood at the window until the vicar was out of sight then turning, canted his cigar at the bottle. 'Another?' he suggested benevolently.

A warning signal ticked over to red in Hammersley's brain, a vague queasiness fluttered through his being like a dead leaf in a breeze. He was aware that his host had not invited him to Four Chimneys for the sheer joy of his company, and he thought it desirable to shake off the slight woolliness that was creeping over him. 'Thank you, no,' he beamed brightly. 'Never spoil a good thing by excess.'

Gabbitas shrugged and said surprisingly, 'Will you excuse me? I have a sudden urge to finish a painting.'

A ghostly hand put a fistful of ice-chippings on Hammersley's neck. 'My dear sir! An Englishman's home!– You're an artist?'

'I was once.' A jagged edge broke the surface.

'I shall be quite happy here with the newspaper,' said Hammersley. Then, 'A picture you were working on when I arrived yesterday?'

'I haven't touched it for a fortnight. A few more strokes should complete it.'

Hammersley did his best to conceal his surprise. There seemed to be a certain lack of balance when one's host suddenly asked to be excused so that he could add the finishing touches to a picture he hadn't touched for a fortnight. But then, all artists were crazy. Perhaps Mr Gabbitas was crazy.

Gabbitas examined the ash on the remains of his cigar. 'Are you interested in art?'

'I know what I like,' said Hammersley cautiously.

'Then see if you like my little gallery-cum-studio.'

Gabbitas led the way through the house. They ascended a dark oak stairway redolent of another age and passed through a door at the end of a short gallery. 'My studio,' said Lew with a flourish. 'The nerve centre, as it were. Where nerves are soothed, where nerves are made.'

Hammersley blinked at the sudden transition from an era of periwigs and linkboys to one of ultra-modern streamlining. The room was long and low and lit by concealed lighting. The floor was covered with broad-loom carpeting. At the far end was an easel, bench and other paraphernalia, and the window was one entire sheet of glass to catch the north light. The walls on either hand were filled with discreetly-lighted oils. There was an air of peace and quiet.

'My dear sir,' exclaimed Hammersley, 'this is wonderful!'

'You like it? I'm so glad! Such compatibility should make our future association so much easier. Understanding, or lack of it, is at the root of most problems. We are going to get on famously together as partners.'

The temperature of the room dropped. A little trickle of ice-water slithered down between Hammersley's shoulder-blades. 'Are all these paintings your own work?' he asked.

Gabbitas beamed. 'You flatter me! My work is on the right; the paintings on the other wall are – um – acquisitions.'

Acquisitions! Hammersley had read all about wealthy collectors who 'acquired' rare works and were not too fussy in the way in which they acquired them. Polishing his spectacles he approached the right-hand wall. 'I can see examples of acquisitions in any art gallery,' he said. 'I am far more interested in what you can do.'

Lew's ego zoomed up into outer space.

'Examine them at your leisure, please do. I'll get on whilst the urge to paint is still with me.'

'First may I see what it is you're working on?' pleaded Hammersley.

'Of course!' Gabbitas led him to the easel and flung aside a cover. For a moment Hammersley stood and drank in the picture in frank admiration. It was a wintry scene of London's river, all deep blues and greys and black. The foreground was occupied by H.M.S. *Discovery,* dark and sombre, and whilst the shrouds were painted in with delicate precision the long vista down river faded into an indeterminate, smudgy haze. In the top right-hand corner the leafless skeletal branches of a plane tree hung down in stark reality, the little bobbles of seed hanging like balls on a Christmas tree.

'Superb!' breathed Hammersley. 'But surely it's finished? To me it's the perfect capturing of a mood.' There was a lupine expression on Lew's face which disturbed him.

'Don't you think it lacks something?'

Hammersley stood back and squinted through his spectacles. 'Not that I can see – or not see.'

'Colour?'

'Possibly colour, but certainly not tone. There's never much colour in the bleakness of winter.'

'Ah! You have it! Never *much* colour. This picture needs a silver lining, a small break in the sky to relieve that heavy pall of haze over the river. Something to show there's always hope.'

'H'm! I appreciate the fine sentiment but it's not necessarily life. If you add to it you'll probably spoil the whole effect.' Hammersley suddenly stopped in confusion. 'I beg your pardon – who am I to offer criticism?'

'I prefer criticism to sycophantic praise irrespective of merit.'

'Then all I can say is that I like it as it stands. I'd buy it any day. Do you sell your pictures?'

Gabbitas was shocked. 'Sell them! My dear Hammersley, this is a hobby, not a means of livelihood. There's too much of me in every picture. Who would sell his soul?'

'Too many people, nowadays,' frowned Hammersley.

'Perhaps you're right,' said Gabbitas. There was a remote sadness in his voice which made the other look over his spectacles at him. 'I sold my soul once,' said Lew. 'A long time ago, during the war. I prostituted my talents and made a small fortune. Afterwards I vowed that I would only use my artistic skill for personal relaxation.'

Hammersley felt uncomfortable. Affecting not to notice the jangling tautness in the other, he leaned forward to within several inches of the painting and adjusted his spectacles. 'Surely, Mr Gabbitas, your original intention was that this picture was complete?'

Lew looked at him sharply. 'What makes you think that?'

'There's a date in the bottom left-hand corner. Surely artists don't date their works until they are finished?'

'That is the date I started.'

'Oh. Isn't that unusual?'

'You will notice the picture at present bears no signature,' went on Lew. 'On some of my works I put *two* dates – one denoting the start, the other the completion. If you examine the examples on this wall you will find two dates on most of them. You will have to look closely at some, but generally speaking the dates will be woven in somewhere.'

'So that if there's only one date the picture isn't finished?'

Gabbitas stared out through the window for a moment. 'That could well be the position,' he said slowly, 'but not necessarily so. If the signature is there, the work is finished.' He turned abruptly. 'And now, if you will permit me' He stripped off his jacket and donned an artist's smock. Selecting a fitch, he set to work with a fiery intensity, translating to the canvas whatever it was that was moving him.

Hammersley moved away discreetly and passed along the line of pictures, examining each one with care. There were seventeen in all, of varying sizes, and true enough the majority bore two dates and a signature. In most cases the second date was difficult to detect, the numbers being cunningly threaded into the general texture of the picture. At first glance there was no second date; and then suddenly it leapt into being, rather like those clever advertisements in shop windows which continually alternate as one walks by.

Gabbitas had a penchant for river scenes – desolate mudflats, dark, sinister barges, brooding warehouses, swirling fog-wraiths and heavy, lowering skies. In Hammersley's humble opinion the paintings were of exceptional skill. And although he found in them tranquillity he was in some way curiously disturbed by them.

Whilst Gabbitas was lost in a world of his own, Hammersley examined and re-examined the canvases, trying to analyse why they had such a powerful effect on him. There was definitely something *odd* about them, something which chilled him. He realised that this said much for the skill of his host, for after all the pictures were only inanimate pigments on a taut flaxen background.

Gabbitas worked obliviously for nearly an hour and Hammersley did not interrupt him. He went over and looked at the valuable collection of modern paintings on the other wall. Up to a point he found them intriguing, but he was no great lover of angular faces with one eye and three ears, or of disproportionate females lifting up the corners of the sea to reveal the harrowing details of disillusionment. He found himself drawn back to the works of Lew Gabbitas as if they possessed some special powers.

One canvas in particular puzzled him considerably. It took pride of place in the centre of the wall. It was square, smallish, and consisted of a background of draped velvet. There was the outline of a necklace in foundation paint. But the gems had not yet been painted in. There was only one date. And there was no signature...

'What do you think of them now that you've really seen them?' asked Gabbitas suddenly.

Hammersley said slowly, 'I think they're exceptionally clever. If you'll permit the implied criticism, they're photographic and real, but I prefer them that way to the multi-eared Cyclops over there.'

Gabbitas preened himself. 'My dear Hammersley, you're too generous!'

'I notice one thing about them,' said Hammersley.

The highlights changed in Lew's eye. 'Oh?'

'They aren't in chronological order.'

This time there was a glint of – relief? Hammersley wondered just what it was the paintings might tell him if only his powers of deduction were sharp enough. That fleeting easing of tension conveyed to his very shrewd brain that his host had been momentarily afraid that a dark secret had been uncovered. But Gabbitas was poised enough when he spoke.

'You're altogether too flattering, Hammersley. Only the works of the great are arranged chronologically, and then mostly in catalogues and biographies. These efforts of mine have been arranged one against the other to show them off to best advantage. One must strive for artistic effect.'

'There's another thing I've noticed.'

Gabbitas tensed. A tiny pulse hammered in his jaw. He seemed about to spring. 'Oh?'

'Something very obvious. You have a great love of the Thames.'

Once again relief flickered in the deep eyes; the feline poise evaporated. 'I get much pleasure out of the sense of timelessness that water induces, especially out of that quiescent period between ebb and flow when all is at peace. And having found a subject at which I am good – I say that in all modesty – then why not capture another mood of that same subject if it gives me pleasure?'

'Van Gogh did much the same thing,' agreed Hammersley. 'He found a subject which sold well and worked a number of pictures of the same subject until it no longer sold.'

'Hammersley, I wish you wouldn't compare my efforts with those of genius – it's most embarrassing.' Gabbitas grinned boyishly. 'I like it!'

'Well, there is a difference – van Gogh was actuated by need. Painting with you is purely a hobby to relieve the tension of your work, whatever that might be.'

Gabbitas was not to be drawn. He said, 'You, too, must have your hobbies.'

'I have, indeed,' declared Hammersley.

'You are, if I remember rightly, a "factor"?'

'That is so.'

'Then I would say that in your case your occupation is purely to relieve the tension of your hobbies. An inversion.'

Hammersley's heart stood still. The warmth of the room was negligible. An amoeba of alarm wriggled up his spine and left an ice-cold trail of jelly. 'Just what do you mean by that?' he asked in a barely audible voice.

Gabbitas regarded him benignly. 'Life is a battle of wits, Hammersley. I, like you, don't care for poverty, but if one is to avoid it, it follows that one must have money. The problem is how to get enough money.' He lit a cigarette. 'I need a man of your calibre.'

'My calibre?' gulped Hammersley.

'Yes. I was very much impressed by the way in which you dislocated your right shoulder. I said to myself, now here is a man of sheer genius.'

'It – it was very painful!' stammered Hammersley.

'Yes, yes, of course!' agreed Lew with a show of sympathy. 'Rather like those percussion fractures one reads about. You know, where one stubs a toe and doesn't break the toe but, by percussion, breaks a kneecap instead.'

'I don't see the parallel.'

'No? Then let me put it this way. You fell off your horse and dealt your left shoulder a severe blow. Curiously enough, by the time you reached hospital you had dislocated your right shoulder. Come now, it must have been by percussion.'

'You vouched for the accident in your signed statement,' said Hammersley quickly. 'You declared it was my right shoulder.'

'I was too much of a gentleman to declare otherwise,' said Lew, showing his teeth. 'I rather admired your courage.'

'I said before, it was painful.'

'I mean your courage in making a false claim.'

Hammersley's Adam's apple refused to function properly. 'It was backed up by

134

medical evidence,' he gulped.

'Ah, yes. Now I wonder what sort of evidence backed up your claim in respect of the horse? It would be most interesting to hazard a guess.'

'Idle speculation will get us nowhere. It's all dead wood now.'

'Unfortunately dead wood, or what we think is dead wood, has a habit of sprouting again at inconvenient moments. One never knows when it is coming to life again. For example, out of all the people who watched you that evening in Knightsbridge, I am probably the only person who remembers that you wrote that telegram with your *right* hand. Do you see what I mean?'

Hammersley saw it only too clearly.

'Now,' went on Lew, 'you are a factor. Would you accept another commission from me?'

'Have I any option?'

'No.'

'I accept. What is it?'

'Do you know Thielt?'

Hammersley looked doubtful. 'The place in Belgium? Where Rommel had an H.Q. when he was put in charge of the West Wall?'

'That's it. I want you to go there. I will meet your first-class expenses and pay you a handsome commission.'

Hammersley was always content to enjoy the best of everything. 'What are the snags?'

'Snags? My dear sir! Do you imagine there'll be any snags?'

'Yes. I'm extra-sensorily perceptive. What do I do?'

'You take a letter to Thielt. You hand it to a man in a café in Tramstraat. He will give you another letter to bring back to me.'

'What's illegal about that?'

'Illegal? My dear Hammersley, why on earth should I want you to do anything illegal?'

'It's my turn to say that that's a good question. Suppose you tell me?'

'All you have to do is to act as my courier. You go to Rijwel's café-restaurant in Tramstraat and make yourself known in a manner that I will describe. You will deliver the letter and receive another in return. You will spend the night in a comfortable little hotel in the market square and will return to England the following day. It's as simple as that.'

'Why not just post the letter – that's even simpler. And cheaper.'

'I run a personal service, cheapness doesn't come into it. After one or two trips you may have to bring back a small parcel. Do you know anyone in Belgium?'

Hammersley thought of Blake's place in the Rue du Dépôt in Brussels. He recalled his meeting there the previous year with the other members of Roag's Syndicate. He remembered Sergeant Blake's phlegmatic calm under blistering fire in World War II; he could still hear his searing tongue when things had gone wrong. He recollected Blake's ability to tackles safes, especially Lumm's safes, for Blake had worked at Lumm's before it was taken over by Rempert's Safes. And he remembered Blake's simple post-war passion for providing sandwich lunches for the masses, a passion which had now developed into a string of high-class restaurants, a club – the Golden Web in Curzon Street, and a hotel – the Golden Fleece, in Brussels. Every one of Blake's places was the Golden-something-or-other, like the Golden Porcupine or the Golden Handshake. Unfortunately Blake was now languishing in Parkwood Jail for his part in trying to help Mr Justice Meddlisome in the Toledano affair. Hammersley remembered all these things. 'No,' he said briefly.

'Good. Do you know anyone in Amsterdam?'

'Amsterdam?' Hammersley thought of Rip Strookman with his Pyx Travel Agency in the thoroughfare known as Rokin. Strookman had been a member of the PIAT team in that fearful holocaust at Hondschouwen, when Major Peter Meek had walked out to certain death smoking his pipe and blazing away with a Bren at the hip position, only to

vanish in a landscape which suddenly mush-
roomed violently. Before the war, Rip, of
partly Dutch extraction, had been through
the diamond trade in Hatton Garden,
London, and Tolstraat, Amsterdam; since
the war he had built up a successful travel
agency, and his interest in diamonds was
now what he chose to call 'academic'. Interpol had other ideas. 'No,' said Hammersley.
'Why?'

'You may have to go to Amsterdam as
well.'

'Oh. It seems I'll be travelling about quite
a bit. Is it essential that I shouldn't know
anyone anywhere?'

'You won't be distracted from the job in
hand.'

'I see. And when do I start?'

'As soon as possible. I'm anxious to
resume my special courier service with the
Continent. My last courier let me down. He
read about that diamond robbery in Hatton
Garden when the Yellow Fire Diamonds
were stolen – on the day of your accident, if
I remember rightly – and one would almost
imagine he thought I had something to do
with it!'

'Whoever did that job won't get away with
it.'

Black frost formed in the depths of Lew's
eyes. 'He won't? He *has*!'

'He thinks he has. But he won't. When a

policeman gets killed the whole force rises up in righteous anger. They'll get him in the end.'

'They haven't been very successful so far. He seems to have got clear away.'

'Could be a "her",' said Hammersley. 'In all that smoke and gas I don't suppose anyone knew precisely what happened. Incidentally, a quarter of a million pounds' worth of diamonds would go a long way towards your million-pound objective – whatever that might be.'

Warmth crept back into Lew Gabbitas. He said, 'Have you ever been in love?'

Hammersley's head jerked round in surprise. 'I've – um – had my moments,' he said modestly. 'Trouble is, I've always been regarded as a sort of kind uncle, no more than that.' The grey eyes twinkled through the thick lenses. There was no hint of regret in his voice. 'Why?'

'Being in love costs money, too,' growled Lew, and it seemed to Hammersley that a veil was being torn aside.

'I wouldn't have said so – basically,' he said gently. 'I've read in books that quite a lot of poor people fall in love.'

'Needs are no longer basic,' said the other. There was a splinter of bitterness in his voice.

'So because you're in love you need even more money? To the extent of a million pounds?' There was a humorous slant in Hammersley's tone.

'To the extent of a million pounds,' responded Gabbitas soberly.

Hammersley was astonished. Even Quenella Mansfield, charming as she was, mercenary as she might be, wouldn't insist on such a dowry. She would jump at Simon for half a million. 'How far have you got to go?'

Not much farther if things work out. I have – earned – a considerable amount on the Continent, both in cash and kind – my target doesn't necessarily have to be in actual cash, but the sterling equivalent. With your help I hope to achieve my object. You'll find me not ungenerous. Unfortunately I lost a great friend in a disastrous fire at Ghent.'

'I'm sorry to hear that. What was his line of country?'

'He was a claims adjuster.'

'What was he doing at the actual fire?'

'Adjusting.'

'The loss?

'No, the fire.'

'Oh.' Hammersley digested this. 'I hope you don't expect me to – er – adjust any fires,' he remarked.

'Of course not, it's a skilled job.'

'Every man to his trade,' agreed Hammersley, beginning to wish he had never come to Four Chimneys. 'And why are you telling me all this?'

'In for a penny, in for a pound,' shrugged Lew, and Hammersley liked him less every moment. 'There's nothing you can do about it, anyway. I've found out a lot about you, my friend.'

'It might pay me to get out even now and take the consequences.'

'On the other hand it might not. I'm utterly ruthless.'

'I can't believe that, Mr Gabbitas,' said Hammersley faintly.

'Don't underestimate me,' pleaded Lew, glancing critically at his fingernails. 'A number of people have done so to their everlasting regret. And I mean everlasting. But let us turn to more positive things. I find the present conversation distressing.'

Hammersley agreed. 'But what am I supposed to *do,* apart from carrying letters like a district messenger-boy.'

'Nothing. And when it's all over you'll be wondering what you were worrying about. Incidentally, it occurred to me – bearing in mind your own little insurance swindles – that either you're very confident and clever, or else you've got someone working with you on the inside. Do you in fact know anyone in insurance?'

'I might,' said Hammersley cautiously. 'Why?'

'Because I want some special cover arranged. I would like any friend of yours to get the commission.'

'I could perhaps put you in touch with someone.'

'Thank you. By the way, have you any dependants?'

Hammersley considered the point. 'Now that's a curious question,' he remarked. 'Why do you want to know?'

'If anything goes wrong I always look after the dependents.'

'How very comforting – although I can't say you've made me the happiest man in the world. Is all this crime-and-goodwill merely to provide off-beats kicks for your mixed-up lady-love?'

'Not entirely; the accidents that occur from time to time are purely incidental. She gets all the kicks she wants from the gradual attainment of the million-pound objective.'

'Her requirements are very modest,' said Hammersley sardonically. 'She must be very fond of you.'

The door suddenly swung open and in burst a young lady in tight sweater and calf-length casuals. She stopped short when she saw Hammersley and turned apologetically to Lew. In a heart-stopping voice of liquid gold she said, 'I'm sorry, darling, I didn't know you had a visitor.'

'That's all right, my dear,' fussed Lew.

'Come and meet Mr Hammersley. Hammersley, this is Veronica. Lady Veronica Tuke'

Hammersley's mind back-somersaulted violently to the day he delivered the packet. 'I think we've met before,' he said.

There was a telephone in his bedroom and that night before he retired he made a call to Richmond and asked Simon Good if he was interested in earning a commission. Simon said possibly, and Hammersley said he would give him further information at a later date.

Lew Gabbitas listened on an extension and took a note of the name and number.

# 11

## Blank Astonishment

It was cold and damp and dark when Hammersley arrived at Thielt after a hectic day's travel, which included a brief stop at Mortlake to pick up his passport and a few other odds and ends. So far as he could tell, from the moment Gabbitas had left him at Victoria after handing him a letter sealed with red sealing wax, he had not been subjected to surveillance.

He peered round the ill-lit station yard with quickening interest, recalling the days of long ago when he had marched in full battle-order with the rest of the regiment. Bags of swank, the C.O. had said; the populace were being liberated, not watching a sanguinary sick-parade.

He made his way along the cobbled road and turned right into Tramstraat. The streets were narrower, the houses smaller than he remembered them. Time made places smaller and only memories larger.

There was Kaiser Bill's one-time H.Q. in World War I, and almost opposite, Rommel's West Wall H.Q. in World War II; and there, on the corner, was Rijwel's café-restaurant. With a sudden flood of memory he realised it was the same little *bistro* where twenty years previously the troops used to absorb the barley beer which had such a salutary effect on the kidneys.

With a feeling near to emotion he pushed open the glass door and took stock of the place. There was the same old Continental stove sticking out into the room, with the foot rest and brass rail; the same old chromium and glitter of the bar; the same old smell of cigar smoke and coffee; the same old Russian billiards and *tabac* advertisements; the same old half-room at the rear with one step up, where Madame's husband did haircutting. The same old every-thing, except the name and Madame. It was a long way to come in time and motion for a cup of coffee.

There were a number of people warming themselves round the stove. Hammersley coughed his way through the haze of cigar smoke and made for the gaudy bar.

Madame eyed him shrewdly. *''Soir, m'sieur.* M'sieur travels?'

'Indeed Madame.' Hammersley mustered his French. *'D'Angleterre.'*

'From England! Then let us talk in Eng-lish. When I was a young lady the Tommies helped me with some of the idiomatic phrases.'

Hammersley shuddered and hoped she had forgotten most of them. Mother tongue taught by any unit of soldiery anywhere inevitably led to embarrassing moments.

'You will have something warm, m'sieur. A *café filtré* with a little something in it, perhaps?'

'I am entirely in your hands, Madame,' said Hammersley gallantly.

'Then sit by the stove and I will join you in a moment. My seat is the one in the corner – nobody sits there but me.'

'It was a place of honour even before your time, Madame,' smiled Hammersley. 'I remember it well.'

Madame's *coiffure* bobbed excitedly.

'M'sieur has been here before? I look forward to reminiscing,' she said, getting busy with the coffee.

Hammersley made his way to a vacant place next to the corner seat. His affable nod to the customers already leaning on the rail round the stove was met with blank stares of appraisal, and he was glad when Madame rejoined him with his coffee. Together they talked of the dark days, and Madame rippled with animated amusement at some of Hammersley's anecdotes.

'I remember the days,' said Hammersley, 'when the roads to Thielt were stripped of trees by the Germans to provide anti-invasion posts in the foreshore of the West Wall.' He warmed his hands. 'Many of the posts never reached the West Wall – some even went to feed this selfsame stove.'

'That is the truth,' she agreed. 'I remember it well, although I was quite small at the time.' She said suddenly, 'Is m'sieur staying in Thielt?'

'Only tonight,' replied Hammersley. 'Tomorrow I return to London.'

*'Quel malheur!'* exclaimed Madame. 'I was looking forward so much to m'sieur's company.'

'I shall be back on other occasions,' said Hammersley casually. 'Tonight, though, I must find a hotel.'

'Then m'sieur has nowhere to stay?'

Hammersley said quietly, 'Mr Gabbitas did recommend a place, but I'm afraid the name escapes me.'

'Then Maurice will take you to it,' said Madame in a matter of fact way, her eyes sliding over to a man who was quaffing a tall glass of *bock* at a table by the door. 'The Hotel Grand Mogador – a name in keeping with the gloss on the outside, but a trifle pretentious for the dreariness inside. So many things in life are pure façade, as m'sieur is well aware. However, the room awaiting you is clean and the cuisine is above average. When you are rested, Maurice will take your bag.'

The words seemed in the nature of a command, and Hammersley finished his coffee. 'I look forward to more meetings, Madame,' he smiled as he got up and made for the door.

Maurice drained his glass with one gulp and relieved Hammersley of his bag. 'It is not far, m'sieur,' he said in passable English. 'In the main square...'

Just short of the *Place*, Maurice pointed out a drab shoe-repair shop squeezed in between two tall buildings on the other side of the road. *'C'est á moi, m'sieur.'*

'Yours?'

*'Oui.* I am a cobbler, m'sieur, as was my father before me. The Mogador is on the other side of the *Place.'*

147

The Hotel Grand Mogador was, as Madame had remarked, pretentious. The royal-blue neon sign cast eerie distortions over the flashy tiled frontage, and the foyer was a Continental riot of chromium plate, brass grilles marked *réception, bureau de change, tourisme,* and the inevitable pygmy lift surrounded by wrought-iron cagework – in all, a spider's invitation to a dingy web. There was no one at the reception desk.

'I will take m'sieur to his room,' said Maurice, and without any of the usual formalities Hammersley found himself in room No. 37 overlooking the square.

'You have the letter, m'sieur?' asked Maurice bluntly.

Hammersley opened his case and produced the red-sealed envelope.

Maurice thrust it into his pocket with scarcely a glance. 'I will give m'sieur the reply in the morning. I hope you will be – tranquil? – the service here is really very good in spite of appearances. Your suit will be collected for pressing when you retire.'

'Oh, that won't be necessary,' said Hammersley.

'The service is all paid for, m'sieur – why not take advantage of it? Besides, if m'sieur hasn't got his trousers we know where he is. Leave your shoes out to be cleaned, too. I would not advise an evening stroll beyond Rijwel's café-restaurant. A chat with Madame can be very pleasant. *Bonne nuit.*'

The following morning Hammersley, suit freshly pressed, shoes shining like a dollar, stood with Maurice on the low platform at Thielt railway station, waiting for the train to clatter reluctantly in. Maurice took his case and found him a corner seat in a compartment which contained only one other passenger. The confusion of people, luggage and trolleys had barely sorted itself out when the engine gave a warning hoot, and Maurice, with an effusive farewell, thrust an envelope into Hammersley's hand. He skipped expertly on to the platform as the juggernaut overcame inertia and gathered speed.

The man in the corner was dozing peacefully, and Hammersley itched to examine the envelope. Like the one Gabbitas had given him, it had one red seal across the flap and was unaddressed. A sixth sense told him not to give it more than a cursory inspection. He opened his case and put it inside, and then placed the case up on the corded rack above his head. As he sat down, the man in the other corner gently closed his half-veiled eyes, but not before Hammersley had caught the brief glint of light across the pupils...

The flat countryside slid by monotonously

until at length his fellow passenger gave a prodigious yawn and proceeded to munch a packet of sandwiches with moody satisfaction. He was so studiously insular that it was obvious his one mission was to keep Hammersley under observation without arousing suspicion.

Hammersley reached up and got down his case. If this cat-and-mouse business was going on all the way back to London it might be as well to have the letter in his pocket, for he wanted an opportunity of examining it. Ostensibly getting out a bar of chocolate, and using the open lid of the case as cover, he slid the envelope inside his jacket, making a show of relocking the case. The man in the other corner screwed up his paper bag and tossed it out of the window; he relapsed once more into a feigned doze and remained thus until the train ground to an exhausted halt at Ostend.

Hammersley made his way to the passenger boat at the quayside, apparently unaware that another gentleman was now tagging along with him. His suspicions were confirmed when, settling in a comfortably-cushioned seat in the saloon, he was joined by that gentleman, who considerately moved along nearer to him to make more room for others. Whatever it was Hammersley was supposed to be doing, Gabbitas obviously now intended to keep him under constant observation. *This* letter was important.

'I hope it will be a smooth crossing,' said Hammersley conversationally.

'My remedy is to eat plenty and drink little,' smiled the other, sympathetically; he settled down with a magazine and made no attempt to open up the conversation.

Ostend soon slid into the background and the vessel once in the open sea, heaved and strained alarmingly. Talk amongst the passengers grew desultory, faces became grey and green, stewards were busy with paper bags at critical moments.

'Would you mind looking after my case?' said Hammersley at length. 'I'm afraid I shall have to – er – retire.'

'By all means,' agreed the other, moving aside to allow Hammersley free passage.

Hammersley made his way to the Gentlemen's and locked himself in a cubicle, and a remarkable change came over him, especially when he saw the small handbasin at the side with a tap which dripped hot water. His sad, woebegone expression vanished completely as he examined the letter carefully. The red seal was thick; he liked thick seals. Easing open a very fine blade of his penknife, he heated it for half a minute in the flame of his cigarette lighter. Quickly wiping off the carbon on a piece of tissue, he gently pressed the hot blade against the edge of the red wax. For a moment it held, and then gradually it began to slide into the underside of the wax like a knife through butter. It was necessary to heat the blade several times before the seal came away intact, if slightly thinner. Laying it carefully aside, he then dabbed hot water along the edge of the stuck-down flap of the envelope; when it had absorbed sufficient moisture he gently eased it open. He examined the double sheet of paper inside with a thoughtful frown...

Replacing the contents of the envelope, he dried off the flap against a hot pipe, applied a smear of gum from a small tube he had collected from his flat, and stuck it down again. He dabbed a little gum where the seal was to be replaced and allowed it to get tacky. Then playing the lighter-flame delicately on the reverse of the intact red medallion, he quickly but gently pressed it back into position. And now, far from looking sick, he was looking puzzled...

'Feeling better?' asked his neighbour, a few moments later.

'I'm feeling – er – curious,' said Hammersley.

'It gets people in different ways,' agreed the other, getting up. 'I think I'll go and get something to eat.'

The vessel dipped, heeled and shuddered from stem to stern.

'Try some pork,' suggested Hammersley.

Whilst the other was gone, Hammersley returned the letter to his case. At Dover, his fellow traveller tagged along with him through Customs and accompanied him in a friendly fashion to the waiting train. And as they parted company at the barrier at Victoria, Hammersley turned and bumped into Lew Gabbitas.

'Fancy meeting you here!' said Lew genially. 'Come and have a coffee. You have the letter?'

'Locked in my case,' acknowledged Hammersley. 'Do you want it now?'

'When we sit down. It has not been out of your possession?'

'Certainly not! At least, I asked a chap to mind my baggage whilst I was – um – not feeling well. I hope that was all right?' he added anxiously.

Lew Gabbitas smiled secretly. 'Of course!' Then, 'Now you know almost the whole procedure. Not difficult, is it?'

'So far as I'm concerned it's money for old rope,' agreed Hammersley. When, a moment later, he handed over the letter, he only hoped Gabbitas would think the expenditure was worth it. The double sheet of paper inside merely said 'O.K.' – that and nothing more. Just 'O.K.' Gabbitas thrust the envelope into his pocket unopened.

Even that letter was more informative than

the one Hammersley had taken to Thielt. In that one the double sheet of paper had been perfectly blank.

It seemed a very expensive postal system.

Expense, however, appeared to be of no account to Lew Gabbitas. Every few days he sent Hammersley over to Thielt, and on the face of it each visit was quite above board. Hammersley discovered – when the seals were thick enough to permit tampering with – that the letters were abstract to the point of nothingness, no longer containing even the black capitals 'O.K.' On each occasion Hammersley kept as tight a rein as possible on his light baggage, checking it carefully to ensure he was not being used as a vehicle for smuggling – not that he minded that, but he liked to know what it was he was smuggling, he had his own code of ethics. The ritual of pressing his suit at Thielt was observed, presumably to keep him in at night after lights out, and each following morning he felt carefully round the seams to see if anything had been stitched in overnight; and each time he found nothing. There was only one alteration to the initial procedure, and that was that on the outward journey Gabbitas now met him at a small hotel near Victoria and stayed with him for a nightcap before retiring. Here, too, Gabbitas insisted on the suit-pressing and shoe-polishing routine, impressing on Hammersley the need for looking smart, and Hammersley had no alternative but to acquiesce with ill-concealed impatience. It seemed that having once embarked on a tour of duty he was under constant surveillance.

'I'm getting a bit fed up with Thielt,' he remarked to Gabbitas. 'I've exhausted all my small talk with madame, and she watches every drink I take in case I get what she calls *zig-zag*. And the only other local inhabitant who understands what I'm talking about is the cobbler opposite. I would like to go to Brussels to see the bright lights for a change.'

'I hope you're not getting restive,' said Gabbitas, and there was an undertone in his voice, which made Hammersley look at him sideways. The veneer was peeling at the edges, and for a moment naked ugliness peeped out. 'The last courier I had got too big for his shoes; he had a most unfortunate accident. He should never have leaned over that fifth-floor balcony. However, you'll soon have a change of venue. Amsterdam. But please remember, my dear Hammersley, that when you're working for me you do what you're told. You are being kept in like a naughty boy as much for your own protection as mine. If anything goes wrong because of something you do, you'll be very much on your own.'

'I've no doubt about that,' agreed Hammersley.

'Nobody earns their money for nothing.'

Hammersley regarded the other thoughtfully. 'I think I must be earning mine. The police were asking me questions about you.'

Gabbitas's left ventricle missed a beat. 'You didn't tell me this before!'

'I think they were really after me about the accident, but they asked when I last saw you and did I know your private address. I told them the circumstances of our meeting, that I didn't know your private address, and that you'd been called away that same evening to a sick friend in Scotland.'

'Why did they want my address?'

'I think it was a gambit for making other inquiries about the Knightsbridge incident. I more than satisfied the officer. Anyway, I didn't know then that Four Chimneys was your property.'

Gabbitas looked relieved. 'You *shall* see the bright lights,' he beamed. 'After your next trip – your last to Thielt. You may spend the following day and night in Brussels – as a free agent. You will not be watched.'

'And where do I have to stay in Brussels?'

'Make your own arrangements. At my expense. Enjoy yourself.'

Hammersley preferred this Lew Gabbitas to the one whose staff had unfortunate accidents.

He spent his day of freedom in Brussels wandering nostalgically around old haunts, and in the evening made his way by tram-car to the Porte de Namur district, where he watched a cabaret in the Avenue Louise. Finally he crossed the main boulevard and went down the gentle slope of the Rue du Dépôt to Blake's place, the Golden Fleece. Accommodation had not been easy to obtain, as it was the first week of the *Exposition Internationale,* and even at the Golden Fleece his inquiry for a room had been met with extreme doubt. The man from Interpol, sitting at the bar of the café-restaurant, was most interested in the sudden change of demeanour of all concerned when Hammersley rather indiscreetly murmured 'Syndicate' and got what he wanted...

Hammersley was becoming more and more conscious of the sinister side of his employer. The gentle flow of events was gathering momentum and he felt he was being swept towards unknown maelstroms. He decided, therefore, to lay the facts before Simon Good, before he was sucked under...

Thus it was that on his return to England he called at Simon's place at Richmond, and he was making his way along the tree-lined road in which the house was situated, when he suddenly stopped and slipped behind the cover of an evergreen shrub. Someone was leaving Simon's house, and although at that distance he could not be absolutely certain, it looked for all the world like Mr Gabbitas...

He watched the figure out of sight and then made his way to the front door and pressed the bell. He waited for half a minute and then pressed again. Simon Good was evidently not at home. He tried again the following evening.

# 12

## Neutralising The Position

Following Simon Good's release from the irksome restrictions of Wormwood Scrubs, his employers (the Tyburn & New York Insurance Company) to avoid embarrassment all round, farmed him out to the Goodwill Insurance Company in St James's Street, where the manager, Mr Bulworthy, held him in high esteem. Simon worked hard – if not entirely in the interests of the company – and therefore was quite prepared to relax, as only one leading a life of blameless piety could, and listen to Hammersley's tale of woe.

'It would seem,' he said at length, 'that this man Gabbitas is putting you in all the right places at the wrong time. One of these days you'll be in the wrong place at the right time.'

'That's what I'm afraid of,' said Hammersley, adjusting his spectacles. *'He's* keeping in the background and I'm the one who's getting known to everybody. The Customs almost regard me as a relation.'

'I can see now why you've been avoiding me like the plague ever since we returned from Portugal,' said Simon. 'Without my guidance your extra-curriculum activities have landed you in a right old mess. You are, as they say, in a cleft stick, being borne aloft at a great height and rushed through the jungle of greed and avarice. If you had not changed shoulders on the way to the hospital, Gabbitas wouldn't have had any hold over you.'

'As a "factor" I had to do a lot of writing,' explained Hammersley petulantly, 'and to get full compensation I had to be fully incapacitated. As I write with my right hand it just *had* to be damage to my right shoulder. The trouble now is that Gabbitas is in the position of being able to blackmail me into being his courier, carrying nothing but blank sheets of paper to and from the Continent. What's worrying me is that it's all so perfectly innocent.'

'And now he wants to involve *me* in one of his commissions,' mused Simon thoughtfully. 'You must be doing *something* for him

– nobody pays anybody for doing precisely nothing. I think he must be waiting for the right opportunity. For all you know, the police may be watching your movements...' Simon's voice trailed off. He said at length, 'And that may be the answer to a number of curious things.'

'What sort of curious things?' blinked Hammersley.

'Before we went to Portugal the police called on Quenella and asked her what she was doing on the Friday before Bank Holiday. And then they called at the Golden Web to check if she was at a party there the night before, like she said she was. During the interview Blake mentioned that he had left for Brussels on the Saturday morning. Something must have happened on that Friday in between. Have the police asked *you* any questions about what you did on that day?'

'Only in connection with my accident – they were really trying to trace Gabbitas.'

'They were? Why?'

'The officer didn't say – although–' Hammersley hesitated, 'I couldn't make up my mind if he was trying to trace Gabbitas or pump me about Fiddler.' He frowned. 'There was something else. It worried me at the time. For a brief second I thought I *knew* him.'

'That's possible, I suppose.'

'Yes, but this was in some other connection, some other place. And then the impression faded and I never recaptured it.'

'Did he give his name?'

'He flashed his warrant card, but I didn't get a good look at it. I could hardly ask him to get it out again.'

'He went away satisfied?'

'Apparently. I haven't seen him since. That was also before we went to Portugal.'

Deep in thought, Simon lit a cigarette. 'I wonder if he was the same chap Blake thought he recognised that day in the Leather Bottle? You know, the superintendent who later turned up to question him at Dorking about that gun the Judge borrowed? Was your man a superintendent?'

Hammersley frowned. 'Yes, I believe he was.'

'Then it looks as if we're being watched like the Judge promised me that day in the dock – and like he subsequently reminded me when I came out of jail. By someone we ought to know. Now who on earth could that be?'

'Search me,' said Hammersley, at a loss. 'Why should he be watching us? What have we done?'

'Perhaps it's a question of what has *Gabbitas* done. They've seen you with him and they're linking up the rest of the Syndicate. Now what startling thing happened on that special Friday? Remember, I was arranging the flowers in the prison chapel at the time.'

Hammersley stirred his brains. An item of news floated sluggishly to the surface. 'There was a diamond robbery in Hatton Garden,' he said doubtfully.

'Hatton Garden! It's a wonder they haven't chased up Dutchy! His stall is just round the corner in Leatherwick Way. Do you happen to know where friend Lew was at the time of the robbery?'

'I'm afraid I don't. I met him for the first time on that Friday evening. Come to think of it, he mentioned the robbery in casual conversation at Four Chimneys. A quarter of a million, so the papers said. Yellow Fire Diamonds. I remember saying it would go a long way towards his ultimate objective, but he didn't seem particularly interested.'

'Get hold of some back numbers of the newspapers from Fleet Street to-morrow, will you?' instructed Simon. 'I'd like to read about this robbery. When does Mr Gabbitas want to see me about his insurances?'

'He didn't enlarge. I thought perhaps he'd already been to discuss the matter. I called here yesterday, but you were out. As I came along the road I saw a man leaving the house. From a distance he looked like Gabbitas.'

'Oh? I expect it was the man from the burglar-alarm company – the system's kaput at the moment.'

'I had the impression he'd been inside.'

'He couldn't have been. Anyway, nothing has been disturbed so far as I'm aware. I keep nothing of importance here, but I'll have a look round later.' Simon dismissed the matter. 'I wonder what Lew's insurance problem is?'

'I expect he'll bring it up when he's ready,' said Hammersley. He took off his spectacles and gave them a nervous polish. 'If you ever get invited down to Four Chimneys, ask to see those pictures of his. There's something about them that's not quite *right*.'

'He needs more practice?'

'No, not that, they're very good paintings. But – there's something about them that's – *queer*. You might be able to put your finger on it.'

'I'll try – if I ever get to Four Chimneys. It's a pity Blake's out of circulation – it sounds a place that might be worth a nocturnal visit.' Simon stubbed out his cigarette. 'You say your next port of call is Amsterdam. When will that be?'

'I'm waiting to hear from Gabbitas.'

'Then we've got to do something in the meantime. The position is fluid and the vantage is with Gabbitas. We must neutralise the position. If the enemy takes a piece of your ground, counter-attack whilst he's trying to consolidate and take a piece of his.

If Gabby is putting you in the right places at the wrong time, it is up to us to put you in the wrong places and the right time. Now.'

'I was only your batman,' said Hammersley apologetically. 'What do we do?'

'*We* don't do anything. You go to the police...'

Hammersley sat as if pole-axed.

'Go to the police?' he gaped.

'Yes. And tell them what's happening?'

Hammersley remained in stunned silence.

'Your record is clean, isn't it?' went on Simon. 'I don't mean in the Book of Gold – you obviously won't beat the well known Abou ben Adhem, whose name led all the rest. But if at C.R.O. the page in respect of *Hammersley, Charles,* is unsullied then you've nothing to fear. Go to Mortlake Police Station and tell them what has been happening to you next week?'

'You mean to go next week and tell them what has been happening?'

'No, I mean go the week after and tell them what has been happening to you next week.'

'Haven't you got your tenses mixed?' asked Hammersley politely.

'Only until the end of next week. You will then tell them about a number of things which will have happened to you by the time you tell them. We are about to neutralise the position.'

The inspector at Mortlake was a fatherly-looking man who listened sympathetically to Hammersley's outpourings. He said pontifically, 'It appears you're being impersonated, sir. Now that could be a serious offence.'

'It seems so pointless.'

'Up till now. But we don't know what it's leading up to. You say the first incident was at your grocer's?'

'Yes, at Mortlake. A small, one-man business. Judd's. Been there for years – you may know it. On Tuesday I went in to buy some cheese and old Judd said, "You forgot to take it with you yesterday, sir." I told him he was mistaken, that I hadn't been in the day before, and he said "Oh, yes, you did, sir, yesterday morning; gave me quite a large order – about twice the amount of everything you usually have.' He wouldn't take the money – said it had already been paid for. He was so insistent. I didn't argue with him. To tell you the truth I wondered if he was going round the bend. By the end of the week I wondered if I was.'

'There was no question of someone attempting to charge this large order to your account, then?'

'No question at all. But everywhere I went this week it was the same story. I go to get a pound of sausages and the butcher asks if the three pounds I bought an hour ago weren't enough. I go to the fishmonger to get some fish for supper, and the manager inquires if the haddock I was doubtful about for lunch was to my liking after all. And then a low table arrived from a local furnishing stores. I went round and asked him why they had sent it, and they said that I'd ordered it for my television set. It was of no use my telling them I hadn't got a television set – the salesman said he distinctly remembered me saying what a wonderful picture my set gave. Do you know, Inspector, I was beginning to get really worried, and worry with me brings on a form of hay fever. I had several severe attacks.'

'I believe they can alleviate that type nowadays with sedative drugs,' ruminated the inspector. 'Did you go to a doctor?'

'I was afraid to,' confessed Hammersley. 'I thought I might discover I'd agreed to wear a truss and a National Health wig.'

'What finally induced you to come and see us?' asked the inspector.

'The thing that got under my skin was the incident at the bank.'

'Ah!' said the other. He leaned forward in anticipation.

'You see, up to that point I had no real grouch. Everything was being paid for by someone else.'

'Quite a consideration, these days,' agreed the inspector.

'Yesterday I called at the branch office of the Mortlake & District Bank, and asked for a note of my balance. The young lady looked surprised and said, "But I've only just given it to you, sir – ten minutes ago." I didn't know what to say! Coming on top of all the other incidents, I just felt confused. I wanted time to think, so I muttered something about I must be getting old and forgetful, and drew some money and left. Now if people choose to send me furniture, all well and good; but if they invade the privacy of my banking account, that's a different matter. I finally decided to come and report the whole business to you. I haven't said anything to the bank manager yet.'

'This last episode is curious,' mused the inspector. 'In all the others you haven't been put to any expense.'

'I haven't been put to any expense at the bank,' pointed out Hammersley.

'Not as yet.'

'I don't follow.'

'Someone could be planning to utter a forged cheque in your name and wanted to see how much you were good for.'

'Then I'm afraid he got a shock when he saw my balance,' declared Hammersley frankly. 'Anyway, it surely wouldn't be necessary for anyone contemplating issuing a forged cheque to go through all this other carry-on with the local tradesmen? Why not just go into the bank and present the cheque?'

'That is very true,' agreed the inspector profoundly, 'unless someone is testing his ability to pass himself off as you.'

'But why pick on me? I haven't an enemy in the whole wide world. I hope,' added Hammersley anxiously, 'that I'm not wasting your time? You must have more than enough to do.'

'Not at all, it makes a change from interminable parking offences.'

'Perhaps it will all finish, as suddenly as it started.'

'It may well do that, sir, but it occurs to me that someone may be planning to do something big in such a manner that you will get the blame.'

Hammersley looked startled. 'I hadn't thought of that!' he blinked. 'You mean like rob a bank in broad daylight, and then half a dozen people will swear it was me?'

'Something like that,' agreed the inspector in happy anticipation. 'What's just been happening is something in the nature of a trial run.'

'But – but that's preposterous! What can I do?'

'You've done the right thing in reporting the matter,' soothed the other. 'Please let me know if any further acts are committed.'

'But I may not get to hear of them all,' said Hammersley, in obvious distress. 'It may be going on over a much wider area, for all I know.'

'Yes, yes, of course, sir. But let me know of those incidents that come to your notice. We'll get him in the end, you know, we always do.'

Hammersley hoped there was a fair margin of error. 'You're very reassuring, officer,' he said. 'After making such a fuss, I only hope the whole thing doesn't turn out to be a hoax.'

The inspector paused fractionally before replying. 'I only hope so, too, sir,' he said deliberately, and Hammersley was not sure that he liked him at that precise moment. The inspector said, 'Would you be kind enough to write down a list of all the places where incidents have occurred?'

This time it was Hammersley who paused, but it was for the briefest of split seconds, and the inspector appeared not to notice it. 'By all means, Inspector. May I borrow your pad?'

'Of course!' The inspector grinned disarmingly. 'Then we'll not only have a list of the places, we'll also have a sample of your handwriting. And your fingerprints.' He was still grinning, and Hammersley wondered if there was a touch of the wolf in his forebears. 'I suppose, sir,' went on the inspector, 'you haven't upset a lady friend who is now having her own back?'

Hammersley was shocked. 'What, at my age!' he said indignantly.

'At any age, sir. You know what they say – *cherchez la femme!*'

'Not my *femme!*' said Hammersley. It had been a very exhausting week, what with going round all the local stores twice, and this was carrying things too far.

'We'll make a few discreet inquiries,' said the inspector.

The discreeter the better, thought Hammersley...

He had managed to fit in that week's work just before Gabbitas instructed him to go to Amsterdam. He was given his air tickets and flight number, and was told to put up at the Hotel Amerikaan.

Hammersley telephoned Simon, who, leading a sedentary life, liked things to keep moving.

'I wish I could come and keep an eye on you,' said Simon regretfully, 'but I've had my passport stolen. I think it *must* have been Gabbitas you saw coming out of my house. Still, not to worry. I've got Monday off, and I shall go bird-watching in Suffolk instead...'

# 13

## The Cobbler Of Thielt

Rip Strookman looked thoughtful as he replaced the receiver in his office in Amsterdam. It was not often that he received a telephone call from his former O.C., Simon Good. His mind slithered back twenty years to a battle-scarred factory in North-West Europe to when Roag's Syndicate was first dreamed up, back to when Major Peter Meek – to use his correct name – had taken hold of their tattered, battle-strained nerves and had deliberately steered their thoughts away from death and destruction by talking of impossible things like Civvy Street and the jobs they were going back to; hinting at the formation of a post-war syndicate which would turn Civvy Street into Easy Street, a scheme which at that stage was nothing but a fantastic pipe-dream born out of the wild thoughts of a handful of men due to be annihilated by man's inhumanity to man. But the little group survived, due to the subsequent bravery of Major Meek, and there was nothing Rip Strookman wouldn't now do for him.

He strode out of the Pyx Travel Agency and walked briskly to a public telephone booth on the corner of Amstelwag and Jaafestraat. There were occasions when he deemed it wisest to use the public services, and this was one of them. He obtained the number he wanted after some delay, and even before Simon Good had started out in his Jaguar for the Suffolk marshes, a Belgian fishing smack chugged sleepily out of Nieuport harbour...

The Jaguar ate the miles out through Epping Forest on the road to the east, and by midday it was snaking down Church Hill into the fashionable fishing resort of Aldeburgh. Turning left at the foot of the hill, Simon found a hotel overlooking the ancient Moot Hall, which in the days when the town was granted a charter was in the middle of the town, but which was now almost in the sea.

Simon booked a room and ordered a meal, making it known to all and sundry that the weather was just right for observing the habits of that rare Scandinavian bird, the *globulating sputgutter* (invented on the spur of the moment) which, for reasons best known to itself, migrated to this country in the winter, thereby proving what a curious creature it was.

Simon asked the waiter which marshes he

recommended – those situated between the North Fields and Thorpeness, or the more desolate tracts south of Slaughden Quay, where the River Alde was separated from the sea by a mere spit of land. The waiter, who had not heard of the *globulating sput-gutter*, strongly recommended the wastes beyond the Martello Tower. Simon thanked him and said he would investigate the area that very afternoon before the light faded; if he found the right conditions he would be up at the crack of dawn, on the job.

Changing, therefore, into more suitable attire, he ambled off along the sea-front, at length turning into the side street where the cable station is situated. He remembered the excitement, when he was a very small boy on holiday, when the original cable was hauled ashore at low tide from the cable-ship and the connection made with the newly-built station. He remembered how years later he crouched in a foxhole in the shadow of a cable station at the other end of the cable at La Panne, waiting for the barrage from the rocket-ships to lift farther inland, wondering if he would ever live to spend the Liberation francs stuffed in his field-dressing pocket...

And now the years had marched even further, turning full circle, and here he was striding along the lower end of the High Street, out past the Mill House, along the desolate road to Slaughden Quay. The grim bulk of the Martello Tower, one of a number built to defend the country against the might of Napoleon, lay ahead.

He crunched along the shingle for perhaps half a mile, taking note of the boats laid up in the river, and of the isolated coastguard's hut on a marram-bound tump of land; and by dusk he was glad to be back in the warmth and friendship of the hotel. He sought out the manager and arranged for a couple of flasks of cocoa and some assorted sandwiches (packed in cellophane bags to keep them moist) to be left for him last thing at night. 'I don't want to disturb anyone in the morning,' he explained.

'You'll find it grim out there on the marshes,' shivered the manager. 'When do you plan to be back? We'll have a hot meal ready for you.'

Simon thoughtfully fingered his book on wild birds. 'That's difficult to say,' he said doubtfully. 'I'd planned on crossing the river by the ferry and exploring the other side. If it gets too late in the day, where's the best place to make for?'

'Well, there's Framlingworth. Or, say, Orfordbury – you'll find a place there. Bed-and-breakfast.'

'In that case, I may be away for a couple of days, so don't worry. You've got my car as collateral.'

'I've always wanted a Jaguar,' grinned the manager.

Early the following morning, the lonely coastguard on the narrow spit of land up past the Martello Tower watched a fishing smack creeping down the Alde on the ebb-tide, its auxiliary engine chug-chugging dreamily. He swung his glass round and took careful note of the Yarmouth Harbour registration number on the bow.

It was not until the boat was well outside the three-mile limit that the skipper went forward and ripped off the strip of adhesive plastic to reveal the Nieuport Harbour letters and number underneath.

Simon Good preferred things that way; it saved all the messing about applying for a new passport. Not that he had anything against the passport system, but Government departments were hard-pressed enough as it was, and this method obviated much clerical work. Even if his passport had not been stolen it was doubtful if he would have used it. An unstamped passport told a negative story of its own. It said one hadn't been anywhere in particular...

Considerably later he strode purposefully down the cobbled street which led from Thielt railway station, past the row of houses where, in the dark days, he had been billeted.

In Tramstraat he eased up his pace as his eye caught the neon sign of Rijwel's café-restaurant. Glancing at his watch he decided he would be just in time for the evening visit of Maurice the cobbler. He sauntered along to the café and examined the framed menu-card in the window. Half turning as if in doubt, he paused and took another look and appeared to make up his mind. He pushed open the plate-glass swing door and went inside.

Madame greeted him with a twinkle in her eye. *"Soir, m'sieur.* Our coffee is not poisoned.'

Simon grinned. 'I am sure it is not, Madame. I was merely debating my needs.'

'A sandwich, perhaps?' With a sweep of her hand she indicated a glass case on the counter, stacked with substantial lengths of crusty bread liberally filled with a variety of savouries.

Simon made his choice and found a corner by the window. The café was well-patronised and idly he watched the flow of customers. So this was the place where Hammersley had met Lew Gabbitas's contact man.

Through the runnels of steam on the window he saw a man cross the road and make for Rijwel's. He was in his fifties, bespectacled, faded, withdrawn, and when he removed his hat as he pushed his way in through the door he revealed thinning mousy hair which added to his general air of dejection. Madame greeted him cheerfully.

''*Soir*, Maurice. You look tired. Trade bad?'

'Not good,' he acknowledged with gloomy satisfaction. 'It's not that I haven't the custom, but I work all the hours heaven has given me merely to earn the overheads. People no longer appreciate the work of the craftsman.'

Madame prepared a coffee. 'Shoes are cheap, nowadays,' she pointed out. 'It's almost as cheap to buy a new pair as it is to have the old one repaired. Sandwich?'

'Please. Beef and gherkin.'

'Nevertheless, the special jobs help you considerably,' said Madame kindly selecting an extra large sandwich.

'That is true,' said Maurice, 'but there is an element of risk. If anything goes wrong the craftsmanship might be traced back to me.'

'*Zut!* That is why our friend pays well.'

'One never knows for how long it will last,' said Maurice, reluctant to look on the bright side. 'Or when the next job will be.'

'The next job will be to-morrow,' said Madame, ringing up the till.

Maurice gulped his coffee in surprise. 'To-morrow?' he jerked. 'Here in Thielt? Or Antwerp?'

'Neither,' said Madame. She ran a damp cloth over the counter. 'Our friend says you

177

are to have your papers ready. They are in order, I presume?'

'*Mais oui.* So I am to go out of the country, yes?'

'It will make a change,' shrugged Madame. 'And the money is good.'

'Where then am I to go? Paris?'

'You will be instructed in due course. It will all be arranged in detail as usual. All I can tell you at present is to pack your bag, check your tools, and see that your papers are in order.'

'Arrangements couldn't be better through a travel agency,' said Maurice, smiling for the first time. 'I must hurry away and finish what urgent repairs I have promised...'

Simon drained his coffee. Although he had not heard every word of the conversation it had been possible, by concentrating, to isolate their voices from the general hubbub, and he had gleaned enough to establish that the morose gentleman finishing off his sandwich was Maurice the cobbler who had escorted Hammersley to the Hotel Grand Mogador.

Maurice pushed aside his plate and climbed down off his stool. '*Au 'voir, Madame,*' he grunted, making for the door.

Simon followed casually, and once outside on the pavement turned in the opposite direction for the benefit of the watchful eye of Madame. Pausing as if he had no particularly direction in mind, he turned about and drifted slowly in the wake of Maurice.

The cobbler crossed the thoroughfare and hurried along the other side. Simon, with deceptive strides, kept pace with him. Suddenly his quarry slid into a dismal little shoe-repair shop jammed between two tall buildings, and Simon had to resist a temptation to follow the man into his shop and ask for a pair of shoe-laces. Patience had to be nicely balanced with urgency and he had no wish to precipitate matters. Things would unfold themselves in the fullness of time, and later he was glad that he had not forced his attentions on Maurice at this stage.

He strolled round into the main square and found the pretentious Hotel Grand Mogador. He asked for room No. 37, solemnly assuring the young lady at the desk that he had stayed in that very room on one of his honeymoons and had found it very comfortable. Without batting an eyelid, she consulted the register, found the room was free, and handed him the key with a brief nod in the direction of the lift. '*Troisième étage, m'sieur,*' she said.

Once past the glittering façade of the foyer, there was an air of crumbling poverty about the place. Patrons paid dearly for the lavish lighting which greeted them outside and lured them in. Room No. 37, with its Continental accoutrements tucked away behind a curtain, was functional, and that was all that could be said about it. It was certainly no bridal chamber.

Nobody came and whisked away Simon's suit for sponging and pressing. And in the morning he found his shoes in precisely the same position in which he had left them outside the door, untouched. It seemed that the special service was for Hammersley only.

Simon had an early breakfast and, as there appeared to be nothing further to be gained in Thielt without drawing attention to himself, made a telephone call and caught a train to Bruges.

A number of interesting trips by motor vessels ply along the canals from Bruges, and a popular itinerary, both in and out of the season, is one which crosses the frontier into Holland at Zaansluis, affording glimpses of windmills, dykes, Dutch national costumes, clogs, meerschaums, the lot.

Simon booked a ticket at an office in the Grande Place and made his way at the appropriate hour to the starting point. Although it was out of season, there were a number of tourists amongst those regular passengers who used the service merely as a means of transportation, and Simon joined the trickle of people boarding the surprisingly large launch. Vessels plied to and from both sides of the frontier, and the launch was a Dutch one with the name *Willem II* painted astern.

A Dutchman at the head of the gangway examined tickets and reminded passengers that passports might be required. Simon presented his ticket and Rip Strookman did not seem to think it necessary to remind him about his passport.

Simon vanished discreetly into a door marked *Toilet*. He emerged a couple of minutes later clad in greasy overalls, and made his way to the engine room. And after a further short interval a mechanic, now wearing Simon's hat and raincoat, came out and joined Rip at the gangway.

Five minutes later, *Willem II* was ready to cast off.

The gangway was hauled aboard, the bow rope unhitched, and the mechanic with whom Simon had changed places jumped to the landing stage and tossed in the stern line. *Willem II* juddered into life, and with a couple of sharp toots on the siren yawed gently away from the staging and began to make way.

For a while Strookman busied himself at the loudhailer, announcing points of interest. One of the reasons for the success of his Pyx Travel Agency, with its head office in Amsterdam, was that he was never too big to take an active part in the business;

and this was a special occasion.

At length, when they were in nondescript country, he announced that coffee was being served at the hatch and made his way to the engine room.

'*Goede morgen, mijnheer*,' grinned Simon. 'I'm sorry to put you to this trouble, but as I explained on the telephone, my passport has been stolen – with the object, I imagine, of preventing me from checking up on Hammersley's activities in Amsterdam. There was no time to sort out the matter with the Passport Office.'

'Perhaps you'll put me in the picture before we reach the frontier,' said Rip. 'Jan did give you his identity papers–? *Goot!*' He slanted his eyes in the direction of another mechanic who was busy with the engine. 'Hans here speaks nothing but Dutch, so you may talk without reserve. Let me tell you here and now that your name is Jan Kippel – don't forget! Now please tell me about Hammersley – I'm sure Hans will be able to dispense with your services for a while.'

With economy of words Simon explained the position.

'So,' said Rip at length, 'friend Charles arrives at being a *dummkoph* carrying blank sheets of paper in heavily sealed envelopes. How very curious. He has done about half a dozen journeys to Thielt, and now starts a new series to Amsterdam. And you want to see what goes on.'

'That's about the measure of it,' agreed Simon. 'Of course, Hammersley hasn't been able to examine every letter, but whatever it is he's doing in all his babe-like innocence, it is something that Gabbitas doesn't want to do himself, and he's found a fall-guy in Charles.'

'Does Charles know you're over here?'

'No.'

'I see. So, my friend, we are on the outside looking in.'

'That's about it. I hope you've laid on transport?'

'The Pyx Travel Agency arranges every-thing. At Meerdijk there is a three-hour interval before *Willem II* puts about for the return journey. Two other men will replace us. We will proceed by car to the West Schelde. There we will cross the ferry to Vlissingen. At Vlissingen my own car awaits ready to whisk us along the motorway to Amsterdam. I myself will see you safely back into Belgium to-morrow.' Rip glanced through the porthole. 'We're not far from the frontier post of Zaansluis. I am regarded there with some respect, and anyway the Customs' examination is usually perfunct-ory. Put some sludge on your face and wrap that muffler round your neck. If you're questioned, hold your throat and I'll explain that you've lost your voice; and when I shout "Papers, Jan!", hand them up with a grin and look the officer straight in the eye. And then turn back to your engine. But please, please don't do anything to it – it cost ten thousand guilders. And now I have an announcement to make to the passengers...'

A few minutes later his voice could be heard over the Tannoy speaker, informing passengers that Holland lay ahead and that passports should be made ready to avoid delay. A sprinkling of houses now began to break the flat, uninspiring vista, and the canal narrowed into a lock with dual frontier controls. They were waved through the first post, and as the man at the helm brought the vessel skilfully into position at the Dutch post a Customs official jumped aboard. Rip greeted him as a long-lost friend, passports were collected and Rip walked with the officer towards the gangway, offering him a cigar *en route*. The other was in the process of accepting a light when he paused and jerked his head over his shoulder at the engine-well.

'And am I not to see the papers of your engineers?'

Rip slapped his forehead and rolled his eyes upwards. 'Oh, *ja, ja*, I forget! Hans!' he bellowed. 'Jan! Your papers, if you please!'

Hans stepped up and handed over his

papers. Simon, rubbing his hands on the seat of his overalls, extracted some papers from his top pocket. The official took them and looked at him briefly, and Simon turned aside once more to the intricacies of the engine.

The official held the papers distastefully between thumb and forefinger.

Rip took him by the arm and pleaded, 'Don't dirty those papers in your grubby office, my friend.' He added, 'You will, I hope, be on duty to-morrow? I am bringing you a small bottle of schnapps...'

The stamping of the passports proceeded with vows of eternal friendship ... at least, until the schnapps arrived.

Simon, spruced up, mingled with the passengers eagerly alighting at Meerdijk to explore the natural charm of the place. There were always tourists with time and money who preferred the off-season in spite of the cold weather, and the local inhabitants saw to it that what they came to see was much in evidence. The quaint costumes (carefully put away after the last boat left) the waterside cafés, the cheese market with its piles of cannonball cheese, the shops filled with meerschaum pipes made in Stepney Green, and lidded beer mugs imported from Sweden, were all there, but Simon had no eye for these attractions...

The Interpol man, sitting on a white-painted bench at the landing-stage, stiffened as he spotted Rip Strookman leaving *Willem II*. Tapping the dottle from his pipe, he followed him at a safe distance into a quayside beer house and ordered a drink next to him at the bar. The landlord served him and turned back to Rip.

'You are on this run regularly again?' he inquired affably.

'No, just a routine check,' replied Rip. 'I return to Amsterdam to-day. I may not be this way again for a month...'

The Interpol man took careful note of this; a few minutes later he watched Rip make for a car parked farther along the quay, and saw him get in and drive away alone.

Strookman had arranged to pick up Simon on the outskirts of the village.

Once clear of Meerdijk, he trod on the accelerator all the way up to the West Schelde. Parking the car at a garage, they crossed the ferry to Vlissingen, picked up Rip's own vehicle and were soon skimming along the main motorway which went through Gorinchem and by-passed Utrecht to Amsterdam.

'I have booked two rooms in this Hotel Amerikaan,' remarked Rip. 'It is a mean little place in the de Walletjes district. I have also checked the time of arrival of Hammersley's

186

flight. I will first install you at the hotel, and that will just about leave me enough time to get back to Schiphol Airport.'

Some hours later he watched Hammersley leave the arrival bay with a very smooth-looking individual who escorted him to a small car and drove him into the heart of Amsterdam. Rip followed at a discreet distance and saw them both safely into the Hotel Amerikaan. He devoutly prayed that Simon was now ensconced behind a newspaper in the foyer as arranged. For a few minutes he sat in his car debating the next move, when out came Hammersley's escort by himself. The man drove off up the narrow street and Rip, acting on the spur of the moment, followed.

His quarry went over what seemed like the best part of Amsterdam's five hundred bridges before pulling up outside some squalid premises in the diamond-cuttery centre. Rip crawled past and, taking note of the doorway into which the man hurried, drove back to the Hotel Amerikaan. He found Simon in his room.

'I've followed Hammersley's driver to a cuttery in the diamond district,' he reported. 'It is not unknown to me. It's a place where they're prepared to do all sorts of clever cutting and polishing without asking questions. You name it, they'll do it. At a price. Where's Hammersley?'

'Eating himself silly in the restaurant. We'll take it in turns to keep watch. There's a café almost opposite – one of us could take up a position there.'

It fell to Simon's lot to follow Hammersley round the dingy streets for an evening stroll. So far as Simon could tell, no attempt was being made by anyone else to keep track of Hammersley, who at length returned to his room and retired.

There were bedrooms on only two floors, and Rip had booked a room on each of them. Rip's room was at the end of the corridor in which Hammersley's was situated, and leaving the door slightly ajar, he sat and watched. At ten o'clock Hammersley put out his shoes in the manner predicted by Simon, although judging by the general standards of the establishment it was doubtful if anything would happen to them. Rip optimistically put his out too, and an hour later he caught a glimpse of a tired, wispy little man in an apron collecting Hammersley's. Rip waited a few seconds before peeping out again. His own shoes were still in position, and the little man was wearily climbing the stairs to the floor above.

Silent as a wraith Rip followed and round the head of the stairs he saw the other enter the room next to Simon's and close the door behind him. Pondering for a moment, Rip went back to his own room and lit a cigarette. He had smoked half of it when he heard movement in the corridor again. Gently easing the door open he squinted through the crack. A blowsy-looking maid was collecting Hammersley's suit for pressing, and she plodded downstairs with it with ill-grace.

Strookman suddenly made up his mind. He hurried up to the floor above and without preamble tried the little man's door. It was not locked. Thrusting it open, he strode boldly in as if he had every right to be there.

The old boy whipped round like a startled buck rabbit. He was seated at a cheap writing desk by the window. Hammersley's shoes were there, as was a cleaning and polishing outfit. There was also an unrolled canvas holdall of tools – awls, knives, screwdrivers and an adjustable hammer. Rip's eye remained on the array of tools for about a thousandth part of a second before looking round the room in feigned bewilderment. 'I beg your pardon!' he exclaimed apologetically. 'I seem to have come to the wrong room.' He hurried out. And reported back to Simon. 'It's the oldest trick in the book,' he said at length. 'Do we tell Hammersley?'

'No,' said Simon. 'Let him carry on in all innocence for once. If we told him, he'd only have a stroke, and I don't think his policies are extended to cover Continental travel...'

Early next morning Simon was slipping back from the bathroom, when the door of the room next to his suddenly opened and out came the wispy little man with Hammersley's shoes. Simon was unable to avoid him.

'*Goede morgen,*' he said.

'*Goede morgen, mijnheer,*' said the cobbler of Thielt.

At first light the following day, a fishing smack bearing Yarmouth Harbour registration letters crept back up the River Alde to draw breath after a severe battering in the North Sea. The coastguard up beyond the Martello Tower put aside his telescope with a shiver, made an entry in his log-book, and reached for a streaming mug of cocoa on the stove

An hour later, Simon Good, his clothing suitably muddied from the rigours of watching the habits of the *globulating sputgutter,* squelched along to the desolate spot where an ancient bell, green with long exposure to salty atmosphere, was suspended from a sort of miniature gallows. Grasping the leather thong on the clapper, he wiggled it vigorously, sending out a joyous clangour which sent the gulls screaming at low level across the water to summon the ferryman.

An old salt rowed out to fetch him, and

Simon tipped him well, but not too well. He wanted to be remembered with affection, not with suspicion. But he wanted to be remembered.

Back at his hotel he had a hot bath and ate a hearty breakfast. At nine-thirty sharp he telephoned his office to tell Mr Bulworthy all about the sudden temperature he had developed which had rendered him virtually bedridden. Then he went to bed and slept as only a man with a clear conscience can.

# 14

## Milk Bottle Tops

'I tried to get you on the telephone yesterday,' said Hammersley, 'but I could get no reply.'

'I was smitten with the palsy,' said Simon blandly, 'and had to take to my bed. I was much too weak to answer the telephone. What's the urgency?'

'I travelled to Amsterdam and went through the same ridiculous caper,' grumbled Hammersley, 'and now Gabbitas wants to see you.'

'Things are moving. When?'

'As soon as possible, here in London. He

met me at Harwich – I came back via the Hook. We stayed overnight at some grubby little hotel, and he's not returning to Exeter for a few days.'

'H'm. I'll see him to-morrow lunch time. One o'clock at the Belvoir in South Molton Street – that is if he's going to foot the bill. If not, make it Fred's Café in Berwick Market. I'll be wearing a white gardenia and toreador jeans'

'Good afternoon, Mr Good. I'm so glad you were able to make it. Hammersley's description of you was perfect. You look extremely fit and well.'

'*Mens sana in corpore sano,*' acknowledged Simon.

'I hope it will stay that way,' said Mr Gabbitas pleasantly. 'Have you been abroad recently?'

'I can't afford such luxury,' said Simon regretfully. 'In any event I've had my passport stolen.'

'How inconvenient! Have you reported it to the police?'

'Not yet.'

'Why not! They'd probably believe you.'

'I may have only mislaid it. Do I need a passport for what you have in mind?'

'To the contrary, I'm glad you haven't one. You might be tempted to check up on what Hammersley's doing.'

'Hammersley tells me very little.'

'He's told you about my million pound objective?'

'Should he have done? It sounds worthy of mention.'

'So far as I'm concerned, the fewer who know about it the better.'

'Then why mention it to me?'

'I mention it only to a few who are in no position to do anything about it. I can be quite ruthless.'

Simon looked into the mild, dreamy eyes. 'I'm sure you can be,' he agreed. 'The only thing Hammersley has dwelt on is your wonderful skill at painting. I would very much like to see your work.'

'Perhaps it can be arranged,' replied Gabbitas, exuding pleasure. 'I understand you are in the insurance business?'

'Your understanding is correct. What can I do for you?'

Lew Gabbitas considered his words carefully. He tapped half an inch of ash off the end of his cigar. 'I am interested in a small furniture depository at Westland Zoy in Somerset,' he said. 'I want to effect some insurance cover.'

'It's not insured already?'

'The building is. But not the contents.'

'You mean to say you have no floating cover on stock? Seems a poor arrangement – or can't you find any company to take you?'

Gabbitas ignored the thrust. 'Perhaps I should explain that the cover I wish to effect is in respect of a special consignment of pictures and antiques from a stately home – whilst the decorators are in. All perfectly straightforward.'

'I'm sure it is,' said Simon, without conviction. 'But why pick on me?'

'I must have an agent,' shrugged Gabbitas. 'You're in the insurance business, you know about these things. And you're a friend of Hammersley's – you might as well have the commission.'

'I'm sure your chief concern is that a friend of Hammersley's should have the commission. What about your present agent?'

'He's – he's no longer in a position to do business.'

'He's in the Scrubs?' suggested Simon sympathetically.

'He's dead.'

'Ah! No doubt there's plenty of scope for fire insurance where he's gone to. He was elderly?'

'No – quite young. He met with an unfortunate accident.'

'Oh. I'm sorry about that.'

'So am I. He was a useful man.' A distant look came into Lew's eyes. 'But too inquisitive.'

'I'm inquisitive, too,' said Simon gently.

'Anyone can meet with an accident,' said

Mr Gabbitas. 'Your friend Hammersley has curious accidents which earn him a lot of money.'

'I'm still listening,' said Simon courteously.

'To get away with it he must have someone on the inside to advise him. You.'

Simon lit a cigarette. 'Hammersley's quite capable of looking after himself – he's over twenty-one.'

Gabbitas shrugged. 'I think it's the kind of thing you'd enjoy doing.'

Simon Good masked his concern behind a smokescreen. 'How come?' he said, at length.

'When I found out your name it rang a bell. I went to Fleet Street and searched back through the file-copies of the national dailies. The account of your trial was most diverting.'

'I'm glad you derived some amusement. I now find it rather embarrassing – instead of remembering the boyish prank which put me in the dock, too many people recollect the unkind things suggested about me in cross-examination. Things, I might add, which were not proven.'

'Yes, you were very lucky,' agreed Gabbitas cynically. 'I take it you are prepared to help me?'

Simon expelled a smoke ring. 'The maximum commission I could hope to get in the market is fifteen per cent. What over-riding have you in mind?'

'Five hundred pounds?'

'Did you say a thousand?' asked Simon. 'In cash?'

'Now *I* must be getting deaf!' smiled Gabbitas. 'Yes, you were perfectly correct, seven-fifty. In cash. All you have to do is to place the insurance.'

'Twelve-fifty,' said Simon. 'In cash. In advance.'

Gabbitas sighed. 'A thousand,' he agreed.

'You drive a hard bargain,' said Simon admiringly, and they settled down to their meal.

In due course the insurance was effected, but not with the Tyburn & New York Group. Simon placed it through a friend of a friend who knew a broker at Lloyd's. And he was to be very glad he had done it that way.

The rates for furniture depositories are fairly steep, not because the incidence of fires in the class as a whole is high, but because furniture depositories either stay up or get burnt down; there is no half-way measure and little or no salvage.

Lew's place was a case in point. A week after the insurance was effected it was completely gutted by fire in the middle of the night.

The Special Investigation Department of New Scotland Yard was very interested. The fire experts were called in, and from the information at their disposal the seat of the fire was established in the packing department. And although the entire building and contents were reduced to twisted angle-iron and charred rubble, at the very centre of the hot-spot was found an ordinary silver foil milk-bottle top. Now milk-bottle tops are to be found all over the civilised world; the most inaccessible beauty spots have their quota; in practically every office throughout the length and breadth of the land there is a filing cabinet behind which may be found an assortment of the gold and silver symbols of contented cows; in every factory, even where there are canteen facilities, there is still the odd cubbyhole where tea is surreptitiously brewed with its aftermath of foil medallions. And in spite of the fact that earnest people collect them for the benefit of the blind and disabled, it takes a war to ensure that all are accounted for. So that to the casual bystander a milk-bottle top would not arouse any undue suspicion even if it was found in the packing department of a furniture depository.

This particular milk-bottle top was standing on a brick under some rubble which was once a wooden rack containing packing material; and near the brick was a badly scorched telephone which had apparently fallen there when the rack burned through. The metal cap, the brick and the telephone were carefully packed up and taken away to the Yard's forensic laboratory.

In the little silver foil bowl they found faint traces of fulminate of mercury ... the stuff used for priming-sets in hand-grenades ... highly explosive and very sensitive to heat. And the porosity of the recess of the brick contained an impregnation of stearin, such as might have come from an ordinary tallow candle. And there was an extra wire on the telephone which should not have been there.

The information at the disposal of the Arson Squad was not, of course, available to Simon Good. Conversely, certain information at the disposal of Simon Good was not available to the Arson Squad...

A week before the fire, Dutchy, at Simon's request, forsook his bulb-stall in Leatherwick Way and went on holiday to Westland Zoy. Such was the power of teaching by numbers that he still found himself obeying almost automatically anything in the nature of a command from his old O.C. He booked in at the Goat & Compass, and by a curious coincidence the room he chose faced across the ancient market square and took in a view of the front gates of the depository in the narrow street opposite.

Nothing much happened at the establishment for several days until one morning business suddenly flourished. Crated antiques and paintings were off-loaded with great care from vans which backed in at the unloading bays. Dutchy strolled over to the main gates and casually watched proceedings. The burly foreman was a frequenter of the Goat & Compass, an ex-sergeant-major type who bellowed instructions in a fluent flow of Middle English.

The job on hand was of some magnitude, and speed seemed to be of the essence. No sooner was a van unloaded than it was driven away through the market place and up the hill to Trent Court for another load. As one such van was being seen safely through the gates Dutchy caught the foreman's eye and flipped him a cigarette. 'Business brisk, chum?' he inquired, as he lit one for himself and extended the match in a cupped hand.

'Yep – got a rush job on up at Trent Court... Ta! Got to clear a couple of wings by termorrer so the decorators can get in. The way some of these local yokels work you'd think they was on a go-slow or something. If they was to go on strike you wouldn't notice the difference. Blimey, what a mob!'

'Trouble with you, me old pal,' said Dutchy sympathetically, 'is that you're more used to the rat-race of "the Smoke".'

'I wish I was there now,' grunted the other. 'Seen you over at the Goat & Compass, ain't I?'

''Sright,' agreed Dutchy. 'Supposed to be on holiday, but it gets a bit of a bore on your own. Wouldn't mind doing a couple of days' work here meself. Anything going?'

The foreman looked him over. 'Can you drive a van?'

'Any make you like to name, chum. *And* my licence is clean.'

'Hop into the office and let's have yer name. I'll rustle up a couple of jokers for you who know the ropes. And out of curiosity I'll have a gander at that clean licence – it's a long time since I've seen one.'

Dutchy worked through the rest of the day till seven p.m. He offered to carry on till later, but the foreman, hesitating briefly, said there was nothing more for him that night; if he'd care to call over at eight a.m. there might be something for him to do in the morning. Dutchy thanked him and went back to the solace of the Goat & Compass.

Work at the depository, however, went on until quite late, and Dutchy, seeking a breath of fresh air before closing time, strolled across the dimly-lit market square and watched the vans roll by.

Suddenly he stiffened. The vehicles now in use were strange ones with new drivers. And their mates were no local yokels, they were far too keen and anxious-looking. From a shadowy corner he watched through some high iron railings and noted the slickness and speed with which the newcomers worked. No bellowed orders were required for these gentlemen ... there was nothing but smooth efficiency. Dutchy took a note of the van number as they moved away – in the opposite direction to Trent Court...

The following morning he reported and was taken on again, and the job was finished by midday. That evening at the Goat & Compass he treated the foreman to a drink for his kindness in giving him some employment.

'Sorry it wasn't longer,' said the foreman, 'we'd have got on well together. You speak my language.'

'I think I'll have an early night,' said Dutchy, draining his tankard. 'I'm not used to hard work! If you get any more rush jobs in the next few days you'll know where to find me.'

He went up to his room but did not go to bed. He turned out the light, made himself comfortable in an armchair by the window, and settled down for a long vigil.

At length the inn closed and the customers drifted away to their lawful beds. Quietness descended, and by half-past-eleven Westland Zoy slept...

Dutchy chain-smoked into the early hours.

He woke with a jerk just before dawn.

There was noise and confusion everywhere. Through a gap in the curtains he was conscious of lurid flames leaping skywards out of a terrifying holocaust of billowing smoke and sparks. For one awful moment his simple soul wondered if he had passed on to the wrong place. He shook himself into full wakefulness and got quite a good view of the fire at the depository...

Later he pressed Button A and waited for the coins to settle in the box.

'Simon?'

'Yes?'

'There's been a fire, you know where.'

'There has? Well, well, whaddya know! Much damage?'

'The damp-course may be left.'

'How very efficient! When did it start?'

Dutchy hedged for a moment and Simon repeated the question.

'I – I must have dropped off for a second,' said Dutchy apologetically. 'It was well on the way when I woke up.'

'Clot! So after all that you wasted your time?'

'Not entirely. A couple of days ago I got a driving job shifting stuff in from Trent Court, and the bric-à-brac was crated and stowed away in the depository under the direction of the foreman.

'And?'

'Although I was laid off in the evening, work went on till past midnight. And the blokes who did the night work weren't locals. And the vans were different.'

'And?'

'The following morning the crates in the depository *looked* the same, but they weren't.'

The silence was deafening.

'You still there?' asked Dutchy.

'Of course I'm still here. How do you know they weren't the same?'

'I chalk-marked 'em – at least, all those I could mark without being seen. They rang the changes all right! I shouldn't mind betting that a load o' rubbish went up in smoke last night.'

'Any idea where the vans went to?'

'No, I had no means of following 'em. I took some numbers, but I expect they rigged the number-plates. There was just one driver's mate I thought I recognised – I'll see if I can find him and loosen him up.'

'You do that,' said Simon...

Lew Gabbitas picked up the receiver and announced himself.

'Sorry to hear about your fire,' said Simon. 'It was on the seven o'clock news.'

'Yes, it was most unfortunate,' agreed Mr Gabbitas. 'Most unfortunate indeed.'

'What was the cause?'

'A complete mystery. Probably a carelessly discarded cigarette-end in the packing department.'

'Smoking is permitted?'

'Of course not! But you know British workmen! I can well imagine a piece of sacking smouldering for hours before bursting into flames. In fact, one of the directors of the firm suggested as much to the Fire Brigade chief.'

'And what did the Fire Brigade say about it?'

'They are entering the cause of the fire as "At present unknown".'

'H'm. It was very wise of you to effect adequate insurance.'

'Indeed, yes! One can't be too careful – though I'm told the insurance will be by no means adequate.'

'So that average will apply?'

'I'm afraid so. The depository will have to find a considerable sum of money to make good the balance of the loss under the removal contract with the trustees of Trent Court. The depository most certainly will have to go into liquidation.'

'That's a very clever move,' agreed Simon Good.

Gabbitas was silent for a moment. Then, 'I'd like to discuss some further insurance business with you. Can you make it at the week-end?'

'I'm sorry, I can't. I'm taking a long week-end in the West country. Honiton.'

'Excellent! Then why not have lunch with me in Exeter on Saturday? Say one o'clock at the Raleigh Hotel – near St David's Station. You could come on to my place and see my pictures.'

Simon thanked him, and they were both very pleased at the way things were turning out. Simon was one step nearer to Lew Gabbitas. And Lew was one step nearer to his million-pound objective; he said as much to Lady Veronica Tuke...

Veronica looked unhappy. 'Don't you think you ought to call it a day?' she said.

A queer look came into Lew's eyes and he gazed at her with deliberation. For the first time since she had known him she felt, for some indefinable reason, *afraid*.

'You wanted a million pounds,' he said coldly, 'and you'll get a million pounds. There's almost half a million in sterling, and when the Yellow Fire Diamonds are finally in my possession there'll be a quarter of a million in kind. Add to that one more job which I have in mind, and then, total one million. And you.'

Veronica looked up at him with misgiving. 'The point is, Lew, will you be able to stop then? Has this acquisition of wealth become an obsession?'

'Whose fault would that be?' he countered. 'You weren't prepared to marry me unless I attained the objective – remember? Your pinnacle was high – why cut it back within sight of the summit?'

She was silent for a moment. Then– 'Lew, do you still love me?'

'Still?'

She nodded mutely, and once again saw the look of cold appraisal creep into the depths; there was little of the warmth of love.

'Yes,' he said briefly, but it was from his lips, not his heart. She swung away and extracted a cigarette from a silver box on the fire-place.

Lew softened. 'Veronica – I meant it!'

'I'm overwhelmed with the display of affection,' she said, fumbling with a table lighter.

'I gave you the answer to an unnecessary question.'

'It was a calculated answer. There's no place for calculation in affection.'

'Everything I do lately is calculated,' growled Lew, putting an arm about her. 'And as for being calculating, weren't you being just that when you gave the police a near description of me in Hatton Garden? There was no need for you to have come forward at all – especially as I had just handed you a quarter of a million pounds' worth of diamonds. That was being calculating to the point of foolishness.'

'I've told you again and again, Lew, I had to make a quick decision, and I still think it was for the best.'

'You could have walked away out of it like I did, but no, with your everlasting search for kicks you couldn't resist attending a line-up with the Yellow Fire Diamonds in your handbag.'

'Listen, Lew. It wasn't done in my ever-lasting search for kicks, as you put it. According to the form, the man left as a rearguard should have trailed along behind the others down Flinders Court. But he didn't, he stayed put. And the only way in which I could cover setting off the igniter was by spilling my handbag near the gully – it was no longer a matter of bending down to flick a piece of grit from the inside of my shoe. And as the guard bent down to pick up the odds and ends he got a good look at me – so there was no question of my walking away out of it as you suggest, that would have made me Number One suspect. For all I knew he subsequently got a good look at you, and you could have been picked up from *his* description. As it happened, he was weeping so much from the tear gas he saw very little, but I didn't know that at the time. It seemed to me, therefore, that the best thing I could do was to give a reason-ably elastic picture of you and then smack it down at any later identify parade. That let you out completely.'

'There might not have been anyone else on the line-up who fitted the description you gave,' objected Lew with considerable feeling.

'My dear Lew,' smiled Veronica, 'the whole idea of the parade is to *have* people roughly fitting the description so that the suspect has every possible chance. And as you were picked up so quickly, all the other men must have been in the vicinity at the same time – any one of them could have done it. It was ironical that the man I actually picked out was a policeman.'

'Ah, yes, the police! Why did you later imply to them that you weren't in Hatton Garden?'

'Because I wanted no part in murder, Lew,' she said coldly. 'As soon as I learnt a man had been killed I had to think in terms of my own alibi. As it happened, the police themselves provided me with it. They saw me on the Chard road.'

'Others have lost their lives,' grated Lew, 'and you know it.'

'I know of accidents which may or may not have been accidental.'

'This was accidental.'

'From an explosion engineered by you in commission of a crime. Followed by cold-blooded shooting. That's sailing too near the wind for my liking.'

'There was still no need for you to have denied being in Hatton Garden. It would have been better to deny any connection with me – that way we would have both been in the clear if we kept well apart; they would have to prove conspiracy. As it is, they've been asking questions all round – of you, of Hammersley, of the car-hire firm–'

'But not of you.'

'No, I only get a courtesy call from the local police to see how I enjoyed my holiday – that in itself is suspicious.'

Lady Veronica's mood changed and she uttered a soft, deep-throated chuckle. 'My darling Lew,' she chided, 'you're far too sensitive! You must always find a motive for everything! They're not asking you questions because there's nothing to ask. Forget all about it and go ahead and paint your picture – have you started a new one yet?'

'I've nearly finished it – a small one commensurate with the job.'

A queer, apprehensive look suddenly came into her eyes. She said, 'I drove out to West-land Zoy last night and watched the fire.'

'You did what?' jerked Lew angrily. 'I told you not to go anywhere near the place!'

'It was safe enough – half the county was there; it could be seen for miles. It depressed me, Lew. As I watched all that smoke and ash I felt I was on the edge of a volcano.

Perhaps both of us are... Was – was any-one–?'

'Hurt?'

'Yes.' Her voice was no more than a gentle susurration of sound.

He regarded her whimsically. 'No, my dear. No casualties at all, this time.'

Fear fled. 'Then only one date,' she said gaily. 'That makes a change! Darling, darling Lew! You were born poor and I was born rich. I've got poorer and you've got richer – we must be near the meeting point!'

'The objective is in sight,' he agreed with satisfaction.

'What happens now – you said there was one more job?'

'I thought of winding up with a burglary. Here.'

'*Here?* At Four Chimneys? You must be mad!'

'Aren't we all? I've asked a friend of Hammersley's down. A certain Mr Good. Simon Good. I think you'll find him interesting.'

The driver's mate that Dutchy thought he recognised on the night they rang the changes at Westland Zoy turned out to be a local man after all, but it cost Dutchy a couple of pounds in the Goat & Compass before he extracted the information that the vanloads of antiques had been whipped away to an ostensibly derelict warehouse in

Banwell Major.

A trip out in the middle of the night in a hired car, followed by a skilful breaking and entering, confirmed that the place was chock-a-block with stuff waiting, no doubt, to be hived off to unscrupulous buyers.

Simon was pleased with the information.

Although the theft of a quarter of a million pounds' worth of diamonds was small fry in these days of two-and-a-half million pounds train robberies, Superintendent Lingard, because of his nagging conviction that Roag's Syndicate was at the bottom of the business, frequently found himself brooding over the details.

The man they were after had calmly walked past the main entrance of the Continental Diamond Exchange and had vanished round the corner into Leatherwick Way – *Leatherwick Way!* With a jolt Lingard thought of the man Dutchy with his stall of bulbs and fertilisers. There was nothing in records about him other than being an old associate of Simon Good, but it might prove interesting to know what he was doing at the time of the robbery. He decided to have a word with him himself. Hammersley hadn't recognised him – would Dutchy? After all these years he doubted it.

He was wrong.

There was no time like the present and the

superintendent ordered his car to drop him off in Holborn. Pushing his way through the hurly-burly of Leather Lane market, he made for the narrow offshoot known as Leatherwick Way, which swings back towards Hatton Garden. Dutchy's two stalls, complete with spielers dressed in picturesque Dutch attire, were doing a roaring trade, and for a few minutes Lingard listened spellbound to the virtues of the fertilisers and bulbs offered for sale. Dutchy himself was taking money and giving change hand over fist, and the superintendent waited for a convenient lull before approaching him from the rear of the stalls and drawing him discreetly aside.

'I'm a police officer,' he said quietly. 'Can I have a word with you?'

'Sure, guv,' said the Cockney easily enough, although his heart jinked alarmingly and his mind back-somersaulted to Banwell Major. 'What d'you want – some bulbs for the cells? Of course, I'd like to have a look at your union card – can't be too careful these days. Ta! Now – what's your beef?'

'Cast your mind back to the Friday before Bank Holiday. What were you doing?'

'Doing?' The question took Dutchy by surprise. 'Same as usual, I suppose. Me and the boys was here about ten o'clock.'

'Is ten o'clock the usual time, then?'

'Well, no – it's a bit earlier than usual. We had a lot of gear to put out for the Bank Holiday trade, see? Why?'

'Did anything unusual happen?'

'Not so far as I can remember. It's going back a bit– Half a mo' – that was the day of the robbery in Hatton Garden. That caused a bit of a stir! I went round and had a gander at the scene of the crime–' Dutchy broke off and looked thoughtful. 'What are you getting at, guv? I was here before the robbery took place, but so was quite a lot of other stall-holders.'

'Of course, of course!' soothed Lingard. 'We shall interview them all, in due course. But the man we're interested in escaped this way and I wondered if you could recollect any small point worthy of mention.'

'No, guv, nothing. Why, did he hide the diamonds in me bulbs?'

Lingard joined in the forced laughter and apologised for having held up the lunch-time trade. 'If you think of anything, let us know,' he said.

'I'll do that,' said Dutchy as the super-intendent drifted away into the crowd. Thoughtfully he lit a cigarette and touched one of his men on the arm. 'I'm going to get a cup of tea,' he said.

'I'll send the lad over for one, guv.'

'No. I want to think. I've just had a shock.'

He went across to a grubby little café and

sat down with a cup of strong tea. He brooded there for perhaps ten minutes, his mind laboriously grinding back into the past. Although relieved to learn that the questioning had nothing to do with his activities in the West country, he had nevertheless been shaken to the core. Lingard! So that was the man who had put Simon down for twelve months! The sixth man, the odd man out! The man described by the judge in court as having a good memory, who would remain in the background and keep an eye on Simon when he came out, the man who said he would tear the Syndicate apart – one at a time if necessary. The man that Blake couldn't place before and after he was arrested for doing a good turn for the selfsame judge.

This was something that Simon would be interested in with a vengeance. With a vengeance.

# 15

## Artists In Crime

When Simon Good arrived at the Raleigh Hotel in Exeter, Lew Gabbitas was already at the bar sipping an aperitif. His eyes were downcast and the corners of his mouth drooped, but as he looked up and saw Simon his face slicked into radiant geniality – so quickly that Simon wondered if he had been mistaken.

'My dear Mr Good! So nice to see you. I was very satisfied with your trial run – I refer, of course, to the depository business.'

'It was to our mutual advantage,' said Simon smoothly as he accepted a drink. 'What is it you want me to do now?'

'Tut, tut! First a meal here and then a pleasant drive out to my place. Then we'll get down to business.'

'At least tell me about your million pound objective – that sounded interesting.'

Lew sipped his drink reflectively. He said, apparently at a tangent, 'I have numerous lady friends.'

'There's safety in numbers,' agreed Simon profoundly.

'But there is one above all others.'

Simon blew a neat smoke ring up at the oak-beamed ceiling. 'I've heard this story before,' he said reflectively.

'Not this one,' replied Lew firmly. 'Before she'll consent to marry me I have to attain a target, in money and kind, of one million pounds sterling. I have almost reached that figure.'

'And you can't wait much longer, Spring is on the way.'

Lew was faintly annoyed. 'My impatience has nothing to do with the urgency of Spring,' he flashed. 'The point is that now the objective is in sight I begin to have certain doubts.'

'Like she doesn't love you?'

'Something like that. I sometimes feel that perhaps after all she is, as the vulgar say, stringing me along, that she set the target merely for kicks. She is considerably younger than I am.'

'It's a large amount of wealth to acquire,' mused Simon. 'Do you think you'll be able to stop at a million?'

The deep-set eyes of Lew Gabbitas clouded for a moment. 'She has expressed the same doubt,' he said unhappily.

'A lot of people must have got hurt.'

'A lot of people did get hurt,' said Mr Gabbitas frankly, and entirely without regret. 'People are always getting hurt, even in the pursuit of happiness.'

'And what does she think about that?'

Once again Lew's eyes slated over. 'She doesn't like it,' he said. 'Even to the extent of instituting a compensation scheme.'

'How very kind. She is, as you say, one above all others. Are you living together in sin?' Simon added offensively.

'No. Suspense.'

'Same thing, in many ways,' said Simon cheerfully. 'Do you know, Mr Gabbitas, I've a feeling she might let you down.'

'That would be a pity,' shrugged Lew. 'She has no near relatives for me to compensate. Shall we eat?'

An excellent lunch mellowed Lew Gabbitas considerably. Later, as they drove into King's Barton, he spotted the vicar at the lich-gate of St Anselm's. That extrovert young man, suddenly recognising Lew, waved his arms frantically. They slowed down.

'Good afternoon, Vicar,' smiled Lew. 'Mr Good, meet the Reverend Theodosius Todd.'

As the name rolled mellifluously off Lew's tongue, Simon thought he detected a faint modulation of malicious humour. Acknowledgements were exchanged and young Mr Todd got down to business with the earnestness of his calling. 'I wondered, Mr Gabbitas, if it would be convenient for me to call this afternoon with the scouts, to collect the articles you promised for their jumble sale?'

'By all means,' beamed Mr Gabbitas. 'They'll need their handcart, there's a considerable amount of stuff. It's all ready in the garage. How is your hand?'

'Almost completely healed now, thank you,' said the Rev Theo. 'I'll be round later, then.'

With a brief nod, Gabbitas instructed the driver to proceed, and for a moment his features relaxed into a fathomless expression as he looked away. And it was then that Simon saw a sudden, startled look come into the eyes of the Reverend Theodosius Todd. It was as though young Todd had seen Gabbitas in some other light for the first time; and that what he had seen had not met with his approval. Incredulity, doubt, distress, all merged in that violent lucent flash of understanding. There was a fractional reflection of something which came and went with the quickness of a high-speed lens-shutter.

The Reverend Theodosius Todd, deep in thought, watched the car snake up the road.

'A charming little village,' remarked Simon, as they drove through the market square with its ancient timbered wool exchange.

'Delightful!' agreed Lew. 'Now, you see that inn – no, not that one – the next one, the Bull & Buffalo. When you help me with my next scheme I would like Hammersley to stay there – and you, too, if possible. The manager is due to go on holiday shortly. Do you think Hammersley could manage the place?'

'I've no doubt at all, but surely the brewers wouldn't let just anyone step in?'

'It's a free house. I'm the licencee. I own it.'

'Well, well! Lew Gabbitas, licensed to sell wines, beers and tobaccos. Your tastes are certainly catholic! What *do* you do for a living?'

'My income-tax form stresses the gentle-man farmer aspect – although really I'm not very good at farming.'

'And you've told the Inland Revenue all about your million pound objective?'

'I've not even told you much about it,' smiled Gabbitas, 'and you're a friend.'

'I shouldn't bank on that,' advised Simon.

'Come now, Mr Good, I only invite my friends to Four Chimneys.' They swept into a drive. 'And here we are...'

Simon remarked as they entered the house, 'I should have thought there was room for both Hammersley and myself to stay here rather than at the Bull & Buffalo. What's the point in farming us out?'

'Servant problem. And it's preferable that we are not seen together too much. If any-thing goes wrong it will be better for you.'

'Nice of you to think along those lines.'

'Nothing will go wrong, of course,' said Lew reassuringly. 'Would you mind very much if I put the finishing touches to a painting before getting down to business? I was in the middle of it when I had to leave to pick you up in Exeter, and I must get it out of my system. You can browse around my pictures whilst I do it.'

This seemed to be the standard method of greeting guests at Four Chimneys.

Simon was vastly impressed by all that he saw in the studio.

'Make yourself at home,' urged Lew, slipping into a smock. 'There's a drink in that cabinet and cigarettes in the box on top. I must get to work whilst the urge is still with me. I shan't be long.' And without further ado he got down to work on a small canvas already set on an easel.

'May I see what it is you're finishing?' inquired Simon.

'Of course.'

Simon gazed in admiration at the picture, one of troubled waters at the mouth of a river. 'Surely it's finished?' he said, squinting at it closely. 'The oil appears to have dried out – except in that corner.'

'I'm adding a bright spot,' smiled Lew. 'Just a break in the clouds with a hint of sunshine.'

'It's your picture,' said Simon. He left

Gabbitas to it and wandered thoughtfully around the gallery, helping himself to a cigarette on the way. He examined the exhibits carefully, paying particular attention to Lew's own works. There was one small vacant space which could have been the resting place of the picture Gabbitas was finishing. Now why should he want to finish a picture which was already finished? It bore a date, and Simon had mentally registered it. Gabbitas was certainly a curious host.

And then Simon pulled up with a jerk; he came to the half-finished canvas which took pride of place on the wall, the canvas to which Hammersley had referred. There was now a difference, however. When Hammersley had seen it the picture had consisted of a piece of carelessly, but carefully, draped velvet, rich in dark purples and black, an inanimate but real, touchable background effect. But now a casually dropped diamond necklace was taking shape, a breath-taking razzle-dazzle of iridescence which seemed three-dimensional in its scintillating brilliance. Surely its reality could be compared with the Flemish master's famous 'tear' picture in Bruges, a picture of a single tear rolling down a female cheek with such effect that generations have waited for it to drip to the floor.

The necklace was not yet complete. Twelve

major stones were in position, as were a host of smaller ones together with the clasp. There were still a number of background spaces in foundation colour waiting to be filled in with the twinkling yellow-fire sparkle from the brush of the man whose very soul was there on the canvas.

Simon stood there transfixed for a full minute before he suddenly bent forward and looked for a date. It was there in the left-hand corner. And then he saw something which puzzled him beyond the periphery of his understanding...

He drew away and pondered for a moment on this strangely moving collection of oils, trying to fathom what it all meant. He sensed a curious, eerie quality about them, as though good and evil were each striving for control.

Without disturbing Gabbitas, he wandered over to the cocktail cabinet and poured himself a drink. There was a folded copy of the *Telegraph* on top of the cabinet, and casually he glanced at an item marked in red ink:

*Copenhagen, Friday:* Lotte Ryngby, widow of a Falck Redningskorps officer who lost his life in a Copenhagen furniture-depository fire in June, yesterday received a packet containing currency to the value of £2,500 in recognition of her husband's devotion to public duty. The gift was anonymous.

A half-formed, elemental idea began to skeeter round Simon's brain like an intoxicated gnat, and in one frangible moment of perception it was suddenly imperative to take down a note of all the dates on all of Lew's pictures.

There was a note-pad on the cabinet and surreptitiously Simon eased off the top sheet, gently folding it into a firmer and more manageable size.

From where he stood he counted the pictures, eighteen hanging and one on the easel – nineteen in all. Using his Biro pen he divided the paper into a rough plan. Then wandering from one painting to another, apparently haphazardly, he gradually took note of the dates where he could do so without attracting the attention of Lew Gabbitas. Occasionally he moved over to the other wall and brooded despondently on some modern atrocity or other, speculating if the artist was now safely locked up.

He had managed, so far as he could make out, to account for the majority of the dates, when Gabbitas suddenly said, 'Well, what do you think of my collection?'

There was genial anticipation in his voice.

Simon Good lit a cigarette. 'Quite good,' he said briefly.

Lew was disappointed. 'No more than

that? That collection of moderns is worth a fortune.'

'Is it now? I wouldn't have thought so. Mind you, I like some of the colour effects. I suppose you haven't hung any of them the wrong way up?'

Lew Gabbitas ignored the question. 'What about these?' he inquired, with a sweep of his arm at his own paintings.

Simon remained silent for a moment. 'I like 'em,' he said at length. 'A different school.'

'The faint praise is damning, Good.'

'Well, I either like them or I don't. What more do you want?'

'I was hoping you'd be a little more enthusiastic.'

'I'm no artist, Gabbitas. What would you have me say? A few sycophantic phrases about luminosity and composition? A few catchwords picked up out of the *Artist & Palette?* Is that what you expected?'

'Perhaps I did,' said Lew slowly.

Simon walked deliberately along the range of Lew's works, taking his time at each one. Thoughtfully he walked over to the workbench and flicked off half-an-inch of ash into the Venetian glass ash tray. Abstractedly he moved back along the collection, mentally absorbing each canvas, striving to detect some more of the dates which were woven into the general texture of each picture, dates

224

which, as Hammersley had remarked, were so skilfully merged that they were there one moment and gone the next. At length he said, 'I can say without hesitation that I prefer these to the monstrosities over there. I like them because I can recognise without effort what they're supposed to be. I like them because the extreme delicacy of the brush-work gives them a photographic quality – which I understand is a *bad* point, but I like it. I prefer it, for example, to those female forms over there which appear to have been nourished on a new food that develops only certain parts of their anatomies, and then not in equal proportions. You have, I notice, collected a large number of pictures of the river – the Thames? – presumably all by the same artist. And I notice several curious facts about them.'

'Curious facts?' Lew's voice came from a long way away.

'Yes. In spite of the *sameness* of them, they're all different. In those where the colour is most brilliant there is a curious suggestion of despair. In those which possess less colour – to the point of being almost only greys and blacks and sombre browns – there is somehow a more vivid, more impressionistic effect carrying a suggestion of hope. In the former, the brushwork is fine; in the latter, it is like gossamer.'

Lew Gabbitas radiated pleasure. 'You are

more analytical than you would care to have me believe, Mr Good. And you were doing yourself an injustice when you said you were no artist.'

Simon blinked in surprise. 'Have I said something?' he inquired mildly.

'You are now speaking of my own work,' oozed Gabbitas, obnoxiously modest.

'Your work?' Simon sounded genuinely astonished. 'Then all I can say is that you've missed your vocation. You perhaps mean all except that magnificent centre canvas – the unfinished necklace? That is obviously by a master.'

'No, no, that is mine, too,' said Gabbitas deprecatingly.

'But with an eye for detail like that you could earn yourself a fortune!'

'I did. A long while ago. During the war. I made a lot of money. I worked for the other side – the Nazis. I was a common collaborator. I was not particularly proud of the fact, but I was determined to avoid poverty and other forms of degradation. I didn't ask for the war, it was forced on me.'

'It was forced on quite a lot of people,' said Simon.

'If you can't beat it, join it.'

'Ah, the worthy vicar and his boy scouts,' said Lew. 'Please excuse me.' He hurried from the studio, and Simon seized the opportunity to make a quick but methodical check of the dates of the pictures. Where only one date was apparent, he put a cross in the appropriate square on his chart to indicate the fact. He marked each *s*, *m* or *l* – small, medium or large – according to the size of each picture. He went over to the painting on the easel.

Gabbitas had, with comparatively slight addition, made considerable alteration to the mood. Whereas previously there was a clever picture of turbulence and despondency, Simon now felt there was a battle of good and evil. Or was it evil and good? The paintings seemed to be the key to Lew Gabbitas. There was now another date, this time in the right-hand corner, that day's date, the date Lew had put in the finishing touches.

Simon jotted it down and moved back swiftly to the unfinished canvas of the necklace. He examined it closely again, peering at it from within a few inches of the bottom right-hand corner, moving his head from left to right in a bird-like motion as he tried to catch the light at different angles.

He was baffled. His theorising was now well and truly out of line. Some of the pictures with only *one* date bore a signature. Every other picture with two dates also bore a signature. But here was an *unfinished* picture, as yet with no signature, but with *two* dates... The second one was only faintly discernible, but it was nevertheless there...

'Looking for something?' asked Lady Veronica Tuke.

Simon whipped round. And if the liquid gold voice had done something to his chemistry, the physical being of Lady Veronica was an even more violent reagent. Together, the transmuting effect was devastating.

'I'm looking for a date,' he said, straightening up.

She sized him up in frank appraisal. 'Will I do?' she asked, in a voice full of sultry promise.

'Yes, sweetheart, you will. Are you the maid or something?'

Lady Veronica gurgled happily. 'I'm something,' she said.

'I can't argue that.'

'You must be Simon Good. I'm Veronica.'

'Oh, I beg your pardon. Lew's–?'

'Yes, Lew's. Full stop. No dash or question mark.'

'I was going to say "Lew's objective", but that didn't seem quite polite. Shall we say that at a million pounds he's got a bargain?' Simon added gallantly.

'I think I'm going to like you,' she said, moving over to him and lightly touching his arm in a feline manner which sent his blood pressure rocketing. 'So Lew has told you about his objective?'

'Not all of it. He's told me *of* it.' Simon gently disengaged himself. 'When you came in I was admiring this picture of the diamonds. It's a brilliant piece of work. But surely it isn't finished?'

'Of course it isn't! Anyone can see that! There are still two major stones to be – to be painted in. To say nothing of a number of smaller ones. Why do you pass such an obvious comment?'

'I noticed it was dated.'

'Lew always dates his work when he starts.'

'But some of the pictures have two dates, one in each corner.'

'Sometimes he adds to the canvas ages afterwards, and then he puts in the date when he finally finishes.'

'The curious thing about this picture, light of my life, is that although it is not finished by any stretch of the imagination, it does in fact already bear two dates.'

Lady Veronica Tuke remained silent for a moment. She said at length, 'There's nothing stereotyped about Lew. He's unpredictable. And here he is!' There was relief in her voice.

Lew Gabbitas hurried into the studio. 'Ah, my dear!' he exclaimed. 'You've introduced yourselves? Fine! I've just been dealing with the vicar. I don't know if I've said something to offend him, but he seems suddenly to have turned rather distant. And once I caught him looking at me in a most curious fashion!'

'You're imagining things again, darling. You get worked up over a painting, and before you can say "turpentine" you're in a state of nervous tension. Shall I make some tea?'

'An excellent idea – and perhaps the scouts would like some lemonade or something before they go. Will you attend to it whilst I have a little chat with Mr Good?'

'Call him Simon,' said Veronica. 'I'm going to!'

The faint glint of jealousy which sparked in Lew's eyes did not go unnoticed by Simon. He realised then what Lady Veronica meant to Gabbitas, realised just how much Lew meant to Lady Veronica; or how little...

'She's very impetuous,' commented Lew, as she shut the door behind her. 'Sometimes I wonder about her.'

So did Simon, but he said, 'What is your plan for the immediate future – another unfortunate fire?'

'I thought perhaps a robbery this time.'

'Your collection of oils?'

'I hadn't thought of that,' said Gabbitas reflectively. 'I had in mind jewellery – jewellery in the safe here at Four Chimneys.'

'You want me to arrange the theft?'

'No, I will take care of that aspect. I want you to arrange the insurance – in the best possible way, with the least possible fuss. I wondered if you knew a valuer whose certificate would be accepted without question, one who would be, shall we say, generous in his valuation to start with.'

'I see. So you not only steal your own property, but you get an enhanced indemnity – if indemnity's the right word?'

'It's not a new idea,' apologised Lew. 'I would, of course, be paying premium on an enhanced sum insured.'

'That should give the judge a giggle,' prophesied Simon, his mind leaping ahead of Gabbitas. 'The insurance company would want to come and inspect your burglary precautions. And they might be suspicious if a burglar got round them too easily.'

'I'd thought of having the burglary in broad daylight when half the alarms aren't switched on anyway – after all, a householder does have to move freely in and out of his house without raising the entire neighbourhood.'

'The company might insist on new precautions – a new safe, for example.'

'I will agree to anything they like to suggest; perhaps my burglary would then occur before the work was completed and suspicion would be cast on the workmen.'

'You think of everything,' said Simon

admiringly. 'But don't forget that the company might not give cover till the precautions are in order.'

'Come, Mr Good, whose side are you on – the company's or mine?'

'Mine,' said Simon. 'Are your valuables already insured?'

'For a totally inadequate amount with the Aldwych Insurance Corporation.'

'In that case we must fix it all up through the Aldwych – it will look more natural that way.'

'Will you be able to do that?' asked Gabbitas in surprise.

'You'd be astonished at what I am able to do,' Simon assured him. 'And now, what do I get out of all this?'

Gabbitas looked at him through slanted eyes. 'To avoid intensive bargaining, you name your price.'

'Five,' said Simon.

'Hundred?'

'Per hundred. Or, as Nero said when he fiddled his celebrated fire, *quinque per centum.*'

'That'll be a lot of money.'

'I've no means of telling – you haven't told me how much is at stake. That's why I thought a percentage would be fairer. To me.'

Gabbitas thrummed his fingers on the cocktail cabinet. 'You mean five per cent on the sum insured?'

'Yes. In cash. In advance. My usual terms.'

Lew made up his mind. 'Agreed,' he said.

'There is another point,' said Simon. 'Should there be any items you particularly don't wish the police to know about – you'll have to give them a list, of course, after your burglary – you'll find the valuer I'll send along very understanding. He'll step up the value of the other items to cover the doubtful ones.'

'I'm glad I consulted you, Mr Good,' said Lew Gabbitas.

'It's all part of the service,' said Mr Good. 'And please do call me Simon – it will please Veronica...'

There were several other points they each wished to discuss, and together they concocted a letter to the Aldwych Insurance Corporation inquiring if that august body could recommend a reliable valuer and requesting the services of their burglary surveyor. Simon kindly offered to post it in Exeter.

The letter never reached the Aldwych Insurance Corporation.

That evening, after Simon had left, Lew and Veronica sat by a log fire sipping a nightcap. Lew broke the silence of contentment.

'Within a few weeks the objective will be reached and you will have to keep your part of the bargain, Veronica,' he said gently. 'You have no regrets?'

Veronica reached for a cigarette to play for time. 'I don't really know,' she confessed. 'I don't think so. You've been so very patient. I think I shall be glad when all this business comes to an end. You're trying your luck just a shade too far, Lew. I'm – I'm afraid. One false step and everything is finished.'

'If anything goes wrong it will be Good and Hammersley who'll be finished,' he promised confidently. 'In fact, they virtually are finished. One more trip to Amsterdam by Hammersley will secure the last of the Yellow Fire Diamonds. I shall then install Hammersley as a temporary manager of the Bull & Buffalo, with Good staying there at the weekend I plan to have the burglary. I shall tell the police that after meeting Hammersley casually as a result of a street accident in London he has looked me up on several occasions, rather presuming on my friendship, and that I found this temporary job for him out of sheer kindness. Everyone locally knows that I am always doing good works earnestly. One of the good works I haven't told you about concerns a Mr J Heathersedge Smith of Yeovil.'

'Do I know him?'

'I doubt it. He was involved in a curious mix-up with the Tyburn & New York Insurance Company over a share dividend warrant. It was all in the papers at the time. He incurred heavy legal costs to prove his point. I've sent him cash to the extent of his costs – anonymously, of course.'

'Why should you do that?'

'Because Simon Good is employed by that Insurance Group. If anyone gets curious about our compensation scheme, the finger will begin to point at him.'

'Why, was he involved in this dividend warrant business?'

'I imagine nobody knows for certain. He involved the company in a lot of undesirable publicity over another matter, and I think you'll appreciate that if anyone starts to get inquisitive about the number of philanthropic gestures publicised in the Press, a process of association will bring in the name of Simon Good.'

Lady Veronica Tuke looked doubtful. 'I don't quite see why,' she said.

'Mr Smith of Yeovil has acknowledged receipt of the gift in the Press in the usual way. If anyone is getting curious about the various amounts of compensation being made, Mr Smith's case will be one in point. His case links with the Tyburn & New York, and the Tyburn & New York links with Simon Good. The implication would be that he is linked with all the other cases.'

'You're a genius for involving people, Lew.'

'Yes. I have already fixed up with Harry Levien to do the burglary. When it takes place, the police will leave no stone unturned and they will doubtless make inquiries about the presence of Good and Hammersley. I will immediately send Hammersley to Amsterdam, and this time he will be caught with some of the missing jewellery – not any of the Yellow Fire Diamonds, of course. Good and Hammersley won't stand a chance with their dubious backgrounds.'

'Won't the police connect your burglary-insurance with Simon Good? Where would that put you?'

'Mr Good is an astute man,' said Lew. 'We can safely assume that the placing of this insurance will be far removed from him – as will the valuer, the surveyor and any inspectors who call.'

Veronica drew deeply on her cigarette. 'I like Simon,' she said.

Lew remained silent. That was just one more reason why Simon Good should be removed. He put aside his glass and said at a tangent, 'I wonder why the vicar gave me such a curious look?'

# 16

## Birth Of An Operation

'When I visited Four Chimneys,' said Simon to Hammersley, 'there was – in the words of Omar – a door to which I found no key; there was a veil past which I could not see. But now I've found the key, and I can almost see past the veil. You know what has been happening, of course?'

'I thought we'd agreed that Lew was building up a background ultimately to involve me in something which will help him to attain his objective, at the same time leaving me in the dirt. But doesn't that quatrain go on to say "Some little talk awhile of me and thee there seemed – and then no more of thee and me"?'

'There may be no more of thee, but there's certainly going to be some more of me. For that reason I've summoned the prey of rogues for a council of war, tonight. Gabbitas's paintings are the key. He has betrayed himself. Look at this chart – I've already explained it to the others.'

Simon produced an elaboration of the hastily scribbled plan made in Gabbitas's studio. The new one showed the approximate sizes of the pictures according to the classification he had made – small, medium or large. Dates were now neatly inscribed in the appropriate corners, and at the side of the chart he had made a list in chronological order, using the commencing dates.

'We'll start by stating the obvious,' said Simon. 'All the pictures have a commencement date in the bottom left-hand corner; more than half have a second date in the bottom right-hand corner. Does that suggest that *less* than half have not been finished?'

'Not necessarily,' said Hammersley swiftly. 'Gabbitas told me he didn't *always* put two dates on his paintings, but if the signature's there the picture is definitely finished.'

'I've put a tick on those with signatures,' said Simon, running his finger over the plan. 'It seems that the second date is not solely a finishing date – it could well mark the happening of some other event.'

'That could be the position,' frowned Hammersley.

'Accepting that premise, some pictures may never receive a second date – if the event on which it hinges never happens. Now what is it he adds to an apparently finished picture before he puts the second date? For example, what did he do the day you were at Four Chimneys?'

'He added what he called a "bright spot" to an otherwise desolate river scene.'

'That is precisely what he did when I was there. Now what is the link? What triggers him off? You told me the pictures possessed a curiously disturbing quality. I had the same impression, it was as though evil and good were waging war. The canvas reflects what's going on within him.'

'Would you say he was – um – kinky?'

'Brother, he would make the circumference of a circle look like the shortest distance between two points. I've got a theory about it all. When you were at Four Chimneys, what bright spot happened – apart from the fact that you were there – that could have given him the sudden urge to paint?'

'None, so far as I can remember. When I arrived we had a pleasant evening. We went for a ride the following morning. He told me about his million pound objective, and blackmailed me into acting as his courier. That's about all. Oh, and the vicar called.'

'The vicar! The Rev Theo Todd?'

'I think that was his name. Curious chap. Had some sort of trouble with his oil-heater. And some virgins. I didn't quite get the drift of it.'

'You should go to church more often. What did he want? A subscription for the leaking font?'

'Not quite, although he was after a sub. Some widow in financial trouble. Quite a touching story.'

'And how did Gabbitas react to the plea? Willingly?'

'Oh, yes. He wrote a cheque for a hundred pounds.'

'A hundred pounds! That was a generous gesture!'

'Well, he's interested in antiques.'

'Antiques? What has that to do with it?'

'The widow lost her husband in a furniture depository fire at a place called – um – let me see, East Lampton. Started in the antique restoration department. Place completely gutted. A lot of valuable stuff from a local stately home went up in smoke. Her husband was a fireman. And an old nightwatchman was severely injured – not likely to recover, I gathered. May have died since... What's the matter?'

Simon was rooted to the spot. 'You didn't tell me of this before,' he reproved.

'It didn't seem important. What's the point?'

'Gabbitas recently had a fire at a depository at Westland Zoy in Somerset.'

'*You* didn't tell *me* about that,' countered Hammersley.

'I'm telling you now. We have the factor we've been looking for. The common factor.'

'Was anyone hurt at Westland Zoy?' asked

Hammersley shrewdly.

'No – that's what makes it interesting. *Now* the pictures really do tell a story. What was the date the vicar called?'

Hammersley consulted his pocket-diary, a book with many misleading entries. 'Here we are!' he said, thumbing the place.

Simon glanced at it and looked at his chart. 'Then this picture,' he said, pointing at a square and at the same time covering up the left-hand corner with his other hand, 'must be the one he completed that day – there's the date. Now, what was the date of the East Lampton fire?'

'It was about a fortnight previously. I don't know precisely. There was talk of it being caused by youths with fireworks.'

'Which would bring us back to the approximate date when Gabbitas started the picture,' said Simon, removing his hand. 'And there it is!' he added triumphantly. 'I was right about these paintings. Evil and good at war. The Devil and Conscience. Sin and atonement. Each picture small, medium or large according to the size of the crime. With one exception.'

'I told you he was nutty,' said Hammersley. 'Does your theory work anywhere else? When was this fire at Westland Zoy?'

Simon knew that date only too well. 'This picture fits the bill exactly,' he said, pointing.

'There's only one date here,' said Hammersley.

'Nobody was hurt. Nobody had to be compensated, there was no question of atonement. Evil won. The Devil got away with it. No bright spot was needed to soothe a guilty conscience.'

'We don't *know* there'll never be a second date,' said Hammersley.

'It's a Strad to a busted G-string there won't be!' shot Simon. 'It has a signature!'

Hammersley was impressed. 'Have we any other data to work on?'

'Yes. When I was at Four Chimneys there was a current copy of the *Telegraph* in Gabbitas's studio. A paragraph relating to the widow of a member of the Falck Redningskorps in Copenhagen was marked either side in red ink.'

'The Falck *what?*'

'Redningskorps. A Danish salvage-corps-cum-fire brigade. The widow had received a large sum in currency from an anonymous well-wisher in recognition of her husband's devotion to duty. Gabbitas put a "bright spot" on *this* picture – there's the date and signature.'

'So that the first date should bring us back to the date of the fire in Copenhagen? I wonder how we can check?'

'Newspaper files – if it was a fire of any magnitude. The *Telegraph* referred to a fire in June. We may be able to get hold of a few back copies of Danish papers. Are there any other titbits you can fill in?'

'Gabbitas did mention the loss of a – friend – in a disastrous fire at Ghent, but he didn't say when it happened.' Hammersley removed his spectacles and gave them a nervous polish. 'You're suggesting that these paintings of Lew's are virtually a record of his misdeeds building up to his million pound objective?'

Simon hedged for a bit. 'That's what I thought,' he said, 'but I'm rather puzzled about that central picture – the one that was almost blank when you saw it.'

'The one with the sketchy outline of a necklace?'

'Yes.'

'Has he finished it now?'

'Not completely, but it *already* bears two dates.'

'Then working on your theory, he has already made amends for any injury done. That means that the unfinished picture has its bright spot – am I right?'

'It's one mass of bright spots. There's sheer genius in every single sparkling diamond.'

'They've turned out to be diamonds, have they? When I saw it I couldn't tell what they were supposed to be. And he hasn't finished it yet?'

'No. And the size of the canvas doesn't seem to fit the value of the crime – unless it's a case of *multum in parvo*. I fancy he's gradually completing the painting as the gems come back from, say, the Continent, a few at a time – refaceted and polished, altered beyond recognition; the only un-alterable factor being the innate quality of them. And he's putting his heart and soul into every single stone.'

'The results of a robbery! And somebody's smuggling them into the country – perhaps they were even smuggled out in the first place. A job like that would require con-siderable nerve.'

Simon favoured him with a long, penetrating look of peculiar significance. 'Not if you didn't know you were doing it,' he said.

From outer space, a million light years away, an infinitesimal splinter of under-standing arrived and impinged itself with a sickening jab behind Hammersley's eyes. His jaw dropped a couple of notches.

'Not me?' he gaped.

'Yes, you,' said Simon.

The door bell rang, and Hammersley didn't even see Simon leave the room to answer it. His mind was still travelling rapidly back-wards along the line of understanding to bleak infinity.

'What's the matter with Charles?' asked Quenella as she came in with Dutchy.

'He's just had a shock,' explained Simon. 'He's only just realised he's been smuggling the Yellow Fire Diamonds.'

Hammersley's bone structure turned to jelly. 'Not the Yellow Fire Diamonds!' he gulped aghast.

'What else? They were stolen on the Friday before Bank Holiday, a man was killed, they had to be dropped like a hot coal – who better to give them to than you? You take them to Exeter for Gabbitas, and he clears off to Scotland till things cool off. He's an opportunist.'

'We've – we've got no proof that they were the Yellow Fire Diamonds, have we?' stuttered Hammersley agitatedly, as a long vista of uncomfortable years reached out to him from the Old Bailey. 'Have we?'

'Not really,' agreed Simon, 'except that there are comparatively few yellow diamonds in circulation, and Rip says that the ones you're smuggling are of the highest water.'

'*Rip* says? How does he know?'

'He's seen samples of what you've been carrying.'

Hammersley stared up at Simon in sheer disbelief. 'When?' he gulped.

'Big Brother is watching all the time,' pronounced Simon.

'That's still no proof that they are *the* Yellow Fire Diamonds,' expostulated Hammersley, clutching at straws.

'Except that the number of spaces allotted on Lew's unfinished picture coincides with the number of diamonds in the stolen rivière – according to the newspaper photographs of the necklace, that is.'

'I could get ten years for this,' groaned Hammersley.

Dutchy said he thought twenty, and Quenella promised to be waiting at the gates when she was old and grey.

'One thing that doesn't fit our theory,' said Simon thoughtfully, 'is the fact that the first date on the picture is not the Friday of the robbery.'

Twin beams of hope shone out through Hammersley's spectacles. 'Well, there you are then...' His voice died. 'Of course, it wouldn't be,' he added dejectedly. 'He was on his way to Scotland.'

Simon looked pleased. 'Then they *are* the Yellow Fire Diamonds,' he concluded. 'It all fits beautifully.'

'I'm glad you think so,' grated Hammersley. 'I shall refuse to go to Amsterdam in a couple of days time.'

'For heaven's sake don't do that! Lew's almost had his ha'p'orth out of you and one or two more trips will complete matters. You've just about reached the point of no return. There'll be one accident for which you will be in no position to make a claim – unless you have an asbestos claim form.'

Hammersley's look of anguish was almost comical.

'Poor, dear Charles,' said Quenella, bestowing a light kiss on his forehead. 'I hate funerals.'

'Don't worry,' said Simon. 'It's my guess that it'll be the trip after next when you won't know what's hit you – when you've brought back the remaining diamonds.'

'I'll never be able to look those Customs chaps in the eye again,' said Hammersley unhappily. 'It's all right when you don't know what you're doing.' A sudden thought struck him. 'How was I doing it, anyway?'

'When you next go to Amsterdam Rip will show you–'

A muted chime sounded, and Simon looked up in surprise. 'Back door!' he said, leaving the room again.

He returned a moment later with Strookman.

'You're under observation at the front,' explained Rip. 'Looks like a plainclothes man.'

'Well, well, things are hotting up! I wonder what they suspect us of? Complicity in the diamond theft? Is it all clear on the towpath?'

'So far as I could tell. I moved with caution

in case not. And how is my dear friend Charles? He doesn't look quite so carefree as he did a short while ago in Amsterdam.'

'Your dear friend Charles isn't at all carefree,' said Hammersley testily. 'You might have kept me in the picture.'

'*Ja, ja,* I tell you all about it one day.'

'I'm only sorry my passport was stolen at the critical time,' said Simon with profound regret. 'What have you found out, Rip?'

'I learn from trade connections in Antwerp that the firm which bought the Yellow Fire rivière is a small one, reputable – although they did work a fast one in purchasing it from an old man who didn't know its true value. They gave him all the money he was likely to need for the rest of his life – that was all he asked for – but nevertheless the deal was slick. The insurance was underwritten in Brussels by an American syndicate.'

'Did they pay up?'

'Yes, but the diamond firm was underinsured, and the insurance was subject to average. They tried to extract an *ex-gratia* payment – on the grounds that the deal was so secret that they didn't wish to disclose a precise amount to their insurers, but the underwriters wouldn't play.'

'I should think not! Was anyone fired from the diamond firm after the robbery? I'm thinking along the lines of the security leak.'

'Nobody was fired *after* the event, but one old employee was under notice for inefficiency – he'd taken suddenly to the bottle, and nobody knew where he was getting his money from.' Strookman lit a cigar and examined the end critically. 'This old boy had been seen once or twice in a café with a well-dressed stranger, whom he referred to as "M'sieur G". He left the firm on the Thursday before the robbery and hasn't been seen since. One concludes that "M'sieur G" was Gabbitas.'

'The jigsaw's almost finished,' commented Simon. 'What are we going to do about it?'

Quenella threw out a suggestion. 'Couldn't we find out, with a little research, what the crimes represented by the pictures were, and hold the information over his head?'

'With the limited means at our disposal I think it would prove quite difficult to track down all the events,' brooded Simon. 'Newspaper files are all right if we know roughly what we are looking for, but mere dates aren't enough. All sorts of crimes happen on the same day all over the place, and all sorts of people get gifts from anonymous donors.'

'Lew's line of action appears to be confined to arson and robbery,' pointed out Quenella. 'I suppose the snag from our angle is that a newspaper wouldn't necessarily relate the good deed to the bad one – although

Gabbitas could have made such reference a condition of the acknowledgement.'

'Doubtless we could trace all the events if we had the time and all the newspapers for the last umpteen months,' mused Simon. 'I imagine we haven't the time, speed is now essential. It's more of a job for the Criminal Records Office.'

Dutchy reached for a cigarette. 'Then why not write to the cops?' he suggested humorously. 'What about Superintendent Lingard?'

Simon Good's jaw swung round. 'You've got something there!' he said.

'Superintendent Lingard? Who's he?' Hammersley sounded irritable. 'Doesn't anyone tell me anything?'

'He's the gent who sampled your grapes,' said Simon gently. 'I thought you knew him.'

Charles Hammersley gripped the arms of his chair and gradually pushed himself upright as his mind slid back down the gentle slope of the years. 'Lingard!' he exploded at length. 'Bless my soul! Lingard! So he's keeping his promise after all these years! I think we should drop the whole business before it's too late.'

'It is too late,' said Simon.

Strookman said, in a calculating manner, 'We're in this Syndicate for what we can get out of it. We've had a spell of crusading with the Judge and Toledano – let's have a go at being infidels for a change.'

'Then how would it be if we relieved Gabbitas of the loot,' suggested Quenella. 'We could realise on it, deduct our usual brokerage, and send the balance to all those who've suffered at his hand. That would satisfy both infidel and crusader among you alike. Everybody would be happy.'

'Except the owners of the property,' said Rip lazily. 'Take, for example, the Yellow Fire Diamonds, with a face value of two and a half million guilders.'

'And who really owns them?' frowned Quenella. 'A slick-jack firm which snapped them up from a doddery old man who didn't appreciate their true value, with the intention of reselling them in London at a fantastic profit.'

'If we sent the old boy an additional cut, everybody, as Quenella says, would be happy,' said Simon.

'Except the insurance syndicate,' yawned Rip. 'And Gabbitas.'

'We don't want to draw too fine a line on it,' remarked Simon. 'Quenny's got something. But even if we could get hold of, say, the diamonds – and that might be difficult with Blake in jail, I don't suppose the Governor would grant him compassionate leave – I'm not sure that Rip would wish to expose himself to the risk of getting rid of them, even with all the peculiar means at his disposal.'

Strookman considered the point. 'I know they're rare stones,' he said, 'but if one string has turned up out of the blue, I see no reason why a second one shouldn't come to light. They've been altered beyond recognition – we might even get away with selling them on the open market.'

Hammersley coughed gently. With great economy he utilised a yawn to polish his spectacles. 'At heart I'm a crusader rather than an infidel,' he remarked. 'A number of policemen have been injured or killed lately in the execution of their duty, and I don't agree with thuggery. Why not let the *police* have the satisfaction of selling the Yellow Fire Diamonds?'

Astonishment sparked from four pairs of eyes.

'My dear fathead,' said Simon. 'If the police recovered the diamonds they wouldn't sell them – they'd return them.'

'To–?'

'Gabbitas, I suppose – if he contended they weren't the Yellow Fire Diamonds but some other necklace.'

'He'd scarcely stick his neck out that far, surely?'

'Well – then they'd be returned to the Antwerp firm. Or the underwriters.'

'The gems have been altered beyond recognition.' Hammersley adjusted his spectacles with the air of one about to give birth to a world-shattering announcement. 'I once picked up an envelope with nine pounds in it. There was absolutely no means of identification either on, or in, the envelope. I handed it to the police.'

'That must have been a long time ago,' said Simon offensively.

'I have a "thing" about picking up money,' went on Hammersley coldly. 'Half a crown in the street, yes. Treasury notes, no. I'm always afraid it may belong to someone who really needs it.'

'What is that strange light shining above your head?' asked Rip Strookman, shading his eyes. 'Can it be a halo?'

'The money wasn't claimed back anyway,' snapped Hammersley frostily. 'After one month the police let me have it.'

'I knew there was a catch somewhere,' said Simon. 'You picked it up in Penzance and the owner didn't think of looking for it at Burton-on-Trent.'

Hammersley ignored the implication. 'You're missing the point,' he said blandly. 'I got to know the procedure regarding handed-in property.'

'And where does that get us?'

'Well, as I see it, the one thing Gabbitas values above all else – possibly even above Lady Veronica – is this necklace. Would you agree?'

'Judging from the masterpiece he's

painted, yes.'

'And if we relieved him of it, his ego would receive the biggest jolt it's ever had.'

'Yes. It probably represents his major crime. So?'

'We do relieve him of it. But there's too much blood dripping off it for us to be left holding the baby. So we drop it like a red-hot clinker.'

'Seems a waste of time. Where do we drop it?'

'At the police station,' said the amazing Mr Hammersley.

His audience sat in rapt astonishment. Simon wiggled his little finger in his ear. 'I must be getting deaf,' he apologised. 'It sounded for all the world as if you said the police station.'

'Perhaps I should have said police *stations*,' said Hammersley firmly. 'It's about time the rest of the Syndicate got to know their local force – like Simon made me. They're quite nice chaps.'

'But I still don't see how that helps anybody.'

Hammersley told them…

At length, when the bits and pieces had joggled into position and assumed the symmetry of understanding, Simon said, 'First we've got to get more proof that Gabbitas is the slug we think he is. We'll write to Superintendent Lingard and ask him if he can help us with this list of ours.'

'What do we do if Lingard approaches any of us again?' asked Hammersley. 'Embrace him as a long-lost friend?'

Simon thought for a moment. 'No. I don't think we do. We'll get more fun if we regard him as a stranger. I imagine he's banking on the fact that we haven't recognised him.'

'He's changed quite a bit,' said Hammersley, at length.

'His memory hasn't,' said Simon.

And so Operation Safe-Deposit was conceived. The period of gestation was quite short – till the day Blake was released from Parkwood Jail. And the actual Operation was born the day after…

# 17

## Letter To Lingard

The commander examined the letter curiously. 'You say this was addressed to your personally, Lingard?'

'Yes, sir. The envelope said "Superintendent Lingard c/o Our Wonderful Police Force, New Scotland Yard. Please forward".'

'Just "Superintendent Lingard"? No initials?'

'No, sir.'

'H'm. Somebody doesn't know you very well – even to the extent of not knowing whether you're actually at the Yard. What are we going to do about it? Comply with the request? I don't think we've had anything quite like this before.'

'It looks as if someone is working on the same lines as you, sir – that is, that there's a link between certain crimes and this wave of philanthropy that's being shown to the people who have suffered.'

The commander tapped the letter with his pencil.

'There's a further link here,' he commented. 'The writer knows what or who binds all the links together, and that's more than we know. He is aware of a number of special dates on which he either knows or suspects crimes were committed. And where he only suspects, he wants us to consult our records and attempt to fill in the gaps.'

'Bit of a job,' grunted Lingard. 'Crimes are happening all over the place, on the same day, at the same time. Where would we start?'

'I surmise that these cases would turn out to be major crimes, Lingard. Our friend goes one step further and indicates dates on which certain compensation – atonement, payment of blood money, call it what you

256

like – was made, and he wants us to confirm, if by using our records we can, that a link actually exists between payment and commission of a crime.'

'Bit of a tall order. We know a lot about the crimes, but not necessarily about the compensation.'

The commander said mildly, 'I thought you knew I'd already been making inquiries along those lines, Lingard.'

'I didn't know how far you'd got, sir,' hastened Lingard.

'This person goes on to suggest,' went on the other, 'that where his list mentions only one date, nobody was hurt; he would be obliged if we could confirm that fact, too. He appears to have in a nutshell a lot of vital information which could possibly eliminate other purely fortuitous philanthropy and point the finger at one master mind – forgive the term! I can't help feeling that the name he appends to your letter is a fictitious one – indeed, the fact that he has forgotten to put his address and then signs himself *R. Dupp* presupposes that no good will come out of it for the Big Boss, whoever he might be, and suggests it would be most unwise to use anything but a pseudonym. Finally, he wants us to insert our findings in tabulated form in the Personal column of *The Times*. What are we going to do – play ball?'

'We're either dealing with a clever chap or

a nutcase,' grumbled Lingard, adding as an afterthought, 'Or a blackmailer.'

The commander flicked a switch on a communications panel at his side. 'Bring me that special "Crime and Compensation" file, please,' he said into the speaker. He knocked back the switch. 'We'll see how far our information coincides, Lingard. And whilst we're on the subject of atonement, the General Manager of the Tyburn & New York telephoned me to-day.'

'Jullien Fane?'

'Yes. You remember that strange episode involving a Mr Smith of Yeovil and a Tyburn & New York dividend warrant which he claimed he never received, and which the bank at St Ives maintained they'd paid?'

'I remember,' said Lingard grimly. 'It was thought that Simon Good had something to do with *that,* but nothing could be proved.'

The commander grinned. 'He was so delightfully innocent that you thought he just had to be the culprit,' he said. 'Now you may recollect that Mr Smith brought an action against the insurance company and, whilst he won the day, he incurred heavy legal expenses. Someone has now sent him a sum of money in old treasury notes which more than covers his outlay.'

'Simon Good!' breathed Lingard.

'I gather the gift was anonymous,' said the other. 'In fairness to Mr Smith, he contacted the Tyburn & New York and suggested they took the balance to offset some of the cost of their defence. And in fairness to the Tyburn & New York, they said they didn't do business that way and good luck to him. Jullien Fane thought I might like to know about the incident. I know what you're thinking, Lingard – if Simon Good is behind that bit of compensation, he's probably linked with the others and the crimes that go with them. You've checked the type-face of this letter of yours with the samples you already have of Good's and Hammersley's typewriters?'

'They're different,' said Lingard testily.

A uniformed man entered the room discreetly and placed a folder in front of the commander, removing himself smoothly before any questions could be asked.

As a result of the commander's earlier hunch regarding the spate of philanthropy which had welled up in a barren world of greed, a wealth of information had been collected, and the commander was pleased to see that since he had last seen the file a neat, chronological summary had been made which rendered comparison with Lingard's letter easy.

The commander's pencil stopped at one particular major crime. 'Does the Friday before August Bank Holiday appear on your list, Lingard?'

'No, sir. Nor the date when the guard's widow received five thousand pounds.'

'H'm. Pity! It seems we're not to blame the Big Boss for the Yellow Fire Diamonds. Incidentally, did you ever find out anything else about the gas and igniter-set in Flinder's Court?'

'We had very little to go on, sir–'

'I said did you find out anything?'

'I'm afraid not, sir,' said Lingard stiffly.

'Don't get huffy, Lingard – just give me the answers.'

'The nearest we could get was that the igniter-set could have been of German origin, because of some initials and the peculiar ersatz quality of the fragments in our possession. There's a fairly good print on one piece. Further, at or about the time of the robbery, the War Office Depot at Clevedon was derequisitioned and was closing down, and stocks of obsolescent war material including weapons and equipment were disposed of to scrap metal merchants.'

The commander raised an eyebrow. 'Not a particularly bright idea,' he grunted.

'It was sold under licence to recognised dealers who undertook to destroy the material within one month,' said Lingard. 'So far as weapons are concerned, the practice is to strip the bolts and breech-blocks and give them to an independent dealer, also under licence.'

'And explosives?'

'Anything obsolescent goes up with a big bang somewhere on Salisbury Plain – although I suppose it's possible that some of it could slip by in error.'

'This W.D. Depot at Clevedon. Is that Clevedon in Somerset?'

'Yes, sir.' The merest flicker of amusement glinted in the superintendent's eye. 'And I've thought along those lines, too.'

'What lines?' asked the commander, with mild interest.

'Why, that Clevedon wouldn't be all that far from friend Gabbitas. But then I thought of what you said about Gabbitas and Lady Veronica Tuke – that to associate those two because one lived in Devon and the other in Somerset was rather like blaming somebody in Brighton for a London bag-snatch.'

'You're still associating Gabbitas with the Yellow Fire Diamonds?'

'I am, sir, although I feel he might be an unwilling pawn in a game played by, say–'

'Simon Good?' grinned the commander wolfishly.

'You said it, sir, I didn't.'

'Unfortunately, the diamond robbery is not listed in your letter,' pointed out the other. 'There's always something to spoil our theories.'

'H'm, but there is some link with the Tuke girl. We're pretty certain she was in Hatton

Garden that day, in spite of the fact she swears she wasn't. And she owns a Jaguar like the one which was at Four Chimneys on the day that Hammersley called.'

'Ah, yes, Hammersley! There's a report in from Mortlake which says that he's being impersonated.'

'Impersonated!' The superintendent cocked an incredulous eye at the commander. 'Now why would anyone want to do that, sir?'

'I can't imagine. Hammersley's lodged a complaint. The suggestion is that someone's building up a situation so that he gets the blame for something he hasn't done.'

'Poor, dear innocent lamb,' clucked Lingard. 'I can't believe it.'

'The suggestion came from Mortlake, not from Hammersley. His complaint is that in every shop he goes into locally he's told he's already ordered what he came to buy; and goods he hasn't ordered arrive at his flat, paid for. He says the shopkeepers think he's going round the bend. And so does he. Most disconcerting.'

Lingard ran his fingers through his hair. He said with a sigh, 'Some say ban the bomb, others keep it. I wish they'd drop the flipping thing and end it all.'

'Don't despair, Lingard – let me give you a flicker of hope. Perhaps the links are becoming apparent, after all. Both our lists have something in common. A furniture depository fire at East Lampton, Devon; and your list shows another furniture depository fire at Westland Zoy, Somerset. The Home Office were interested in both fires. Fulminate of mercury was used in each case – you know, the stuff used in hand-grenades.'

Superintendent Lingard suddenly smiled happily. 'Kings Barton, Devon. The Mullions, Somerset. Clevedon, Somerset. East Lampton, Devon. Westland Zoy, Somerset. East Lampton, explosives. Westland Zoy, explosives. Hatton Garden, explosives. Gabbitas, dear Lady Veronica and Hammersley.'

'And crime and compensation including the Tyburn & New York case of Mr Smith of Yeovil, Somerset.'

'And that brings in' (the superintendent drew a deep breath) '–Simon Good.'

'Add to that lot retribution,' said the commander softly. 'I haven't forgotten that Leicestershire copper, Lingard. You're watching Simon Good & Co. of course?'

'Like a mother hawk, sir. Mr Good was visited by his old friends the other night – Hammersley, Dutch and Quenella Mansfield.'

'What about Rip Strookman?'

'He didn't show up.'

'Oh. He was recently seen in company with a man who fits Simon Good's description.'

'In Richmond?'

'No. Amsterdam.'

'Amsterdam! What were they up to there?'

'Watching a man who looked like Hammersley.'

'*Looked* like?'

'Hammersley says he's being impersonated. If this man in Amsterdam *was* Hammersley, surely the chances are they'd be *with* him, not watching him?'

'Then perhaps he is being impersonated after all, and they're trying to find out what the game is.'

'Nothing would surprise me, Lingard. If somebody is taking Hammersley's good name in vain, then we may rest assured that the intention is to pin something on him. The man they were watching was staying at a doubtful hotel on the fringe of the diamond quarter– Don't say it, Lingard, I know! The Yellow Fire Diamonds! We've also had a belated report from Interpol about Blake's place in Brussels, the Golden Fleece. A man has been seen there who fits Hammersley's description.'

'If it was Hammersley he couldn't have been calling on Blake,' said Lingard quickly. 'Blake's still in jail.'

'Quite so. And almost due to come out – like Good was when the Yellow Fire Diamonds were stolen. Do you ever feel you're losing your grip, Lingard? We seem to be going round in well-oiled circles. However, I think the Big Boss's downfall is imminent; and it is going to be brought about by his philanthropy. Ironical, ain't it?' The commander thrummed his desk thoughtfully. 'We'll play ball with this Mr R. Dupp. See what information we have that fits his questionnaire and try to do something about the gaps. And then draft something for *The Times* Agony column... Oh, by the way, I had an idea in bed the other night – do you ever get ideas in bed? It occurred to me that if Gabbitas *was* the man in Flinder's Court, and he happened to pass close enough to those gas ejectors, then the lab boys would be able to find traces of chemical on his clothing. The scent is getting a bit stale, but it might be worth following up...'

Simon Good left the office one night and was confronted by a large man who bore the stamp of plainclothes detective.

'May I have a word with you, sir?'

'No,' said Simon, turning away.

'I'm afraid I must insist,' said the other.

Simon regarded him coolly. 'Before I call a policeman, who might you be?'

Superintendent Lingard flashed his warrant card, and found his wrist in a grip of steel whilst the other examined the card carefully.

'I'm sorry, Superintendent, I had no idea.

I thought you were about to touch me for a bob. And what is your pleasure?'

For all his flippancy, Simon's mind was racing back in time and distance along the battle-bashed road to Hondschouwen. So this was Lingard. The man who would have nothing to do with Roag's Syndicate when it was mooted. The odd man out. The man whose post-war hunch had put him away for twelve months. Simon couldn't honestly say he recognised him; the street lighting was bad, and as Dutchy and Hammersley had remarked, he had filled out a lot since the lean years.

Lingard himself gave no sign of recognition; he was confident his face and name meant nothing to Simon Good. 'We had a report recently to the effect that you were seen with another man in Amsterdam watching the movements of your ex-batman, Charles Hammersley.'

'In Amsterdam? Don't say they've started to impersonate him in Holland!'

Lingard was not to be side-tracked. 'Was it you, sir?'

'Why should I be watching Hammersley?'

'Was it you?' repeated Lingard stonily.

'When exactly was this?'

Lingard told him.

'That weekend I wasn't Hammersley-watching – I was bird-watching. In Suffolk. At Aldeburgh. Nice place. You'd like it.'

'Oh, yes?' There was naked disbelief in Lingard's voice. He tried a new tack. 'Either somebody is impersonating Hammersley, or somebody is impersonating you.'

'Or both. But I don't think it could have been Hammersley in Amsterdam – he was telling me only recently that he'd mislaid his passport after coming back from Portugal, and he couldn't think what he'd done with it. It was due for renewal anyway.'

'And your passport, sir – I suppose that's been stolen?' Lingard's voice was charged with heavy sarcasm.

'That's right,' said Simon.

'Eh?' blinked Lingard.

'Yes. About a week before I went bird-watching. I reported it to the Richmond police. Didn't they tell you? Somebody broke into my place when the burglar-alarm system was out of commission. It happened during the week when the burglar-alarm firm were putting it right. The only thing that was missing was my passport. So it couldn't have been me in Amsterdam, could it? Would you care for a cup of tea?'

Superintendent Lingard ungraciously said that he wouldn't.

# 18

## A Couple Of Heels

The steel and concrete monstrosity which was the head office of the Aldwych Insurance Corporation in the Strand was a hive of activity. This did not mean that more work, much work, or even any work was being done to gladden the hearts of the directors. It was ten minutes to one, when the twelve o'clock luncheon shift was returning and the next shift was making ready for a prompt getaway to spend its money on anything but lunch. The takeover period was always one of bustle, high spirits, examination of purchases, meeting in the main hall, hurried alterations of arrangements, unanswered telephones, and frustrated clients at the counter who were wasting their lunch hour, too.

It was into this state of highly organised confusion that a somewhat harassed-looking middle-aged man wandered, making little headway against the babbling stream. He wandered through the main office with his battered attaché case, obviously at a loss, until he was obliged to make a direct inquiry. 'Excuse me, miss, which is the typists' room?'

'Oh, you're the mechanic? Last room on the right – although I think they're all out.'

'That's all right, I've got the number of the machine. This is the Fire Department?'

'That's right.'

He would have been surprised if she had said otherwise, for there was a notice proclaiming the fact on the glass swing doors through which he had just passed. He thanked her and wandered along to the typists' room. There was in fact one typist present, reading, knitting and eating but not typing.

'Hallo!' she said. 'Come to look at the machines?'

'Only one of them, miss. You carry on with your work – I've got the number here, I'll soon find it.'

He consulted his notebook and settled on the third machine. Clearing a space for his attaché case, he produced an array of screwdrivers, oilcans, a piece of rag and a small square of emery cloth to roughen up the roller. With a long-handled brush he prodded vigorously at the mechanism for about eight minutes. 'All right if I use some of this paper to test out on, miss?'

'Help yourself,' said the typist affably, wondering if she was altogether wise in attempting a Fair-Isle pattern.

Mr Hammersley polished his glasses and selected a sheet of headed notepaper. He typed quite a nice letter, and it must have been important because he took carbon copies. He packed his paraphernalia away and, shielded by the open lid of his case, purloined an assortment of stationery embossed with the corporation's crest

Mr Gabbitas received a letter from the Aldwych Insurance Corporation the following day.

It recommended a valuer whose certificate would be acceptable to them and gave an Exeter telephone number to ring to fix up a visit at Mr Gabbitas's early convenience. It appeared that the valuer, who did much business for the corporation, was in the locality for the next few days. Mr Gabbitas fixed an appointment without delay.

In due course he was being impressed by the business acumen of the well-dressed man who called at Four Chimneys. He paid but scant attention to the handsomely embellished visiting card and a letter of introduction on Aldwych paper, to which was attached a carbon copy of the letter he had already received.

'Come into my study, Mr Van de Meer,' he boomed expansively, 'and we'll get down to business right away – I gather you're a very busy man.'

'That is very true,' agreed Rip Strookman, extracting some inventory forms from his pigskin briefcase. 'I am, as you might say, here to-day and gone to-morrow.'

In spite of his high-speed ubiquity, they wasted ten minutes fencing about the weather, business in general, the cost of living and the fact that nowadays everybody seemed to be making something on the side. It was at this stage that they really got down to business.'

'My problem,' said Lew, 'is that I have a great deal of expensive jewellery and I want it to be adequately insured. You will appreciate the difficulty in arriving at a compromise between intrinsic worth and, shall we say, a sentimental or false value.'

'The margin is often great,' agreed Rip pontifically, 'I myself am always inclined to take into account what I prefer to call the "artistic" value of any object. Such objects of merit cannot be replaced if stolen.'

'I'm glad you see it that way,' said Lew, pushing over the cigars, '–as indeed I thought you might.' He added significantly, 'I believe – though I don't pretend to know how – that your services were obtained through the good offices of a friend of mine, a certain Mr Good.'

'A number of people have expressed satisfaction over my valuations,' nodded Rip, 'although I can't say the name Good means anything to me.' He added slowly, 'I think you must appreciate that?'

Gabbitas examined the end of his cigar carefully. 'Foolish of me to mention names,' he said. 'The point is well taken. I think we understand each other, Mr Van de Meer. Let us get down to business.' He got up and went over to a large safe in the corner, and Rip watched him like a lynx, watched the manipulation of the dial, watched Lew produce two keys on a ring and unlock two locks, watched the door swing open weightily, watched Lew extract much wealth in small bulk. With a sense of frustration he eyed the two keys on the ring, one in the bottom lock, the other dangling.

For the next two hours all the items from the safe were carefully examined and entered on the inventory ... until they came to the Yellow Fire Diamonds. Rip examined the rivière critically through his glass, and Gabbitas watched him closely.

Removing the glass from his right eye, Rip blinked once or twice and laid down the necklace on the green baize square he had spread out on the desk. 'Let us first replace these other items, Mr Gabbitas,' he said. 'I will give you a hand.' He rose and going round to the other side of the desk handed the small trays of articles one by one to Lew. As he held out one tray and half turned for the next, Lew, turning abruptly, knocked against it and a few small articles fell to the floor. It seemed accidental, but Rip had made it seem that way. 'I beg your pardon!' he said, bending to retrieve the objects.

'My fault – allow me!' said Gabbitas, beating him to it.

In that brief moment Rip had pressed the wax against the dangling key under cover of the open safe door.

'And now, sir,' he said, sitting down again. 'This rivière. These are yellow diamonds of the highest water, worth a fortune. There are very few of these in circulation.' He picked up his glass and had another look. Gabbitas remained tense and silent. 'It appears to be incomplete.'

'I'm waiting for two more stones – together with a few of the trimmings,' said Gabbitas.

'Ah!' Rip Strookman leaned back in his chair. 'I suggest we don't put this on the inventory, Mr Gabbitas. There would be too many questions asked if you were – um – unfortunate enough to have a burglary.'

'You know best,' said Lew shortly. 'Have another cigar.'

'Thank you. They're very good. I was wondering if perhaps I've been a little conservative in some of the other valuations. If I stepped them up a little it would at least go part of the way to offset not mentioning this particular item.'

'I am entirely in your hands,' said Lew. 'I expect your valuation fee is quite high?' he hinted.

'No, just the normal fee,' said Rip blandly. 'Unless you happen to have a burglary. And then I would expect a little gift of some sort – nothing ostentatious, you understand. A new car, perhaps. Not cash, that looks bad.'

'You're too kind,' said Lew. A sudden, disturbing though rippled home. 'You want something in writing?' he asked.

'My dear sir, of course not! You're speaking as if you were anticipating a burglary! I merely rely on you to show your appreciation. If you don't, well, you don't, that's all. I'm sure you wouldn't want me to lose faith in humanity. Now,' added Rip briskly, 'I will go back and make the necessary adjustments and forward my official certificate to the insurance company, sending you a duplicate to keep with your papers in the meantime. I'm afraid the company won't give you cover until they've sent their surveyor along to look at your anti-burglary arrangements – they may even insist on improvements. Now when would it be convenient for him to come along – I happen to know he's in the area at the moment.'

'As soon as possible.'

'Very wise of you. One never knows when calamity will strike. May I use your phone?'

'By all means.'

Strookman rang a number, spoke for a few moments and then looked up at Lew. 'Next Thursday all right, Mr Gabbitas? Some time in the afternoon? It's difficult to make a precise time.'

Gabbitas nodded and Rip confirmed the appointment. He replaced the receiver. 'Oh, and Mr Gabbitas. The man they're sending along is named Atkinson. He's quite well-paid by the insurance company, but unimaginative. He might misunderstand any talk about little gifts on the side.'

'The arrangements suit me fine, Mr Van de Meer.'

The arrangements also suited Roag's Syndicate. Blake was due to come out of Parkwood Jail on Thursday.

The readers of the Personal Column of *The Times* were puzzled by an unusual list of statistics which appeared one day, consisting of numbers, events and dates, and although they did not know it, a lot of things began to happen at considerable speed...

Lady Veronica Tuke received a letter postmarked Manchester. She opened it wonderingly, for she knew nobody in that town, and immediately turned pallid under her careful tan make-up. Even her lips, accentuated by a fashionable off-beat shade of lipstick, seemed to bleach themselves of all colouring.

The envelope contained a cutting from *The Times*. She read through the data twice and telephoned Lew Gabbitas.

Mr Gabbitas was thunderstruck. Ice-cold maggots crawled up his spine. Somebody knew his secret, and it was there for all the world to read, even if the people who read it did not understand the significance of what they read.

'Simon Good, do you think?' breathed Veronica in a scarcely audible voice.

'He's in it as much as we are,' said Lew thoughtfully. 'But I don't see how he could have collected all this information. In any event, Good fixed the insurance on the Westland Zoy depository, to say nothing of introducing me to a most co-operative valuer – who is also in it right up to his neck. What could he expect to gain? No, it can't be Simon Good.'

'But why send the cutting to *me!*' expostulated Veronica.

'You're in it as much as everybody else,' said Lew, not without satisfaction. 'You say every event is listed except – except the one on the Friday before Bank Holiday?'

'Yes– Could Mr Hammersley be at the bottom of it?'

'He's altogether too naïve, my dear. I'll get him over to Amsterdam for the last few stones without delay. And I'll see that the yacht is victualled up at Torquay – we may have to leave in a hurry...'

In response to peremptory instructions from Mr Gabbitas, Hammersley took the first available flight to Amsterdam, and Lew, if he had been at the airport, would have been very surprised to observe that his co-operative valuer was on the same plane; he would perhaps have been more than a little perturbed if he had known that both gentlemen stayed at the same sleazy hotel on the fringe of the diamond quarter. It was significant that although they did not arrive at the hotel together, or have their meals together, or spend the evening together, they were nevertheless both waiting in Hammersley's room at the crack of dawn.

Hammersley stood on tiptoe on a chair by the door, peering cautiously through the fanlight into the corridor whilst Rip Strookman, indolently smoking a cigarette, was propped up by pillows on the ancient brass-knobbed bedstead.

At length there was a slight movement in the corridor and the cobbler of Thielt came into view bearing Hammersley's shoes. Hammersley froze. He got down from the chair looking very thoughtful indeed.

'Do you know him?' grinned Rip.

Hammersley nodded mutely. Then, 'It's

Maurice. The chap who gave me the letters at Thielt. What's he doing here, cleaning shoes!'

'Working for Gabbitas.'

'But the man who meets me at Schiphol Airport has been exchanging the Amsterdam letters.'

'Get your shoes, my friend, and let us see what sort of a job he's made of them...'

Hammersley retrieved his shoes and examined the highly polished leather. 'An excellent job,' he commented, handing them to Rip.

Rip scrutinised the composite-rubber heels. 'The heels aren't new,' he remarked.

'Of course not. They've never been repaired.'

'Usually, you know, when heels like these begin to wear, one sees the shiny stubs of the screws where they've worn down beyond the head and washer. What strikes you here?'

'No shiny stubs,' said Hammersley.

From a small case on the bed, Rip produced a canvas holdall which he unrolled to reveal a set of tools. Selecting a thin screwdriver, he prised it down into the rubber heel like a probe until he came up against a metal stub. Forcing back the rubber, he exposed the gleaming head of a new screw. 'You see?' he said, with satisfaction.

Hammersley was unimpressed. 'They're

always countersunk,' he said.

'Not to that depth.'

'The rubber has merely closed over it with wear.'

'You think so?' said Rip, beginning to unscrew.

'Here!' objected Hammersley.

The screw came out with comparative ease, as did two others, enabling Rip to lever off the rubber heel. For a moment he looked disappointed as he revealed a layer of leather. Then he was happy again as he noticed the brand new tacks round the edges. Digging in his screwdriver between the layers of leather, he gently separated the top layer, and clucked with satisfaction as he saw the neatly hollowed-out cavity rammed tight with plasticine. Probing out the wad of clay and squeezing it between thumb and forefinger, he produced two yellow diamonds of considerable size.

Hammersley sat on the end of the bed in stunned and rueful silence.

'I imagine you took them to Thielt in their original form,' said Rip, 'and then they were smuggled to Amsterdam – possibly by your friend Maurice – and after alteration you took them back to Gabbitas.'

'Why not straight to Amsterdam?'

'Perhaps the original intention was to have them altered in Belgium and somebody got cold feet. Doubtless the relatives are now receiving compensation.'

'But why umpteen visits? Why not all at once?'

'My dear Charles, you have big feet, but not that big. Besides, if you were caught, Gabbitas wouldn't lose so much.'

'I *knew* all that business of the letters was crazy!'

'And he knew that a man of your peculiar talents was bound to be inquisitive, and he gave you something to think about. Let's have a look at the other shoe.'

The plasticine in this shoe produced a number of smaller yellow diamonds. 'The trimmings,' explained Rip. 'And how very artistic! Maurice has even bedded them in traditional blue clay.'

'If I took them over to Thielt I suppose they were planted in my shoes at the hotel near Victoria,' mused Hammersley. 'Lew must have a shoe-repairer working for him there, too. Yes, and that's why Lew has stayed overnight with me on the return trips from Amsterdam.'

Strookman turned to his case again and extracted a chamois leather bag which he emptied on to the bedspread. Hammersley goggled at the assortment of gems.

'All paste,' said Rip, as he began a matching-up process. 'We'll ring the changes – these diamonds are much too good to walk on, and we might as well have the last few for ourselves as commission.'

'Mr Gabbitas is not going to like this,' said Hammersley unhappily.

'He may not even notice it,' said Rip. 'And besides, if you get caught, you'll only be carrying paste...'

On his return to London, Hammersley made his usual overnight stay at the hotel with Gabbitas. In the morning Lew was very much on edge and anxious to get away.

'The manager at the Bull & Buffalo is snatching that holiday I told you about,' he said. 'Perhaps you would kindly stand in for him as you promised. I would like you to come down to-morrow.'

'Of course!' agreed Hammersley with a show of enthusiasm.

'You have one more Continental visit to make at the end of next week, but your friend Mr Good has agreed to lend a hand whilst you're away. And then our association finishes. You have done very well, you will receive a bonus. You did say you had no relatives?'

'No relatives,' agreed Hammersley flatly...

Before returning to his Mortlake flat, Hammersley visited the large Woolworth store near Bond Street and purchased a number of bead necklaces which he asked to be wrapped in separate bags. He also bought a number of cards of nylon thread used for rethreading beads, and an assortment of gaily coloured cardboard gift boxes. Operation Safe-Deposit was on the way.

Hammersley went home and wrote a number of letters in a large, childlike hand. The letters began 'Dear Auntie Mabel' or 'Dear Auntie Ethel' or 'Dear Auntie Maud', and by the time he had finished he was heartily sick of Dear Auntie.

The Press reported that a retired village shoe-repairer from East Lampton, Devon, was found dead from an overdose of sleeping pills in a London hotel. It happened to be the same hotel where Gabbitas and Hammersley stayed. Foul play was not suspected. The old man had no relatives, but Mr Gabbitas saw to it that he got a wonderful funeral.

By process of simple deduction, Simon decided that Gabbitas had reached the end of the line and would be planning something unpleasant for both him and Hammersley in the immediate future. Speedy avoiding action by Roag's Syndicate seemed to be of the very essence. Unfortunately Simon had received a summons from the Sheriff of the County to attend court for jury service on Thursday, and in the quaint and urgent words of the demand – which implied that the well-being of the county depended on his attendance – he was to fail not at his peril. Mr Good was well aware that in calling him the Sheriff's Office had made a mistake, for gentlemen who have been convicted of a felony are not invited to give their services for this duty – presumably because they might have a tendency to deal leniently with the accused irrespective of the merits of the case. Simon mulled over the circumstances carefully and decided the Sheriff's error should be put right by a personal appearance at court.

On Thursday, too, Blake was due to come out of Parkwood Jail. He had one visiting day owing, so whilst on Wednesday Hammersley was making his way down to the Bull & Buffalo, Simon visited Blake in Parkwood and gave him a heart to heart talk. From the earnestness of their conversation other visitors naturally thought Blake was being visited by the clergy.

# 19

## Blake's Jerusalem

It was a little after eight a.m. on Thursday when Blake stepped through the wicket gate in the massive main doors of Parkwood Jail. He turned and profusely thanked the prison officer for all the little kindnesses that had not been bestowed upon him.

'Keep out of trouble,' advised the other laconically.

'That is my one ambition,' Blake assured him. The door closed with an emphatic clang, and he found himself locked out in the freedom of a land of milk and honey. At least, in a land waiting to be milked. Blake's Jerusalem.

The morning was raw, with a hint of wispy drizzle in the air. He made his way by public transport back to his flat over the Golden Web in Curzon Street, calling *en route* at the local police station to report.

'When do I report again?' he inquired.

'Same time next week. Unless we've roped you in for something else.'

'That won't be likely. I'm going home to sleep for a week.'

'You do that,' advised the other. 'You can't go wrong in bed.'

Blake was sceptical but said nothing. He went home to the Golden Web and gave instructions that he was going to sleep all day and was not to be disturbed. Half an hour later, considerably spruced up, he slipped out into the cobbled mews at the rear of the premises, where Quenella Mansfield was waiting with a fast hired car. They were soon speeding on their way to Exeter.

Blake presented himself at Four Chimneys, and the austere visiting card (produced on a home printing press in Simon's garage at Richmond) announced that he was William Atkinson, Surveyor, from the Aldwych Insurance Corporation. Lew Gabbitas examined it cursorily. Clipped to the card was a further carbon copy of the original letter Gabbitas had received recommending the valuer, and attached to that was the valuation certificate.

'You already have a copy of that, I believe,' said Blake, as Lew led him inside to his study. 'I won't detain you for long, sir, I'll be round the house in a couple of jiffies. Ah, there's the safe – quite a hefty one, too. A Masterlock. Is it post-war?'

'No, pre-war. I purchased it second-hand a few years ago.'

'H'm,' mused Blake, taking a note of the

serial number, 'then it's doubtful if it's fitted with anti-explosion bolts – unless you've had it modified. Have you the maker's specification?'

'I'm afraid not. It has twin locks, but I don't know about anti-explosion bolts – I've had nothing done to it, anyway.'

'May I have a squint at the inside?'

'By all means.' Gabbitas manipulated the four-number combination and Blake watched intently. Under the top sheet of his note-pad he had a series of small clock-faces drawn, and as he stood behind Gabbitas he smoothly ticked off the dial positions. He watched Gabbitas use the two keys.

'There it is,' said Lew, as he turned the twin handles and swung open the heavy door.

Blake appeared not to notice the glittering trays of jewellery. He devoted his attention to the door. 'H'm,' he said critically, 'this hasn't been modified.' He swung the door at right-angles to the body of the safe, and turning the handles back and forth, tested the bolt actions. He turned the lower key and the relative bolts became immovable. 'Do you mind if I test the top key?' he asked.

'Carry on,' shrugged Lew, his eyes fixed on the contents of the safe.

Blake removed the keys, which were linked together, fumbled with them and dropped them. The wax impression of the key to the lower lock took a couple of seconds. It was rough, but it would help. 'I'm afraid I've mixed them up,' he said apologetically.

Gabbitas took them from him and extended the one to the upper lock, which Blake duly tested.

'Well, that seems all right, sir. It's a bit ancient but it's substantial. Do you always carry the keys on your person?'

'Except when I'm in bed, and then I put them in a place known only to myself.'

'You can rely on the servants, of course, sir?'

'I only have an old housekeeper who knows when she's well paid for rearranging the dust.'

'Quite so, sir,' laughed Blake. 'Chauffeur?'

'When I need a car I usually hire one from the village or Exeter – it saves me a lot of trouble. I can drive, and hold a licence, but I consider myself something of a menace on the road.'

'I wish half our motor clients would be so frank, sir,' grinned Blake. 'Now I wonder if I could measure the inside depth? The backs of some of these older safes leave much to be desired. They're all right if they're built into a wall, but otherwise an amateur could have the back off in half an hour with a do-it-yourself kit. Would you mind removing a few trays from the middle shelf, sir?'

Gabbitas obliged, and Blake got busy with a sprung steel rule. 'Oh, there's a good four inches of laminations in the back wall, that's all right. Mind you, I'm not suggesting that a modern safe wouldn't be better, with all that jewellery.'

'That would cost money.'

'Everything costs money, sir. The insurance will.'

Gabbitas looked thoughtful. 'Will they rate me up because of this safe?'

For a moment Blake gave the matter grave consideration. 'I imagine not,' he said. 'I'm only thinking of your property. The burglar is only indirectly interested in your safe – he's after your valuables.'

'Still, I suppose if I do have a burglary I'd be fully indemnified, that's what I'm insured for.'

'Oh, quite. But often reimbursement is not enough.'

'You insurance men all speak the same language.'

Blake chuckled. 'An inspector I know could induce the Ministry of Works to take out a fire insurance on Stonehenge,' he declared. 'Seriously, though, it's not necessarily the intrinsic value that counts, it's the irreplaceable sentimental value. The thief knows no sentiment, he'll dispose of the loot for the best price. For example, have you any items you wouldn't care to lose?'

'I wouldn't care to lose any of them!'

'Of course not, silly of me to put it like that! But you know what I mean.'

Gabbitas fingered the Yellow Fire rivière, and the avaricious gleam of the collector sparked in his eyes. 'I wouldn't care to lose *that*,' he said. 'Do you know how much it is worth?'

'I haven't a clue, sir. Please put it away before I'm tempted to do you an injury. And please don't tell me the value – I'd only be envious.'

Gabbitas replaced the jewellery and locked the safe.

'You've dropped something on the floor,' said Blake, pointing, and Gabbitas looked down in mild astonishment – he was usually so careful. He picked up the diamond ring which Blake had managed to knock from one of the trays, and reopened the safe. Blake took a second set of readings.

'That was careless of me,' said Lew. 'And now perhaps you'd like to see the burglar alarm arrangements?'

Blake said he would, very much so. And when he had finished he asked if he could ring his office. He gave the man at the other end details of the safe and the burglar alarms; and informed Mr Gabbitas he could give him a temporary cover-note.

Gabbitas thanked him and apologised for not being able to offer him afternoon tea as it was his housekeeper's day off.

The bit about the housekeeper made Blake's day.

Less than two hours later, Gabbitas received a telephone call in a muffled feminine voice which he assumed to be Veronica's, urging him to meet her without delay at the Bull & Buffalo.

'But why, my dear?' he asked, puzzled. 'Why not come straight on to Four Chimneys? What brings you here, anyway?'

'Please don't ask questions,' entreated Quenella, through her handkerchief. 'I can't talk here – just come.'

A quiver of anxiety slicked through Lew as he grabbed his hat. He switched on the burglar alarms and locked up. He prayed that nothing had gone wrong, that Veronica had not received another spine-jolting newspaper cutting. He walked briskly to the village, thanking heaven he would soon be out of the country with her.

The detective watching the house followed discreetly. And Blake, having hurriedly matched up the second safe key from a series of partly-shaped blanks at the Bull & Buffalo, and armed with additional information from the man he had telephoned from Lew's, broke and entered Four Chimneys...

Gabbitas strode into the Bull & Buffalo.

He pushed his way through a fair sprinkling of customers and spoke to Hammersley, who looked quite professional behind the bar coping with the orders. 'Has anyone made a phone call for me from here?' he demanded curtly.

'Lady Veronica?' suggested Hammersley, keeping his voice low.

'Yes.'

'The lady said don't go away, she'll be back shortly. What'll you have while you wait?'

If Lew had not been so agitated he would have noticed that this was a slightly different Hammersley. The suit didn't fit so well, his hair was slightly darker, his dentures ill-fitting, his spectacles were not the ancient National Health pair he favoured but of a more modern conception. And as he moved about behind the counter, he walked with a slight limp. But if Lew failed to notice the minor differences, the detective in the corner, trained to observe, took mental note of them and a sudden gleam came into his eyes as he wondered if this was in fact Hammersley. The Hammersley he knew, for example, had no limp. He wasn't to know that it was induced by a ball-bearing in Hammersley's shoe.

Mr Gabbitas spent an hour of seething frustration in the Bull & Buffalo before deciding to return to Four Chimneys...

Hammersley immediately handed over the inn to the tender care of the potman, and was soon speeding out of King's Barton with Quenella and Blake. They struck north-eastward to Taunton and thence to Banwell Major, where Blake had one more job to perform. The safe in the office of the disused depository presented no difficulty, and before long they were snaking back across Salisbury Plain to London, pausing only to take turns at the wheel.

Quenella dropped Hammersley and Blake at different places and drove the car back to the car-hire firm. She called at a friend's place in Brook Street, collected some parcels and bags prominently labelled Selfridges, and returned to Shepherdess Walk as though from a wearying late evening's shopping and supper in the West End. Blake slipped into the Golden Web by the back door, changed, and immediately mingled with club members, making it known that he was no longer being detained at Her Majesty's pleasure. Hammersley returned to his Mortlake flat a picture of cherubic innocence, accidentally dropping a theatre programme as he entered the vestibule. Simon returned to Richmond after a harrowing day at the Sessions; he had attended in waiting but was not called, and was due to return the following day: he was in no hurry to explain to the Clerk to the Justices the error of the Sheriff's Office in empanelling him for jury service, for two days at court was as good an alibi as any: failure to attend would indeed have been to his peril. The police did not recognise the gentleman Simon bumped into near the towpath because Rip Strookman was well muffled up, but they took note of all the outward manifestations of the guilelessness of Roag's Syndicate.

By devious routes the Syndicate met well after midnight at a dismal yard off Leatherwick Way, and one by one they slid unobserved into a back room which Dutchy used as an office.

Rip and Quenella got to work swiftly rethreading Hammersley's cheap strings of beads, interlarding each string with one large and several small diamonds from the Yellow Fire rivière. Simon got busy with a quick-drying cellulose lacquer spray, and as each string dried out Hammersley made up packages which contained a necklace, some small change, and a note to Dear Auntie Ethel. They all wore thin-leather gloves. Dutchy made several brews of hot sweet tea. They slunk back to their homes in the early hours.

The following morning Operation Safe-Deposit went into full swing.

# 20

## Operation Safe-Deposit

It was cold and wintry, with a thick pall of mist spreading outwards from the river. Hammersley, forsaking the lambent glow of the Strand, turned left into the smudgy bleakness of Wellington Street and proceeded up the gentle incline to Bow Street Police Station.

The raw fog clutched at his throat as he eyed the policeman at the top of the steps. This particular officer was one of the old-fashioned, full-sized ones who never failed to induce in him a feeling of guilt.

Swallowing hard, he ascended the steps between the lamps with what he could only hope was an air of quiet confidence. A restraining hand almost turned him to jelly, and he looked up into the speculative eye of the policeman.

'Can I help you, sir?'

Mr Hammersley blinked through his spectacles. The fog was getting at his eyes now. He produced a small packet from his greatcoat pocket. 'I want the – um – Lost Property Department,' he said in a voice which was not his own.

'Ah, yes, sir.' The atmosphere was very friendly now. 'Front office. First door on the right.'

He found himself in a hive of activity, and was surprised to note in this wicked world of ours that two other people were also in the process of handing in lost property. Waiting his turn he drank in his surroundings, admiring the many silver trophies in cabinets round the walls. He noted the box for a police charity on the counter. With a slight constriction of his chest muscles he observed the tiny side-room where someone was being interviewed, no doubt 'assisting the police in their inquiries'. He admired the brisk efficiency with which an endless string of telephone calls at the desk were being disposed of. He tried to sort out some of the mysterious messages being relayed by a disembodied voice from a room at the rear. He spotted the safe in the corner and wondered if Blake could open that too.

It was with a sudden start that he realised there was now a vacant place at the counter and that the sergeant was eyeing him quizzically.

'I've come to hand this in,' said Hammersley, handing over the packet.

'What have we got here, sir – the Crown Jewels?'

A little spasm of alarm went flippertyjiggle up Hammersley's spine. 'I'm afraid not,' he said. 'It's a string of beads – I don't think they're worth much. And there's a small sum of money – twenty-five shillings and eightpence, to be precise.'

The sergeant opened the wrapping-paper and extracted a single loop of large, brightly coloured beads. He held them up critically. 'H'm, not worth a light,' he grunted. 'Only a cheap clasp – look.'

Hammersley looked. 'Is it?' he said innocently. 'I'm afraid I don't know much about this sort of thing. I did notice that the surface of some of the beads is rubbed off. Sort of lacquer, I suppose. I don't think I would have handed them in, if it wasn't for the money. I have a "thing" about finding money.'

'So have I,' agreed the sergeant pleasantly. 'I'm on the look out all the time.'

'No, I mean that I don't mind picking up half-a-crown, but I don't like finding treasury notes – I always have an uncomfortable feeling that they may have been lost by someone who can ill afford it.' Hammersley spoke with some asperity. 'The money is in the envelope.'

'Well, I suppose we'd better enter it in the book,' said the other, groping for the ledger. 'Where did you find it?'

'In the Strand. Last night. About five-thirty p.m. Opposite the Civil Service Stores.'

The sergeant wrote it all down. 'I'd better check the money. How much did you say? Twenty-five and eight?'

'Yes. And there's a letter with it which may explain things.'

The officer tipped the money on to the counter, checked it, and entered the amount in the book. He directed his attention to a folded sheet of notepaper. '"Dear Auntie Mabel",' he read, '"I am sorry to hear you are in hospital, and have bought you a necklace to wear when you come out. Mummy sends her love. Hope you will be well soon. Lots of love and kisses from Pauline." H'm, looks as if a doting niece was sending Auntie a get-well gift. Probably wrote the note whilst she was having tea and buns in a cafeteria, judging from the stickiness of it. No address at the top.' He examined the envelope. 'And no address on the envelope. Ah, there's a crest on the flap.' He screwed it round to the light. 'Intrepid Club, Pall Mall.'

'Yes, I've telephoned the secretary and told him I'd found some money in one of their envelopes which was otherwise un-addressed, and said that if anyone reported the matter to him the packet would be at Bow Street. I didn't tell him how much, or describe the beads in detail.'

The sergeant picked up his pen. 'What name shall I put, sir?'

'Justice,' said Hammersley. 'Norman Oswald Justice.'

'N. O. Justice,' wrote the officer; he grinned to himself. 'Address?'

'Baker Street, W.1. 221b.'

The sergeant wrote it down without comment, he was not a great reader, he was far too busy picking up people who sat down in Trafalgar Square. 'Right, sir. I'll give you a receipt. If the packet isn't claimed within a month, you can come and collect it for yourself. It's all on the form.'

'The necklace wouldn't be of much use to me,' said Hammersley doubtfully.

'You could give it to your girl-friend for a birthday present,' grinned the other. 'And there's still the matter of the money – you might as well have it as the next man.'

'Ah, yes. What happens if I don't make a claim?'

'The property may be disposed of and the proceeds paid to the credit of the Police Fund. It's all on the form, sir,' reiterated the sergeant. 'And there's always this box for the Police Orphanage. There are too many orphans these days.'

'A good idea,' said Hammersley, and the officer was not sure if Hammersley meant the box or the police orphans. His mind was set at rest as Hammersley discreetly slipped half-a-crown in the slot provided.

It may have been that the wispy fog had

lifted a little when Hammersley made his way down the steps into Bow Street, or that his face was suffused with an all-pervading glow of self-righteousness; or that he was just relieved.

A Covent Garden van, moving slowly down towards the Strand, effectively covered his exit from the view of a man who was standing casually by the portico of the Opera House, a man whose alert eyes belied his general air of tiredness. This gentleman smoked two or three cigarettes before giving up his vigil...

Hammersley hailed a taxi in Aldwych, went to Victoria, walked through the station, hopped quickly into another cab and asked for Chelsea Embankment. There he paid his fare, added a neutral tip which evoked neither gloom nor rapture, and then ambled round to Cheyne Road Police Station. He made his way into the front office.

'I've come to hand in a small packet I picked up on the Chelsea Embankment,' he explained to the duty sergeant. He produced a plain, brown paper bag and placed it on the counter. The sergeant untwisted the corners and tipped out the contents, picking up the bead necklace between thumb and forefinger.

'Ah! What's this?' he said gloomily. 'The Crown Jewels?'

It seemed to be a stock joke, and Hammersley wished they wouldn't make it. 'I imagine the necklace is scarcely worth handing in,' he said frostily. 'If you look at the clasp you'll see it's only a cheap one. I don't think I would have made the journey if it wasn't for the money in that little gift-box.'

'H'm. Glass beads covered with cellulose. If you look closely you'll see some of them are scratched.'

Hammersley craned forward and peered through his spectacles. 'So they are! That was very quick of you!'

'We're trained to be observant, sir.'

'Of course! I expect you've been through Hendon Police College. So that's how they do it, is it? A sort of cellulose spray on glass. Quite effective.'

'Bit garish,' said the other critically. 'Worth about four-and-eleven.' He looked at the plain paper bag. 'Woolworth's. You can buy the gift-boxes there, too. What have we got in this one? Three pounds ten. And what's this? A covering note – no address at the top.'

'I think the note explains the whole thing,' said Hammersley.

'"Dear Auntie Em,"' read the officer aloud. '"I am glad to hear you are out of hospital. I hope you are well. I have bought you a present for your birthday and hope you will like it. With lots of love from Valerie. P.S. Love from Mum. P.P.S. And Dad." H'm, looks as if some child has had her good intentions thwarted and Auntie Em saved from a fate worse than death. I'll enter it in the book, sir, and if it isn't claimed within a month you can claim it back for yourself. Have you just picked it up?'

'Yes,' said Hammersley. 'On the Embankment.'

The sergeant wrote down the information. 'What name is it, sir?'

'Judge. Geoffrey.'

The officer looked at him keenly; he was slightly hard of hearing, but the name seemed to ring a bell. 'Judge Jeffreys?'

'No. Geoffrey Judge.'

'Oh. Funny name, sir.'

'It's a funny world.'

'You're dead right there, sir. Address?'

'Fountain View, Bushy Park, Hampton Court. There's no *e* in Bushy.' Hammersley appeared to have an aversion to giving his Mortlake address. He glanced at the form of receipt which the sergeant pushed over, and commented, 'I see that if the property is restored to me after one month, I may have to sign a form indemnifying the Commissioner in case the owner subsequently claims it.'

'Just a formality, sir. It won't be required for a few beads and a small sum of money like this.'

'It seems that the easiest way out would be to put it straight in the charity box.'

'That's what they all say, sir, but they usually turn up for it on the dot and they don't notice the box any more.'

'In that case I'll patronise it now,' said Hammersley, fishing for another half-a-crown.

'Thank you very much, sir. I wish there were a few more like you. The world would be a better place.'

Mr Hammersley doubted this very much, and he went out once more into the raw fog whilst he still had strength. He was fortunate enough to commandeer another taxi which was crawling down to Chelsea Embankment. He called at another police station, and in different parts of London Blake, Dutchy, Rip Strookman and Quenella were engaged on similar errands. It was significant that throughout the proceedings they all kept their gloves on, and it was not necessarily because of the cold weather. By eleven-fifty a.m. Operation Safe-Deposit was complete.

It was not until after lunch that Lew Gabbitas discovered the loss of the Yellow Fire Diamonds.

# 21

## Dear Lady Veronica

'I'm sorry to hear about your burglary, Mr Gabbitas,' said Superintendent Lingard.

'So am I,' grunted Lew Gabbitas ungraciously.

'I understand you've given the local inspector a full list of the stolen articles,' went on Lingard smoothly. 'You were very fortunate in having such a precise and up-to-date list.'

'I only had the inventory and valuation made a short while before the burglary,' snapped Lew. 'For insurance purposes.'

'Oh, yes, I'm told you were fully insured, sir.'

'Yes, the company only came on cover the previous afternoon – I know it looks bad, but what can I do about it?'

'Make a claim, sir. That's what insurance is for – security. I saw it on the television.'

'I've already written them in the matter – and advised them by phone. I must say they were a bit off-hand – they didn't seem to know what I was talking about.'

'Things will sort themselves out. You've

got a cover-note, sir?'

'Oh, I've got a cover-note, all right. Here's my file. There's the letter they sent recommending a valuer, there's the card of the valuer, *and* of the surveyor, *and* the copy of the inventory, *and* the copy of the valuation certificate, *and* the cover-note which the surveyor gave me after consulting his office. I hope that satisfies you.'

'Oh, I'm satisfied, sir. I hope you will be.'

Lingard examined the papers casually. Frowning, he read through them again. Something was eluding him. 'Do you suspect anyone, sir?'

'How can I?' grated Lew irritably. 'The keys have never been out of my sight and the safe wasn't damaged in any way. It looks bad for me!' he snarled.

Lingard agreed. 'I suppose it does,' he said unhelpfully. 'But do you suspect anyone?'

Gabbitas thought quickly. The one thing of which he was certain was that Harry Levien, the peterman with whom he had planned his own proposed burglary, was not responsible, for the safe was to have been blown open, and nothing of the sort had happened; it had been relocked and bore no outward signs of having been tampered with. Further, Levien didn't get dates mixed up and do jobs ahead of schedule. Nevertheless, somebody had got clean away with a safeful of jewellery including the Yellow

Fire Diamonds, and it occurred to Lew that – although it meant advancing his plans – this might be an ideal opportunity to swing a delicately balanced situation on someone else's shoulders. 'There is one thing, Superintendent. Some while ago I met a man named Hammersley – he was involved in a horse-riding accident in Knightsbridge and I saw him safely to hospital. Subsequently he rather presumed on my friendship and called down here once or twice. Something of a scrounger. I actually got him a temporary job in one of the local inns, the Bull & Buffalo.'

'I'll have a word with him, sir.'

'He's no longer there. He left hurriedly the night before I discovered the loss.'

'We know all about this man Hammersley, sir. We've had our eyes on him ever since his accident, and we happen to know that someone has been impersonating him. We've already come to the conclusion that the man at the Bull & Buffalo that night was not Hammersley. A good likeness, but still not Hammersley. However, we'll look into it.'

Gabbitas's jaw dropped a notch. He was too confused to pursue the matter. Instead, he said, 'This Hammersley at the Bull & Buffalo has a friend called Simon Good. *He* came down here, too – not a likeable character. Too smooth. I believe he worked for that insurance company which had a court case over a dividend warrant – the Tyburn & New York – you may recall it.'

'I don't think he could have had anything to do with the robbery, sir. You see, he was called for jury service for two days at the material time and was, you might say, under the full surveillance of the law. Still, we'll look into that, too. You've thought of nothing else that you might wish to add to the list of stolen property?'

'Nothing at all,' growled Lew shortly.

Lingard was disappointed. There was no item remotely resembling the Yellow Fire rivière on the inventory.

Gabbitas made an effort to cover his sense of frustration. 'There was one other curious thing, Superintendent.'

'Yes?' Lingard held his breath.

'A picture was stolen from my studio. I didn't mention it before because the value was sentimental – my own work. *And* un-insured. I'll show you where it hung.'

Lingard followed Lew up to the picture gallery and looked at the paintings with perfunctory admiration. He halted at a blank space in the middle of the collection. 'What was it a picture of?' he asked curiously.

'Oh, just an impression of a – a necklace,' said Lew casually, and Lingard's heart nearly stopped.

'Strange,' he said, and as he said it a star-shell suddenly ripped up into outer darkness

306

and burst in a razzle-dazzle of understanding; for his eye was registering a picture with two dates, both of which struck home like incendiary bullets. And in that quick flash of brilliance the elusive something about Lew's insurance papers clarified itself; the letter from the Aldwych Insurance Corporation was signed *R. Dupp*, Accident Manager. He said, concealing his excitement, 'He must have taken a fancy to it, sir.' Glancing casually at some of the other pictures, his inward tenseness mounted. 'Don't touch anything round this space, sir – I'll send a man along to test for prints. We'll have to take yours, of course, for elimination purposes. And now, sir, on the Friday before Bank Holiday you were questioned in London about being in Hatton Garden.'

Gabbitas looked up sharply.

Lingard went on, 'We now have a very good conception of the man we want, but it would help if we could have another look at the suit you were wearing so that we may complete our picture. It could be that someone tried to victimise *you*. A man very much your size and wearing similar clothing.'

Gabbitas tried to cope with this new twist, and he wished to appear co-operative. 'I'd got rid of the suit only recently, Superintendent. The vicar took it with some other stuff for a jumble sale which was held – what? – a fortnight ago.'

'A pity! We so much wanted to refresh our recollection of it. You will appreciate the need for precise detail in these matters, nothing must be left to chance. You see, the courier, who was at death's door for so long is now fit and well and is prepared to identify his assailant. Still, not to worry, we'll get our man sooner or later...'

The Reverend Theodosius Todd opened the door with a welcoming smile, and glanced at Lingard's credentials. 'Come in, Superintendent. What can I do for you?'

'I've just been having a word with Mr Gabbitas up at Four Chimneys.'

A strange look briefly clouded the eyes of young Mr Todd. 'Oh, yes,' he said guardedly. 'What about Mr Gabbitas?'

'He was telling me he gave you amongst other things some discarded clothing for your jumble sale. Did you dispose of everything?'

'Oh, yes. The sale was about a fortnight ago.'

'You had nothing left at all?'

'No. After the sale a dealer made a bid for the remnants. Was there something you were interested in?'

'Yes. One of Mr Gabbitas's suits. A light summer suit. I think I may tell you in confidence that a short while ago Mr Gabbitas was put up for identification in connection with an incident in London.'

Mr Todd looked distressed. 'He's in no sort of trouble, is he?'

The superintendent was shocked. 'My dear sir, he wasn't picked out – he was perfectly free to go. This was back in August!'

'Then why are you interested in the suit?'

'Because it would help us to build up a more accurate picture of the man we're after.'

Mr Todd thought for a moment. 'What colour was it?' he asked.

'A sort of beigy-tan; in light-weight material, expensive. Why?'

'By a curious coincidence, I think I may still have it.'

The superintendent's heart misfired happily. 'Perhaps I could have a look at it,' he said offhandedly.

'I'm not saying it is necessarily the one you have in mind – Mr Gabbitas gives much to our church bazaars. The fact is, Superintendent, it was such a nice suit – almost brand new – that I thought I might make use of it myself. And then I noticed that unfortunately the trousers were stained round the bottoms – almost as though he'd walked past a workman using a spray-gun.' (Lingard's heart now jiggle-joggled madly.) 'I intended to have them dry-cleaned, but when I actually got round to it the bottoms were worse than I thought – they were pockmarked with reddish-brown spots. I suppose he'd passed by a chemical spray, and in the course of time the chemical had reacted on the cloth. You know what these artificial fibres are like.'

'Indeed, yes,' agreed Lingard. 'Perhaps we could take a look at this suit?'

'Of course. It's in the shed. I decided to wear it for gardening.'

They went out to the garden shed and Lingard examined the jacket and trousers which hung on a peg. 'May I take this clothing away?' he asked; he would have taken it anyway, but he wished to observe the courtesies with this earnest young man.

The vicar's eyes were perturbed. 'Superintendent,' he asked quietly, 'you're quite sure Mr Gabbitas is not in any sort of trouble?'

Superintendent Lingard regarded him kindly. 'We're all in some sort of trouble, sir,' he said. 'My trouble is trying to build up a precise picture of the man we want. We could, for example, be after *you* – if the suit really fits you! What a wonderful front you would have here as the Vicar of St Anselm's! – the man behind all the unsolved mysteries at the Yard! By the way, how are your hands? I understand they were badly burned in the fire at East Lampton.'

The Reverend Theo Todd looked uncomfortable. 'Oh, they're all right now, thank you.' A ghostly nagging worry crept stealthily through his eyes. He suddenly made up his mind. 'Superintendent. I think I ought to tell you something. It has been troubling me for some time.'

'Yes?' prompted Lingard gently.

'When I was in the heart of that fire at the depository I saw Jack Bowling – the fireman who lost his life – attempting, as I thought, to save another man from the flames. I didn't pay much attention to them, I was far too busy with my own little problem of trying to rescue the nightwatchman. But I happened to whip round as a rafter fell and I saw what looked like this other man with his arm upraised – as if he were *attacking* Jack Bowling. I knew I must have been mistaken. The flames and smoke swirled round and Bowling seemed to fall back into the holocaust. The other man rushed wildly towards me, incoherently urging me to leave the building, pausing only to lend a hand to drag the nightwatchman clear of the falling debris. I caught only a brief look at his face, black with smoke and grime. I came to the conclusion that the wild impression I'd had of him apparently grappling with the fireman was born out of the nightmare of the moment, that he was in fact trying to rescue him and had failed. His attempt to help me, however, was singularly clumsy – I could have managed better myself. I am no weakling – in spite of my back-to-front collar.' He paused again.

'Yes?' said Lingard. 'So?'

'I've wondered since if in fact he was trying to *impede* me.' (Lingard scarcely breathed.) 'At the time I dismissed such a thought as being uncharitable,' went on the vicar quietly, 'and didn't mention that aspect to the police. They never discovered who the other man was, he vanished into thin air in the confusion. I now think I *know* who he was.'

Lingard held his breath. 'Who?' he said, so gently this time that he almost never said it.

'Mr Gabbitas. But I can't be sure.'

The superintendent broke the spell. 'Oh, come, sir! He doesn't strike me as being that sort of a man at all. What prompts you to come to this conclusion?'

For a moment the vicar chewed his lower lip. 'A few weekends ago Mr Gabbitas was driving past the church, and I stopped him to inquire about the material he'd promised for the jumble sale. After we'd made arrangements for its collection, he turned aside to order the chauffeur to drive on. I experienced one of those brief moments of understanding when you *know* without knowing *why* you know. There was just something in the tone of his voice, the set of his jaw, the look in his eye, which told me that the man who was in that burning building *was* Gabbitas.'

'Well, sir, what's so wrong about that if he was trying to rescue a man, failing, and then not coming forward? Perhaps his natural modesty forbade him. I understand you're not without modesty yourself.'

The vicar made a grimace. 'Natural modesty is not one of Mr Gabbitas's strong points, Superintendent, although he likes to do good in an unobtrusive fashion. He gave one hundred pounds to the collection for the fireman's widow.'

'Did he now, sir? That was more than generous. But what really convinces you it was he in the burning building?'

'Curiously enough, a negative point. In conversation he has let it be known to me, several times – too many times – that he was *nowhere near the fire.*'

Superintendent Lingard coughed and cleared his throat. 'Negative leads can be very misleading, sir. I've been caught out myself, in my time. Don't worry about it – in your job you become much too introspective.'

'In my own mind, Superintendent, I *know* that Gabbitas was attacking Jack Bowling, and that he *did* in fact endeavour to hamper my efforts to save the nightwatchman.'

'Now that's a serious allegation, Mr Todd,' said Lingard.

Young Todd remained silent. He shifted uneasily from one foot to the other.

Lingard said, 'Why should Mr Gabbitas wish to attack the fireman? Come, be reasonable!'

The Reverend Theo Todd grew pink about the cheeks. 'I don't know, I'm sure. Unless he was caught doing something he shouldn't have been doing.'

'I should forget about it, sir, if I were you,' said Lingard kindly. 'Now if you don't mind, I'll borrow this suit for a while. I shouldn't mention the matter to Mr Gabbitas.'

The Reverend Theo Todd was pleased to leave it that way. He went back to his study and scrapped his draft of Sunday's sermon. The text was now apparent to him. *Proverbs, 13, 15... The way of transgressors is hard...*

The Aldwych Insurance Corporation looked into Gabbitas's claim and denied liability. They would have liked to deny all knowledge of Mr Gabbitas. They denied recommending a valuer, sending a surveyor and issuing a cover-note. When confronted with Lew's papers, they informed him they had no employee named R. Dupp, let alone an Accident Manager of that name, and the *Insurance Almanac* added weight to their contention. They were of the opinion that the whole thing was a hoax, perhaps perpetrated by a member of the staff with an axe to grind, and they called in an expert from the typewriter company to test all the machines. Somewhat to their horror the machine on which the original letter was typed was located, and in due course the typists in that room were questioned, but they were obviously innocent of all malice and not likely to move in the same circles as Lew Gabbitas.

Nobody remembered the harassed mechanic who had wandered in one lunch hour to service the machine.

Superintendent Lingard received another letter from R. Dupp, Esq., advising him to get a warrant and search a derelict furniture depository at Banwell Major, where he would find antiques allegedly destroyed by fire at East Lampton and Westland Zoy; on no account was he to overlook the contents of the safe in the office.

Lingard, in conjunction with the local police, acted with speed. They found not only the antiques but also, in the safe, all the jewellery stolen from Four Chimneys. That is, all the jewellery shown on the inventory; not the Yellow Fire Diamonds.

Lew Gabbitas was flabbergasted when he received a request to step round to the local police station to identify his stolen property. He hurried up the front steps into the front office, his mind seething with disquiet. He stopped short when he saw Superintendent

Lingard, but recovered quickly. 'You've caught the culprit?' he jerked.

'Not yet, sir, but I think we've recovered all your jewellery. Perhaps you'd be good enough to check it over.'

Apprehensively, Lew checked it against the list, his mind working overtime. It was all there, all except the Yellow Fire Diamonds, and they were not listed anyway. He was not sure if he was glad or sorry.

'Anything missing, sir?' asked Lingard, at length.

To Gabbitas the question was charged with electricity. He paused a fraction of a second too long before answering, and Lingard, deceptively casual, noticed the fact.

'It's all there,' said Gabbitas shortly.

'You've thought of nothing else since I last spoke to you?'

'No. Like I said, it's all there. May I take it?'

'Not yet, if you don't mind, sir,' said Lingard. 'You see, we found it in a safe in a disused warehouse over at Banwell Major – a warehouse full of antiques and pictures which were supposed to have been destroyed in fires at Westland Zoy and East Lampton, so it looks as if the same person was behind all three crimes. We've only got to find *him*, and we've caught your man. And we've got an unexpected lead for which we have to thank you, sir.'

Gabbitas refrigerated into perfect stillness. Time stood still. *'Me?'* he breathed.

'Yes, sir. You remember I told you about that courier who was involved in the diamond robbery in Hatton Garden – you know, the one who is now well enough to worry about who attacked him? Well, we've had another stroke of luck. It seems the old nightwatchman, who wasn't expected to live after his experience in the East Lampton fire, is not going to leave us after all. He's remembering all sorts of things about a man he found setting fire to the premises – a man who knocked him out and apparently left him to die.'

The only parts of Gabbitas which moved where his lips. 'And where do I come in?' he said.

'Oh, come, sir, there's no need to be modest – it's an open secret in East Lampton. If it wasn't for all the kindness you bestowed on him whilst he was lying there in hospital, staring vacantly back into the horror of that fire, he would have been dead long ago. Your gifts revived his faith in humanity and gave him something to live for. But as the vicar would say– "Cast thy bread upon the waters: for thou shalt find it after many days." When we've pieced together the nightwatchman's story we'll find the link we're looking for – and there must be a link, otherwise how would your jewellery come to be with all the other stuff at Banwell Major?'

It was then that Lew Gabbitas decided to cut his losses and leave the country; he was glad he had had the foresight to put his yacht in order.

Lady Veronica Tuke was very upset when she heard about the insurance company and about the police holding the jewellery.

She refused to go with him.

'You on the verge of a breakdown, Lingard?' asked the commander sourly. 'I haven't seen you so soppily happy for a long time.'

The superintendent straightened his face. 'I am happy, sir,' he said stiffly. 'A print on the fragment of the igniter-set found in Flinder's Court matches with one of Lew Gabbitas's. And Interpol have the same print on their files. Gabbitas's strong point in the old days was etching, and during the war he collaborated with the Nazis in making plates for spurious currency.'

'Nice chap.'

'Yes – although up till now he appears to have kept out of trouble. But he's right in it now – there are identifiable trace-elements of tear gas and chemical smoke on that suit I picked up from the vicar.'

'So it *was* Gabbitas in Flinder's Court,' breathed the commander gently. His eyes slated bleakly as he remembered the Interpol man who died in the line of duty, and black frost formed as he thought of a widow and two children at Leicester. 'Go and get him,' he said softly.

But Lingard was too late. Firemen were still playing hoses on the smouldering debris that was once Four Chimneys. Lew Gabbitas had carried out his last act of fire-raising, the evidence of his malefaction was in ashes. All, that is, except Simon Good's passport, which was found cockled with heat in the fireproof Masterlock safe, and Lingard would have preferred not to find it.

There was no trace of Lew Gabbitas and the police had no means of establishing that he was now on the high seas, his mind a bubbling, boiling, seething cauldron of hate for Charles Hammersley and Simon Good.

# 22

## Operation Police-Benefit

About a month after Operation Safe-Deposit a number of police stations each received a curious letter referring to a string of beads which had been handed in, and one or two local stations began to report to New

Scotland Yard. The commander (Crime) was so intrigued that he gave an order for all stations to be circularised in the matter and to forward any information and evidence to the Yard.

'Well, Lingard,' he growled irritably, 'have we got the Yellow Fire Diamonds, or haven't we?'

'We've got *some* yellow fire diamonds,' replied Lingard cautiously, 'but whether we've got *the* Yellow Fire Diamonds, I wouldn't know.'

'Let us analyse the position. The rivière was stolen on the Friday before August Bank Holiday. Although you – we – thought Roag's Syndicate was implicated, we can now be virtually certain that Gabbitas stole it. Just as we're about to pin him down, he has a robbery which went wrong, where everything he alleged was stolen was recovered and has since been returned to the rightful owners where identifiable. He didn't mention, or insure, any Yellow Fire Diamonds. In some oblique way Good and Hammersley were tied up in the business. Hammersley alleged he was being impersonated, and this was substantiated to a certain degree by the fact that one of your own men says that the man at the Bull & Buffalo was not *quite* the Hammersley we know. And now the matter of Hammersley's passport; he says he had mislaid it, so how could he have been in

Amsterdam? And how can you prove a man *hasn't* mislaid his passport? It was due for renewal – all he had to do was to shove it on the boiler. Good said *his* passport was stolen; and in fact it turns up in Gabbitas's safe. Perhaps Hammersley had had his stolen, too. All in all it looks very much as if Gabbitas *was* trying to shift a measure of blame on Roag's Syndicate. Don't you agree?'

Lingard remained silent. And sceptical.

'We now come to the point,' went on the commander, 'when on the day that Gabbitas discovered Four Chimneys had been robbed, a number of people called at different police stations – *before* he discovered the theft – and handed in cheap strings of beads alleged to have been found in the street, all packed up in Woolworth gift boxes and bags, all with a letter to Dear Auntie Eth. Here before us we have all the letters, all the boxes and bags, all the strings of beads, all the shillings and pennies change and all the sticky smears of cream buns from tea at Lyons Corner House. All very artistic and not a fingerprint other than those of the policemen handling the articles.

'And now, a month later, we have a series of letters purporting to come from the people who handed the articles in. The tenor of each letter is the same. Let us take one at random. This one, for example: "Dear Sir, With reference to the attached form of receipt for a string of beads and cash found in Pimlico, I beg to inform you that if these are not claimed back by the owner within the prescribed time I do not intend to claim them for myself. Kindly therefore dispose of them for the benefit of any Police Charity or Police Fund. Although I may have omitted to mention it at the time, it seemed to me that some of the individual beads might be of value and well worth careful examination by a qualified jeweller. Yours ever so truly, Mrs Sippi." Huh! Mrs Sippi! River View, Pimlico! There ain't no River View, Pimlico, Lingard. And now take this one from Geoffrey Judge of Fountain View, Bushy Park. We've all heard of Judge Jeffreys, but we can't trace Geoffrey Judge, although we got a good view of the fountain in the middle of Bushy Park. And N. O. Justice – who lives at 221b, Baker Street – we can't find him either; he must have moved when Sherlock Holmes died. Nor can we find half a dozen others with similar names – not forgetting our old friend, R. Dupp. So what have we got? A list of spurious names and addresses and diamonds worth a fortune. What do we do about it?'

'Well, sir, although we know Gabbitas stole the Yellow Fire Diamonds, we don't know *these* are the Yellow Fire Diamonds. If they are, they must have been stolen in turn from Gabbitas.'

'But he didn't say so,' pointed out the commander.

'We recovered *all that he said was missing.*'

'Then they belong to the diamond firm in Antwerp.'

'If they *are* the Yellow Fire Diamonds. But we've no proof. And the Antwerp firm have no proof, and they're doubtful. In any event, they've been indemnified by the insurers for slightly more than the present reduced value.'

'Then the diamonds belong to the insurers as salvage,' said Lingard reluctantly.

'But the insurers, too, are hesitant to lay claim to them – the stones have been altered beyond recognition, and there's not enough of them, some are missing.'

'Then it looks as if we'll have to advertise them in case they're some other recognisable collection of diamonds,' said Lingard. 'So far, nobody has reported the loss of any other yellow stones. What happens if nobody comes forward for them?'

The commander avoided the superintendent's eye. 'Then we'll auction them in the usual way – for the benefit of the Police Fund, as the letters suggest,' he said. Then– 'What about Lady Veronica Tuke?'

Lingard shrugged his shoulders hopelessly. 'She still maintains she was nowhere near Hatton Garden; that she didn't know Gabbitas; that if her car was seen at Four

Chimneys then it must have been borrowed by her Austrian maid, who has since gone back to Austria. Oh, she agreed that it was most unlikely, but how else would her car be at Four Chimneys? She also claims that the maid was of her own build, with green eyes just like hers. Precisely what she was doing at Four Chimneys she just can't imagine, and as Gabbitas is no longer with us, we can't tackle him about it.'

'Ah, yes, Gabbitas. I wonder where he is – I don't suppose he was considerate enough to perish in the fire. The Aldwych Insurance Corporation would like a word with him – although I don't suppose they'd press him too hard in view of the fact that that first letter was typed on one of their own type-writers. But if Gabbitas ever comes back, I should hate to be in either Simon Good's or Hammersley's shoes!'

'Then you're coming round to my way of thinking, sir,' said the superintendent quickly, '–that Roag's Syndicate *are* mixed up in this! You know, there was one hint of a clue we've almost overlooked. On the day all these necklaces were handed in, one of my men tailed a man he thought was Hammersley to Bow Street. When he saw his quarry was making for a police station – Bow Street, at that! – he thought he must have been mistaken. He didn't see him come out, anyway. But that was the very morning Mr

N. O. Justice called there. We could see if the station officer could identify him as Hammersley.'

The commander looked stonily out of the window. 'When did you learn this?' he asked.

'Only yesterday, when trying to check up who actually handed these necklaces in.'

'So that if it was Hammersley your man saw, you'd feel obliged to reprimand him for not reporting the point at the time.'

'He needs choking off,' grunted the superintendent.

'I think these plainclothes men fall for enough criticism as it is,' said the commander. 'We must remember that Hammersley was – um – being impersonated – it need not have been him. Advertise the diamonds in the usual way, Lingard. I imagine we won't find a claimant with definite proof of identity. The Police Fund can do with the money.' Once again the commander avoided Lingard's eye. 'I don't think I want to know if it was Hammersley or not, Superintendent,' he said vaguely.

But for all the vagueness, Lingard detected an instruction...

# 23

## Die for your Country

Superintendent Lingard called on Simon Good at Richmond.

'Oh, hallo,' said Simon, as he opened the door and peered out into the night. 'I remember you – you were the man who asked me some questions about being in Amsterdam, although I can't recall your name. Come right on in. What can I do for you?'

'I've come to return your passport, sir.'

Simon was surprised. 'Really? Where did you find it?'

'In a safe belonging to a gentleman named Gabbitas. His house, Four Chimneys, was burned to the ground. We hoped to find certain evidence in connection with a number of crimes, but it was all lost in the fire. There were a lot of pictures we wanted.'

'Pictures?– Photographs?'

'Paintings,' said Lingard patiently. 'Oil paintings.'

'Oh. Scarcely my line. Where was this Four Chimneys?'

'Devonshire, sir.'

'Well, what do you know! Why should a

bloke in Devonshire steal *my* passport?'

'I was hoping you could tell me,' said Lingard. 'It seems likely he's the man who has been trying to implicate both you and your ex-batman in his shady activities.'

'I'm just as puzzled as you are, Inspector – or is it Superintendent?'

'They say confession is good for the soul.'

'Not my soul,' said Simon. 'Different model altogether.'

The telephone rang out stridently. Simon answered it. 'For you,' he said briefly.

'They knew I'd be here,' said Lingard, taking the receiver. He listened for a moment and stiffened. 'That your car outside?'

'Yes. Anything wrong?'

Lingard snapped out an order into the handset and slammed it back on the bracket. 'Come on, quickly!' he rapped. 'Unless I'm mistaken, your friend Hammersley's in trouble. Gabbitas has been seen at a garage in a fast car. He was asking the way to Marlow…'

Hammersley received a cheque for £800 from the Wyvern Insurance Company, and he wasted no time in paying it into the bank. So much had happened since his pseudo accident in Knightsbridge that he had almost overlooked the fact that the company had not met the claim for the horse immediately. That same evening, he attended to his outstanding account with Tim Tweedy, horse-doctor of Esher.

The account rendered gave a detailed analysis of how the twenty-five guineas was arrived at, and, considering the number of items ranging through consulting-fee, use of horse-box and humane killer, knacker's-yard fee less salvage, the whole operation was cheap at twice the price. Hammersley therefore wrote the cheque for £26.5.0d. gladly. He pinned it to the account, placed it in a stout manila envelope, and addressed the envelope to Mr Tweedy's private residence.

The account omitted one item: To loan of one horse similar in appearance to Fiddler, but worth £850, for insurance valuation purposes.

Mr Tweedy had obviously overlooked the item, but Hammersley was perfectly fair in such matters, even though the account was not marked E. & O. E. Before sealing the envelope, therefore, he popped in a further £100 in five-pound notes for the additional services rendered ... and went out into the night to post it.

And met Lew Gabbitas coming up the garden path.

Lew Gabbitas saw in Simon Good and Charles Hammersley the men responsible for the failure of his million pound objective and for his shattering loss of Veronica. He felt he might even yet induce Veronica to go away with him when he told her the extent of the salvage value of his sadly splintered dream, for his salted-away wealth was still considerable, and life could be very pleasant in his chalet in Switzerland. His immediate plan, however, was to settle with Good and Hammersley, and by a circuitous route he re-entered the U.K. filled with bitter thoughts of revenge. Hammersley was his first objective, for in the gentle, amazing Mr Hammersley he saw a devil incarnate. Hiring a fast car, he swept on from the coast *en route* for London and Mortlake, but found nobody at home in Hammersley's flat. He remembered the address at Marlow, and seething with hatred he pressed on relentlessly, the gun in his side pocket a constant spur. And then he had trouble with the car. He was obliged to stop at some traffic lights and the engine faded and cut out, and he had difficulty in restarting. He didn't know it, but the idling jet was clogged. After several such occurrences he was driving on the choke. On the outskirts of Marlow he gave it up as a bad job, and set out on foot in the dark to Hammersley's cottage. Grim determination was etched in every line of his face as he turned down the rutted lane leading to the cottage. Reaching the garden gate, he saw Hammersley coming towards him, letter in hand. Hammersley stopped and they faced each other for a moment in silence.

'I've come to get you, Hammersley!' said Lew softly, reaching for his gun.

Charles Hammersley hated anything approaching violence. Even more he hated violence approaching. This was one of those occasions. With commendable speed, he whipped into the shadows at the side of the house and made for the kitchen garden like a startled bat. Slamming the greenhouse door as a feint, he slid noiselessly over the low wall into the compost heap and burrowed in like a wart-hog.

Lithe as a leopard, Gabbitas rounded the corner of the cottage like one possessed. And then pulled up in a quandary. He said softly, 'I'll get you, Hammersley, even if I have to wait till daylight!' His voice was the essence of refrigerated hate.

A low whinnying sound answered him, and Hammersley wished Fiddler would keep quiet.

And then a car bucketed madly down the lane and screeched to a halt. In alarm, Gabbitas slipped round to the front of the cottage, foolishly exposing himself against the porch light.

Two men came rushing up the path towards him, and the first one he recognised as being Superintendent Lingard. This was a different Lingard from the deceptively inert superintendent he already knew. This was a policeman who was also hunting with hate.

'I want you, Gabbitas!' roared Lingard in full throttle.

For a split second Gabbitas stood rooted to the spot. Then his itchy finger squeezed the trigger, and Lingard and Simon parted and dived for cover.

Gabbitas saw that the way to the lane was blocked. In a flash of inspiration he remembered the horse. One way to travel over broken country back to the road presented itself to the horseman in him. He fled to the rear, and Fiddler, trustful as ever to mankind, came over in answer to his low whistle. Mounting in one desperate leap, Gabbitas urged the animal into a gallop, away from the cottage, away from the hellhounds now converging from either side. About fifty yards away in the gloom was a sparse copse and Gabbitas made for it, Fiddler entering into the spirit of the thing.

And then Hammersley arose in all his glory from the compost heap.

'*Die for your country!*' he yelled, and it was at that precise moment that Gabbitas slapped Fiddler's flank.

Surprised, Fiddler pulled up with a sudden jerk. Gabbitas was flung headlong. He tried to neck-roll, but the side of his neck hit a tree stump. He lay perfectly still, his body sprawled in an unnatural position.

Simon Good and Lingard raced past Fiddler. They briefly examined Gabbitas by the light of a pencil-torch. It did not require an expert to see that his neck was broken.

'He's dead,' said Hammersley behind them. Lingard and Simon whipped round in surprise, for there was *grief* in his voice. But Hammersley was looking at Fiddler, not at Gabbitas.

Fiddler's war was well and truly over. That last sinew-breaking, heart-stopping jolt had been too much. There would be no getting up this time … no more applause … no more bows.

Fiddler had died for his country for the last time ever.

The publishers hope that this book has given you enjoyable reading. Large Print Books are especially designed to be as easy to see and hold as possible. If you wish a complete list of our books please ask at your local library or write directly to:

**Dales Large Print Books**
Magna House, Long Preston,
Skipton, North Yorkshire.
BD23 4ND

This Large Print Book, for people
who cannot read normal print,
is published under the auspices of

**THE ULVERSCROFT FOUNDATION**

... we hope you have enjoyed this book.
Please think for a moment about those
who have worse eyesight than you ...
and are unable to even read or enjoy
Large Print without great difficulty.

You can help them by sending a
donation, large or small, to:

**The Ulverscroft Foundation,
1, The Green, Bradgate Road,
Anstey, Leicestershire, LE7 7FU,
England.**
or request a copy of our brochure for
more details.

The Foundation will use all donations
to assist those people who are visually
impaired and need special attention
with medical research, diagnosis
and treatment.

Thank you very much for your help.

| 1 | 2 | 3 | 4 | 5 | 6 | 7 | 8 | 9 | 10 | 11 | 12 |
|---|---|---|---|---|---|---|---|---|---|---|---|
| 13 | 14 | 15 | 16 | 17 | 18 | 19 | 20 | 21 | 22 | 23 | 24 |
| 25 | 26 | 27 | 28 | 29 | 30 | 31 | 32 | 33 | 34 | 35 | 36 |
| 37 | 38 | 39 | 40 | 41 | 42 | 43 | 44 | 45 | 46 | 47 | 48 |
| 49 | 50 | 51 | 52 | 53 | 54 | 55 | 56 | 57 | 58 | 59 | 60 |
| 61 | 62 | 63 | 64 | 65 | 66 | 67 | 68 | 69 | 70 | 71 | 72 |
| 73 | 74 | 75 | 76 | 77 | 78 | 79 | 80 | 81 | 82 | 83 | 84 |
| 85 | 86 | 87 | 88 | 89 | 90 | 91 | 92 | 93 | 94 | 95 | 96 |
| 97 | 98 | 99 | 100 | 101 | 102 | 103 | 104 | 105 | 106 | 107 | 108 |
| 109 | 110 | 111 | 112 | 113 | 114 | 115 | 116 | 117 | 118 | 119 | 120 |
| 121 | 122 | 123 | 124 | 125 | 126 | 127 | 128 | 129 | 130 | 131 | 132 |
| 133 | 134 | 135 | 136 | 137 | 138 | 139 | 140 | 141 | 142 | 143 | 144 |
| 145 | 146 | 147 | 148 | 149 | 150 | 151 | 152 | 153 | 154 | 155 | 156 |
| 157 | 158 | 159 | 160 | 161 | 162 | 163 | 164 | 165 | 166 | 167 | 168 |
| 169 | 170 | 171 | 172 | 173 | 174 | 175 | 176 | 177 | 178 | 179 | 180 |
| 181 | 182 | 183 | 184 | 185 | 186 | 187 | 188 | 189 | 190 | 191 | 192 |
| 193 | 194 | 195 | 196 | 197 | 198 | 199 | 200 | 201 | 202 | 203 | 204 |
| 205 | 206 | 207 | 208 | 209 | 210 | 211 | 212 | 213 | 214 | 215 | 216 |
| 217 | 218 | 219 | 220 | 221 | 222 | 223 | 224 | 225 | 226 | 227 | 228 |
| 229 | 230 | 231 | 232 | 233 | 234 | 235 | 236 | 237 | 238 | 239 | 240 |
| 241 | 242 | 243 | 244 | 245 | 246 | 247 | 248 | 249 | 250 | 251 | 252 |
| 253 | 254 | 255 | 256 | 257 | 258 | 259 | 260 | 261 | 262 | 263 | 264 |
| 265 | 266 | 267 | 268 | 269 | 270 | 271 | 272 | 273 | 274 | 275 | 276 |
| 277 | 278 | 279 | 280 | 281 | 282 | 283 | 284 | 285 | 286 | 287 | 288 |
| 289 | 290 | 291 | 292 | 293 | 294 | 295 | 296 | 297 | 298 | 299 | 300 |
| 301 | 302 | 303 | 304 | 305 | 306 | 307 | 308 | 309 | 310 | 311 | 312 |
| 313 | 314 | 315 | 316 | 317 | 318 | 319 | 320 | 321 | 322 | 323 | 324 |
| 325 | 326 | 327 | 328 | 329 | 330 | 331 | 332 | 333 | 334 | 335 | 336 |
| 337 | 338 | 339 | 340 | 341 | 342 | 343 | 344 | 345 | 346 | 347 | 348 |
| 349 | 350 | 351 | 352 | 353 | 354 | 355 | 356 | 357 | 358 | 359 | 360 |
| 361 | 362 | 363 | 364 | 365 | 366 | 367 | 368 | 369 | 370 | 371 | 372 |
| 373 | 374 | 375 | 376 | 377 | 378 | 379 | 380 | 381 | 382 | 383 | 384 |
| 385 | 386 | 387 | 388 | 389 | 390 | 391 | 392 | 393 | 394 | 395 | 396 |
| 397 | 398 | 399 | 400 | 401 | 402 | 403 | 404 | 405 | 406 | 407 | 408 |
| 409 | 410 | 411 | 412 | 413 | 414 | 415 | 416 | 417 | 418 | 419 | 420 |